The Laura Black Scottsdale Mystery Series

The Laura Black
Scottsdale Mystery Series
by B A Trimmer

~~~~

Scottsdale Heat

Scottsdale Squeeze

Scottsdale Sizzle

Scottsdale Scorcher

Scottsdale Sting

Scottsdale Shuffle

Scottsdale Shadow
~~~~

Scottsdale Shuffle

Scottsdale Shuffle

B A Trimmer

Saguaro Sky Media Co.

SCOTTSDALE SHUFFLE

Editors: 'Andi' Anderson and Kimberly Mathews
Cover Design: Tammy Malunas
ISBN-13: 978-1-951052-07-2
Saguaro Sky Media Co.
070119

E-mail the author at:
LauraBlackScottsdale@gmail.com

To my baby sister Stacey.
Of the three of us, she's always
been the brilliant one.
Now I know, she's also
the strong one as well.

Thanks to Tammy for her ideas,
Andi for her wisdom and patience,
and Kim for her enthusiasm and inspirations.

Thanks also to Bonnie Costilow,
Kendall Cusick, Jeanette Ellmer,
Melinda Fowler, Barbra Hackel,
Katie Hilbert, and Carol Lustfeldt
for their help and encouragement.

Scottsdale Shuffle

Introduction

If you've never read a Laura Black Scottsdale mystery, you can start with *Scottsdale Heat*, the first book in the series. If you'd rather start with this book, here are a few of the people you'll need to know:

Laura Black – Laura grew up in Arizona and currently works as an investigator in a Scottsdale law firm. She'd love to make the world a better place but she also has bills to pay.

Sophia Rodriguez – Laura's best friend who works in the law office as the receptionist and paralegal. She sometimes gets to help Laura in her investigations. Sophie's a former California surfer chick and a free spirit who enjoys dating multiple men at the same time.

Gina Rondinelli – Laura's other best friend. She's a former Scottsdale police detective and the law firm's senior investigator. She has a strict moral code and likes playing by the rules.

Leonard Shapiro – Lenny is head of the law firm. He has no people skills but with the help of Laura, Sophie, and Gina, he usually wins his cases.

Anthony "Tough Tony" DiCenzo – Current head of the local crime family. Through events over the last several months, he's become quite close to Laura.

Maximilien – The current number-two man in the local crime family. Through a long series of adventures, he's become Laura's secret boyfriend.

Gabriella – A former government operative from somewhere in eastern Europe. She currently works as a bodyguard for Tough Tony and Max. She takes pleasure in hurting men.

Danielle Ortega – Laura's former friend. Her father is Escobar Salazar, the ruthless head of an international drug cartel called the Black Death.

Milo and Snake – Sophie's main boyfriends. Milo works as a mid-level minion for Tough Tony DiCenzo while Snake is the third string quarterback for the Arizona Cardinals.

Raul – Henchman at the Black Death drug cartel. He and Laura have had several confrontations but, so far, she's always come out on top.

Grandma Peckham – Laura's longtime neighbor who's recently been dating a man named Grandpa Bob.

The Cougars – A group of wealthy, sexy, and fashionable women who like to troll the clubs of Scottsdale looking for athletic younger men for hook-up relationships. Through a series of adventures, Laura, Sophie, and Gina have become unofficial members of their group.

Chapter One

Most people love October in Scottsdale. The brutal summer temperatures have started to fade into memory and the paradise weather Scottsdale is known for returns. While most of the country is bracing for the first snows of winter, October temperatures in Scottsdale are still comfortably in the eighties and nineties.

October is also the unofficial start of Snowbird Season and I'm not thrilled when it rolls around each year. I think of the summer heat as a protective shield, keeping out the hordes of winter visitors in their huge cars and RV's. I know traffic will get bad, I'll have to get to the movies an extra fifteen minutes early to get a good seat, and any decent restaurant in the city will again require a reservation. Prices across The Valley will again go up, in some cases, two or three times what they were.

I think I prefer summer.

~~~~

It was Monday afternoon. I was sitting in my car doing surveillance on a cheating spouse, when my cell phone rang with Rihanna's song *S&M.*

"Hey, Laura," Sophie said when I answered. "Hate to do this, but Lenny wants you to come in for a meeting."

Sophie was not only my best friend, she was the paralegal and
~~~~

admin for my boss, Lenny.

"What's it about?" I asked.

"I think he wants to give you and Gina an assignment."

"But I already have an assignment."

"Well, I guess now you've got two. You know how this works, you're an investigator in the best law office in Scottsdale. It's feast or famine. Now that everybody's coming back into town, it's going to start getting busy again."

"Fine, when does he want us there?"

"Right away. Gina's already here, so we're waiting on you."

"It's not another cheating spouse, is it? I'm starting to lose faith in humanity."

"I don't think so. Lenny had the client in this morning and she's here again now for the follow-up meeting. She doesn't look like the jealous wife type."

"What *does* she look like?"

"Indiana Jones."

"Seriously? Okay, I'll be there in fifteen minutes. I've always wanted to meet Indiana Jones."

~~~~

"Gold?" Sophie asked. "Really? How much gold are we talking about?"

"Don't know," Gina responded. "But she said she found a nugget of solid gold the size of her finger."

I'd walked up to the front reception area of the law office in time to listen to Sophie and the law firm's senior investigator, Gina, in the middle of a discussion.

"Did she happen to say if there was more than only the one big
~~~~

nugget?" Sophie asked.

"Well," Gina said, "she didn't directly come out and say it, but she certainly implied there could be."

"That's good enough for me," Sophie said. "When are we going up to get it?"

"We're going up to get nuggets of gold?" I asked. "Really? Where are we going to get them?"

"The Lost Dutchman Mine," Sophie said.

"What?" I asked. "You mean the mythical mine in the Superstition Mountains that's supposed to be loaded with gold? Everyone knows it doesn't exist. People have been looking for it for hundreds of years."

"Well," Sophie said, "the woman who's in with Lenny says she's found it."

I gave Sophie my best skeptical look, making it look even more skeptical by raising an eyebrow.

"Fine," Sophie said, "don't believe me, ask Gina. She was in the office this morning when the client told Lenny she'd found it."

I turned my skeptical look towards Gina.

"Well, yes, she did say she'd found a cave and there was at least one big piece of solid gold in it. She wants to know if she can officially place a claim on it so that she can legally take possession of the gold. Look, I'm as skeptical as you are about this. I've been hearing about the Lost Dutchman Mine all my life and it seems every few years somebody new says they've found it."

"Well, Lenny wants you both to meet with the client when he's done talking to her," Sophie said, glancing over at the closed door to Lenny's office. "She's still in there, listening while Lenny tells her how much this all will cost. Maybe she'll tell us about the gold mine too."

"Okay," Gina said. "I'll be back at my cube. Let me know when Lenny's ready for us."

Gina took off to the back and I flopped down on one of the wing chairs next to Sophie's desk.

"Did you say you're working on a cheating spouse today?" Sophie asked. "Is this the aerobics instructor one? I'm still behind on my paperwork. What's the story?"

"The wife thinks he's having an affair with his aerobics instructor. She's found some suggestive notes and emails, not enough for proof, but enough to make her suspect. He also never wants to have sex with her on the days he goes to the gym."

"I didn't know anyone still did aerobics. Didn't that fade out about the time we were in high school? Besides, a married guy not wanting sex with his wife doesn't seem like such a big deal. From what I've heard, most married guys only want sex once or twice a week anyway."

"According to the wife, this guy's been a steady five or six times a week since they got married. Over the past couple of months, it's down to twice a week, and never on a Monday, Wednesday, or a Friday. The wife put two and two together and figured out her husband is having sex with the aerobics instructor on the days he goes to her classes."

"Well?"

"Well, I followed him to the gym and I had someone from the membership department walk me around while he was in class. And, I guess you're right. They're called fitness instructors now and the class he's taking is called Guerrilla Bootcamp, or something like that. But to me, it looked a lot like an aerobics class. After that, I sat in the lobby until class was over and he left."

"Did he have sex with her?"

"I don't see how he could have. The class must have had fifteen or twenty people in it. Everyone left the class room at the same time and went into the locker rooms. My guy was dressed and left the club within about fifteen or twenty minutes."

"Did they get together after he came out? Maybe they snuck over to her place or something?"

"That's what I was thinking too, but he got in his car and drove straight to his office. I was still in his office parking lot when you called me. It's possible they're meeting after work somewhere, but then they could meet any day of the week. Why is it only Mondays, Wednesdays, and Fridays he isn't interested in his wife? I'm thinking maybe I'll need to spend all day Wednesday following him around."

"You've been quiet about Max the past few days. Did you two get a chance to go out over the weekend?"

"No," I said, still feeling grumpy about it. "We made plans for Saturday, but he had to cancel. Something happened at work."

"So, what's going on with you two? You dated Reno for almost a year and that whole thing crapped out. I guess that's what happens when you let Gina set you up with a cop. Then you finally hooked up with Max for a weekend, and now it's been a whole lot of nothing."

"I don't know. We spent the entire weekend together in San Diego last month. But now I'm lucky if I see him once a week. When we do get together, it's usually only a quick dinner over at the Tropical Paradise. Tony isn't coming back anytime soon, and Max's workload keeps growing. He gets to work every day by eight and he's at the office most nights until ten or eleven."

"You mean you haven't been, um, together with him, except for the one weekend?"

"Well, I wouldn't say that. There're advantages to meeting in a hotel, even if it's only for a quick dinner. Lots of nice rooms at your disposal."

"You're such a bad girl. I imagine being head of the local mafia is a lot of work. Why doesn't Max hire some people and delegate that stuff, like all those rich CEO's do. You never see Mark Zuckerberg sitting behind a desk with piles of reports to sort through. He has staff to do that."

"When I asked Max about letting someone else take on part of the workload, he said he didn't want to make a lot of major staffing moves that Tony would need to switch around when he comes back. Mostly I think it's because Max is very detail oriented and I don't think he wants to have anyone else making decisions. It's a big company and it's keeping him busy."

"Yeah, but too busy for you?"

"I'm hoping it'll get better after Tony comes back."

"How's he doing? He went from being the boss of the largest crime family in Arizona to being shot and in rehab."

"He's doing great, considering Carlos the Butcher almost killed him. He's out of the wheelchair part of the time and starting to walk with a cane. He's still slow, but he's getting better every time I see him."

"Was he pissed when he found out you blew up his car?"

Thinking about my beautiful convertible brought instant feelings of sadness and anger. "I didn't blow up his car, Colonel Wu did. I haven't talked to Tony since it happened, but Max told him. Tony said not to worry about it, these things happen."

"You know, at this rate, you could have stayed with Reno and still have gone out with Max on the side."

"I couldn't do that. I felt guilty when I kissed Max, I wasn't going to try to juggle two boyfriends. I don't know how you do it. You've dated Milo for nine months and you've been with Snake since the summer."

"It's not hard, all you have to do is tell them up front you aren't going to be exclusive. Most guys take it as a challenge to make me so happy I won't want to be with anyone else."

"Is that still working?"

"Pretty much. Saturday, I was with Milo. We drove over to the Boyce Thompson Arboretum, out by Globe."

"How was it? I haven't been there since my fifth-grade class took a field trip."

"It was nice. I'd like to go back sometime. Milo seemed to know all about the history of the place and he knew the names of most of the trees there. For a hired henchman, he keeps surprising me."

"What about Snake? Have you been spending time with him too?"

"He had a game in Glendale yesterday. Snake was able to get me a ticket, so I went. If he could have gotten two tickets, I would have asked you to come along too. But since he's only the third-string quarterback, the number of free seats he gets is kinda limited."

"How was the game? Did he get to play?"

"Well, the Cardinals won, but Snake didn't play. He's only been in for three plays all year. The starting quarterback took a hit in the first quarter and left the game. If he'd gotten a concussion, it would have maybe given Snake a chance to go in for at least a few plays if the second-string quarterback also went down. Unfortunately, the starter wasn't severely injured and was back in by the third quarter."

"That's a shame."

"Yeah, but Snake and I went out after the game, so that part was nice."

"How was it being at the game with all of the football wives?"

"It kinda sucked. It was sorta like being with the cougars, but these women aren't so nice. There's a pecking order based on how much money their husbands got in their last contract. All the wives of the big money players formed a group. Then there was a group of the wives of the guys who were starting, but don't make as much."

"That doesn't sound so great."

"It wasn't. I ended up with the wife of the backup kicker. He's only been in for one play this year, so Snake has him beat. Unfortunately, she's from South Africa and I hardly understood a word she said the entire game."

The door to Lenny's office opened. He stuck his head out and looked at us. "Where's Gina?"

"She's in the back," I said.

"Well, go get her and come in. Sophie, you'd better come in too and take notes, in case there are any more names. I always get lost after three or four names in a new case."

~~~~

We gathered up Gina and we all went into Lenny's office. The client had a drink in her hand and she stood while Lenny made introductions.

She was pretty much as Sophie had described her. She was tall, athletic, and outdoorsy-looking. Her age was somewhere between late thirties and early forties. She had on dusty brown boots, light brown cargo pants, a khaki shirt with big pockets in the front, and a brown leather vest. I'm not sure if she was going for the Indiana Jones look or not, but she had it nailed.

"Professor Parker," Lenny said, "you've already met Gina. This is Laura Black, who's another one of our investigators, and Sophia Rodriguez who's our paralegal. Ladies, this is Professor Parker from the archeology department at Arizona State. We'll be helping her work out some issues around a discovery she's made in the Superstition Mountains."

The woman held out her hand and we shook.

"It's Mindy," she said, "and I'm only an Assistant Professor. It's sort of an honorary title they give to postdocs if they continue to hang out at the university after they get their Ph.D.'s."
~~~~

I got a chance to look at her while she was talking. Her reddish-blonde hair was parted down the middle and hung to her shoulders. She was using her ears to keep it from falling into her face. The only makeup she wore was around her eyes, which were partially hidden behind a pair of big black glasses. She had a lot of sun freckles on her face, something I've seen a lot growing up in Arizona.

She seemed a little out of sorts at being in an attorney's office. A lot of clients seem to feel nervous as they start off on a legal process. I think it's one of the reasons Lenny always gives them drinks. We all sat in front of Lenny's desk and he began to fill us in.

"Dr. Parker seems to have made a rather important archeological discovery in the Superstition Mountains. She's come to us to help her obtain a legal claim to it."

"Did you really find the Lost Dutchman Mine?" Sophie asked.

"Well, maybe," Mindy said. "But if it isn't the actual Lost Dutchman, it's probably close enough not to make a difference."

"Professor," Lenny said, "I'm sorry, but I'm originally from New Jersey. I've heard of the mine, but I don't know a lot about it. Could you give us the short version?"

"Well, the Spanish have been exploring the area since 1540, that's when a Spanish explorer named Coronado led an expedition of two thousand men, along the Arizona-New Mexico border, to search for Cíbola, a land with seven cities of gold. If we skip forward a couple of centuries, the first hard evidence of the mine's existence was in 1748, when the Superstition Mountains were given to a Mexican cattle-baron, Don Miguel Peralta of Sonora. The land reportedly not only contained a rich gold mine, but several silver mines as well. The last official mention of the mine was in 1847, when a descendant of Don Miguel Peralta led an expedition into Arizona. After taking as much gold as could be carried, the group reportedly concealed the entrance to the mine, then began to make their way back to Mexico. The group was attacked, supposedly by the Apache. Most of the group members were killed and the gold was scattered. The area where they were killed is now referred to as the Massacre Grounds."

"I hiked the Massacre Grounds trail with a group back in college," Gina said. "We only got as far as the waterfall, then no one wanted to go any further. I didn't know it had anything to do with the Lost Dutchman mine."

"Ever since the massacre," Mindy continued, "several people claim to have found the location of the mine. The last credible tale was in the 1870's. Jacob Waltz was a German prospector who was apparently shown the location of the mine by an Apache woman he was dating. He spent the next several years coming down from the mountains with large solid nuggets, but he died without telling anyone the mine's location. Locals began calling it the Deutsch-man's Mine, Deutsch meaning German. Of course, over the years it simply became the Lost Dutchman's Mine."

"How many times have you been there?" Lenny asked.

"Twice, so far. When I originally found the cave, it was late in the day and I didn't have more than about twenty minutes to look around. Last week, I spent several hours in the cave, performing mineral surveys and gathering samples. This is an example of what I've managed to find so far. I would assume there's more."

She reached into her pocket and pulled out a shiny piece of gold, about twice as wide as my thumb and as long as my index finger. She held it out and I took it. It was surprisingly heavy for something that wasn't very big. I passed it to Gina, who carefully examined it, then gave it to Sophie. I could see the look of excitement on her face as she felt how heavy it was. After holding it for about ten seconds, Sophie reluctantly placed it on Lenny's desk.

"How valuable is something like that?" Gina asked.

"The piece is a little over ten troy ounces," Mindy said. "In terms of the gold itself, it's about thirteen thousand dollars. But the value to a museum of having a nugget pulled from the Lost Dutchman Mine would likely make it much higher. ASU has an archeology museum and I can envision a themed exhibit with twenty or thirty items in it."

There was a brief stillness in the office as everyone looked down at the lump of solid gold. It was strange but hearing about the gold mine and holding the nugget in my hand seemed to awaken something in me that spoke of adventure and the possibility of sudden wealth.

"Ordinarily," Lenny said, breaking the silence, "obtaining a mineral claim would be a straightforward process. But since the area you're describing has been taken out of public use, we'll need to acquire a treasure-trove permit from the U.S. Forest Service. That will allow you to dig in the wilderness area. However, those aren't granted without verifiable evidence for what will be recovered. In other words, you basically must show them what you're planning on digging up before they'll consider granting you permission to do so. Even with the permit, anything taken out of the wilderness area would likely remain property of the government."

"It's funny," Mindy said. "I've spent years tracking down the mine and it turns out the most difficult part will be the paperwork."

"Have you told anyone else about this discovery?" Lenny asked.

"I've started a petition through the university for an archeological site to be established, so my thesis advisor, Professor Babcock, and the department chairman know about it. Fortunately, setting up a dig site is pretty common, and I was a little vague about what I hoped to find there. Since the university is a state agency, they have a lot of authority when it comes to permitting, even in a wilderness area. I've only told a few close colleagues what I've found, but honestly, everyone in the department knows I've spent years hunting around the Superstitions for treasures, particularly for one called the Lost Sister."

"What's that?" Lenny asked.

"It's one of seven gold statues that were stolen from a temple in southern Mexico back in the 1520's. I've been doing research where I hope to show the Lost Sister is the source of the original curse legend of the Superstition Mountains. But it's a long story and may not have anything to do with what I've found in the cave."

"It would be best if you don't mention this to anyone else until we can establish some legal rights to it," Lenny said. "As part of gathering the verifiable evidence for the permit, it would be helpful if we went up to confirm what you've found. We can then provide an independent validation to your story. The contract we've both already signed contains a non-disclosure clause, so anything we learn from you must be held strictly confidential."

"Alright," Mindy said. "Why don't we meet early tomorrow morning? That way, we can get up to the cave before it gets too hot. The first part of the hike is an easy public trail, but the last part is steep and rocky. I'd suggest we leave here by five-thirty."

Lenny looked at Gina. "Tomorrow will be tough," she said. "I'm booked until at least three o'clock, maybe four."

Lenny then looked at me and I nodded my head. "I shouldn't have any activity on the aerobics instructor until Wednesday. That leaves tomorrow free. Of course, for something like this, I could probably use some extra help." I looked over at Sophie and when Lenny didn't object, Sophie perked up.

"Well, I'm up for it," she said. "I've never been inside a mythical gold mine before."

"Great," Mindy said. She then started counting items on her fingers. "Bring some sturdy hiking boots, a broad brim hat, a bicycle helmet, a day-pack, and a couple of big water bottles for each of you. Stop by a sporting goods store and get a light you can clip onto your helmet. Oh, and bring some leather gloves. It will make the hike easier and when we get up to the cave, we're going to need to move some rocks."

~~~~

Sophie and I drove to the Walmart at Pima and Chaparral. We
~~~~

went down the list and picked up the bicycle helmets, gloves, hats, water bottles, and clip-on lights. I already had a day-pack, but Sophie got a new one. I also remembered to get a fresh bottle of sunscreen and a small first aid kit. We then made sure to put everything on Lenny's credit card.

"I love gearing up for an adventure," Sophie said. "I'm not sure about the helmets though, they sort of give out a creepy danger vibe."

"I'm thinking more about the hike tomorrow," I said. "It's been years since I've crawled around on the mountains. I'll need to dig out my old hiking boots."

"Thanks for reminding me. I'll need to stop by somewhere tonight and get some boots to hike in. I don't think Professor Mindy will be impressed if I show up in my old cross trainers."

~~~~

I dropped Sophie off at the office, then headed back towards my apartment. I stopped by a Filibertos drive-through and got a carne asada burrito and a bag of warm tortilla chips. It filled my car with the wonderful aroma of grilled steak and I munched from the bag of chips the entire way home.

I walked into my apartment and placed the sack on the coffee table in front of my couch, when my phone rang with the old Eurythmics song *Would I Lie to You?* It took me a moment to place the ringtone, then I remembered it was Danielle's. My stomach tightened, and I suddenly wasn't hungry anymore.

I debated whether I should answer it or not. She'd likely want to set up another in a series of meetings where she and I would be negotiating terms of an agreement between the Black Death and Tony's organization. Now that work was starting to get busy again, I really didn't have time for another meeting. Unfortunately, Danielle was the secret head of the Black Death. I couldn't stop the bad news and delaying always made it worse. I hit the accept button.
~~~~

"Laura," Danielle said, "I really need your help. I need somewhere I can hide for a couple of days where no one can find me. I know this is a terrible imposition, but can I stay at your place?"

What?

"How can you even ask something like that? Don't you remember how you left me to die in a torture chamber at the hands of that sick fuck Raul? Why do you think I'd want to help you?"

"I know we have some history, but you're the only person in Arizona I can trust with this. I found out this afternoon Sergio's trying to kill me."

As she was talking, I realized her voice was shaking and it sounded like she was crying.

"Okay," I said. "Start at the beginning."

"Sergio thinks I want to remove him as head of the group. I found out he's going to have me killed and make it look like Tough Tony was the one who did it. Sergio not only wants to consolidate his power in the Black Death, he also wants to use my execution as a pretext to wipe out Tony, Max, and their entire organization."

I'm so going to regret this.

"Where can I meet you?" I asked.

"I'm in the parking lot at Tempe Beach Park."

It figures.

"Okay, I know where you are. Stay there and I'll be down in twenty minutes."

Despite my twisting stomach, I still took three or four bites of the burrito before wrapping it up and popping it into the fridge.

~~~~

When I pulled into Tempe Beach Park, I found Danielle's white Camaro convertible, but she wasn't in it. I parked and walked down
~~~~

toward the lake. The sun was sitting low in the west. It reminded me of the last time I was here, saying goodbye to Digga.

I found Danielle on a stone bench, underneath a mesquite tree, overlooking the water. Three teams of rowers were practicing and she was watching them as they glided across the lake. Next to her on the bench was a big black bag. It reminded me a lot of Tony DiCenzo's personal bodyguard Gabriella and her bag. I knew she carried an Uzi and several pounds of bullets. I imagined Danielle had a similar arsenal in hers. I walked over to the bench and sat next to her.

"I'm sorry," she quietly said. "Maybe I shouldn't have called you. I know you hate me and I understand why. But I didn't know who else I could turn to. Sophie doesn't know who I really am, and I don't want to get her involved in the Black Death."

"I don't hate you," I said. "But you did hurt me, and I was almost killed because of you. I thought we were friends and then everything happened."

Danielle looked up. Her eyes were red, and she looked terrible. She was about to speak when I held up my hand and stopped her.

"You can stay at my place," I said. "I'm not sure why, but we seem to be stuck with each other. I don't want to see anything happen to you."

Danielle didn't say anything, but tears began to roll down her face. Overcome with an emotion I couldn't describe, I held out my arms and Danielle fell against me sobbing.

~~~~

At my suggestion, Danielle dropped her car off in long-term parking at Sky Harbor. She hadn't had dinner yet, so we stopped off at Carolina's Mexican. Even though I still had most of a burrito at home in the fridge, I got a shredded beef burrito, enchilada-style with green chili sauce. I then dumped several cups of their wonderful salsa over the top of it. Neither Danielle nor I said a lot as we ate.
~~~~

~~~~

After dinner, I drove us back to my place. We took the elevator to the third floor, then walked down the hall to my apartment.

I was pulling the keys out of my bag when Grandma Peckham's door opened and she stuck her head out.

"Well, Laura," she said. "I thought I heard you coming down the hall."

Grandma stopped short, seeing Danielle standing next to me. She looked at Danielle, then at me, and then back to Danielle.

"Laura, I didn't think you had a sister," Grandma said.

"Oh, no, I don't," I said. "This is Danielle. She's, um, my cousin from New Mexico. I haven't seen her in years and she'll be here for a few days."

"It's good to meet you," Grandma said. "I'm Mary Peckham, but everyone here calls me Grandma. I've been Laura's neighbor since she moved in. We seem to share a cat and Laura's been helping me with dating advice. Speaking of that, I really need your help with this one. Grandpa Bob proposed to me last night."

"Wow," I said. "That's good news, right?"

"Well, I'm not sure. I really don't want to give up my independence, but I also don't know if I want to live alone for the rest of my life."

"Did you give him an answer?"

"Not yet. I told him I'd need to sleep on it. We're going out on Sunday to meet his kids, so that gives me a few days to decide."

~~~~

I opened the door to my apartment and showed Danielle around. I had some extra sheets and we made up the couch into a bed. I'd often slept on the couch, so I knew it should be comfortable for her.

I went to my junk drawer and pulled out the spare apartment key. As soon as I gave it to Danielle, I knew I'd need to rekey the lock as soon as she moved out.

"I need to be at the office by five-thirty tomorrow morning, so I'll be up early. I'll do my best not to wake you, but I'm not used to having anyone in the apartment. I'm not sure when I'll be back tomorrow night. There isn't a lot of food, so you'll probably have to go out and get something. There's a market two blocks to the north and a bunch of fast food places on Scottsdale Road. They might already be looking for you, so pay with cash. They might be able to trace your credit cards."

"Um, cash?" Danielle stammered.

"No cash?"

"After I found out about Sergio's plans to murder me today, I just left. I have a few dollars in my purse, but that's it. I have money in my bank account, but if you think they could trace the transaction, I shouldn't use my card anywhere around here."

I dug into my purse and pulled out thirty-eight dollars. "This should keep you going until tomorrow night. When I get home, we can drive somewhere and hit up an ATM."

As Danielle flipped through channels on the TV, I spent a few minutes pulling labels off the water bottles, the clip-on light, and the bike helmet. I then filled and tossed both water bottles in the freezer.

I said my goodnights and went into the bedroom. I closed the door and felt annoyed that it didn't have a lock. I tried to think of a better hiding place for my jewelry, other than the box at the top of the closet, but there was nowhere that would be safe if Danielle decided to ransack my room. I briefly considered putting something heavy against the door for the night, but in the end, I left it alone.

~~~~

I crawled into bed and started to get comfortable when my phone
~~~~

rang with the theme to *The Love Boat.*

"Hey you," I said to Max when I answered. "I wasn't sure if you'd be able to call tonight. How's your week starting?"

"It's been busy," he said. As always, hearing his deep and powerful voice both relaxed and excited me. "It's after ten and I'm only now starting to pack up for the night."

"I'm sure Tony appreciates what you're doing."

"He does, but you know how much I'm looking forward to him returning to work. These long hours are starting to wear me down. What's been going on today with you?"

"Well, nothing so far on the cheating spouse, but I'm hoping for a breakthrough on Wednesday. It also looks like I've got a new assignment. This one involves a gold mine."

"Really? We should trade jobs for a few days. All I'm doing tonight is reviewing financial statements."

"I'll take the gold mine. When can we see each other? I'm still disappointed the weekend didn't work out."

"So am I. Right now, it looks like Wednesday for dinner is a possibility. What do you think?"

"I think dinner would make a good start for the evening. Think there'll be time for anything other than dinner? Don't forget, we're a couple now, even if you're only my secret boyfriend. That comes with certain, um, responsibilities on your part."

"I can't wait to fulfill my responsibilities. We need to plan an actual weekend. It's already been a month since we were in San Diego. This weekend doesn't look good, but what about the next?"

"Well, you know my schedule, but yes, let's plan on it. Do you have anywhere in mind?"

"No, but I'm currently in charge of some of the best resorts in Arizona. I'm sure I can find us a room someplace."

Chapter Two

I woke up to the sound of my alarm going off. I felt around on the nightstand until I found the clock and shut it off. I then got up and took a quick shower. When I walked into the living room, Danielle was already up, and she'd made a pot of coffee. I noticed her black bag was sitting on the coffee table, unzipped and within easy reach. It again made me a little uncomfortable thinking about the arsenal she likely had in there.

"I thought you might need this," she said as she poured a cup and handed it to me.

"Thanks," I said. "You know, I can't get involved in anything between you and Sergio, but I was thinking. I'll be out towards Apache Junction today. If you give me your card, I'll stop by an ATM and get you some cash. It should be far enough away to throw anyone off the scent, especially if they haven't found your car at the airport yet. Make sure not to turn your cell phone on, otherwise they'll be able to track you."

Danielle hunted through her purse and handed me a card. "Honestly, it will probably take Sergio a day or two to realize I'm gone. But then, they might do a records search to find out where I've been. If they think I'm hiding in Apache Junction, it'll certainly distract them for a few days."

~~~~

I grabbed the water bottles from the freezer and loaded everything
~~~~

into my pack. I walked down to the lot and used the beeper to unlock my car. Looking at my old beat up vehicle in the parking lot hit me with a fresh wave of sadness. It had been over a month since my beautiful convertible had been destroyed, but it was taking me a long time to get over it. For about the hundredth time, I told myself I'd get a new car, as soon as I could afford it.

~~~~

I drove down to the office and parked in the back. I'd stopped off at McDonald's and got a Sausage McGriddle and another coffee. The sandwich was already gone, but I was still sipping the coffee.

I pulled out the day-pack and headed in. Sophie had beaten me to the office and was up front at her desk, flipping through pages on her tablet. She had a big gas station coffee in front of her and looked like she hadn't gotten a lot of sleep.

"It's too early," she moaned, as I sat in one of the chairs next to her desk.

"How was your night?" I asked.

"I got home about eight and Milo was off work until ten, so we had a quick dinner."

"How was it?"

"It was a little rushed. He brought take-out over to my place and didn't have his clothes back on until after nine-thirty."

"Did you find any hiking boots?"

"Sure did," Sophie said, as she stood up and walked around her desk. She was wearing a pair of bright pink boots with purple laces.

"Hey, those look nice."

"I like them too. They were sort of expensive, but they're real lightweight. They came with boring black laces, so I got something to give them a little color."
~~~~

"Are they comfortable?"

"More or less. I think I'll need to walk around in them for a while. What kind of hike do you think it'll be? I'm hoping for an easy hike."

"I don't know. From the way our client talked, I don't think it'll be easy. I'm only hoping it won't be too hard. I haven't done anything like this in a long time."

There was a knock at the front door to the street. We looked up and saw Professor Mindy waving at us through the glass.

"Didn't I tell you she looks like Indiana Jones?" Sophie asked.

Mindy had on a similar outfit to the one she'd worn the day before, complete with the same leather vest. Today, she was also wearing a broad brimmed leather hat. All she needed was a whip and a pistol hanging from her belt, and the look would have been complete.

I unlocked the door and Mindy briskly walked in. Unlike Sophie and me, she looked alert and had a spring in her step.

"Well ladies," she said. "Are you ready for a hike? Did you both get everything on the list?"

"We're as ready as we're going to get," I said.

"Why don't we take my Jeep," the professor said. "The road's fine, but I already know the way."

"Perfect," I said. "Lead on."

Sophie and I grabbed our packs and headed out the door. Mindy had a dark red Wrangler Unlimited parked directly in front of the office, on the otherwise empty street. I offered to let Sophie take the front, but she said she'd rather have the back and maybe catch a nap before the hike. Mindy then started the Jeep and we took off.

We got on US-60, drove east through Mesa, then into Apache Junction. As we drove, I got a chance to ask some questions about where we were going.

"You said we'll start off on a public trail. Which one is it? Is it the Dutchman's Trail or maybe the Peralta Trail? I've always thought those would be the most likely locations for the mine."

"Yes, you'd think so," Mindy said. "Most of the historic literature describes locations for the mine immediately surrounding Weaver's Needle, which you can most easily get to on the Peralta Trail. But it turns out, those sources had it slightly off. Actually, we'll start off on the Hieroglyphic Trail."

"Really? I've been on that one before. It's pretty up there and it's only about a mile and a half to the petroglyphs. My parents took me up there when I was a kid. How did you ever find the Lost Dutchman's Mine?"

"It's funny," Mindy said. "I wasn't looking for the gold mine, exactly. For the past ten years, I've been looking for an artifact called the Lost Sister. Finding the mine was sort of an accident."

"What's the Lost Sister?" I asked. "Is that what you were talking about in Lenny's office yesterday?"

"Yes, it's mostly a legend. The Seven Sisters are pre-Columbian gold statues from central Mexico, each in the likeness of a different young woman. The story goes that they were stolen from a temple during the original conquests by the Spanish in about 1520. The priestess who oversaw the Sisters laid a curse on the men who possessed the statues. Over the last five hundred years, six of the seven sisters have been found and are in museums."

"And the seventh sister?"

"The legend says the Seventh Sister, along with many gold offerings, were taken north to Santa Fe and buried under the San Miguel Chapel in about 1610. From what I've been able to piece together, the Spanish thought keeping the Sister in a church, far away from where it originally came from, would stop the curse. In 1640, there was a landowners' revolt in the area around Santa Fe. The Spanish ordered everything of value in the chapel be moved to a safer location. A group of a hundred and fifty men of faith were given instructions to go deep into the wilderness and hide the statue where no one could ever again find it."

"Well, what happened to it?"

"No one knows for sure. It seems to have disappeared. 1640 is the last record of it even existing. But I'll tell you what I suspect once we get up to the cave."

We stayed on the Superstition Freeway until a few miles east of Apache Junction, then we turned north into the village of Gold Canyon. We snaked our way up King's Ranch Road until we got to Cloudview Avenue. The trailhead was a large paved parking lot where the road came to a dead end to the east. As we pulled into the lot, the sun climbed over the eastern horizon.

Although I'd assumed we'd be the only car in the lot, there were already four sedans and a van. Mindy parked away from the others and we climbed out. Sophie had fallen asleep on the drive and was still a little groggy.

We stood next to the car and smeared on sunblock. We then grabbed our day-packs from the Jeep and slowly pulled them on. I wasn't used to wearing a pack and it seemed heavy. Mindy slipped on a much larger pack and this seemed to energize her.

"That's a big pack," I said. "What's in it?"

"Oh, a little of everything. Mostly things for when we get to the cave. But I also have some first-aid and emergency gear, just in case. And I always carry some climbing equipment, but we shouldn't need anything like that for this trip."

Sophie's eyes grew wide at the mention of climbing equipment, but she didn't say anything.

"Are we ready?" Mindy asked. She had a broad grin and you could tell she was ready for an adventure. I nodded my head and Sophie gave out a small moan.

"Alright, put on your hats and follow me," Mindy said. With that, she briskly walked through the parking lot and onto the dirt trail.

~~~~

As I remembered from hiking this as a kid, the trail was relatively flat as it wound toward a wide valley called Hieroglyphic Canyon. The trail gradually became steeper the farther we went.

As we walked, Mindy gave us a lecture on the petroglyphs and the history of the people who were thought to have made them.

"A petroglyph is simply a carving in rock or stone," she said, sounding like a professor lecturing to a room full of students. "Ancient people all over the world made them. Sometimes they did it for art, sometimes to tell their history, and sometimes for religious purposes. The petroglyphs we'll be seeing today are thought to be carved by the ancient Hohokam Indians, who lived in this part of the desert until about five-hundred years ago. They carved hundreds of petroglyphs into the basalt cliffs above the pools, about a third of the way up the canyon, some with very intricate designs."

After Mindy's talk, we walked in silence. As the walls of the canyon gradually rose on either side, the trail became steeper, and the valley began to narrow. Fortunately, temperatures were still in the seventies and it was a beautiful morning for a hike.

After about an hour, we came to the petroglyphs. They were carved onto a small cliff-face above several wide rock basins. I'd never seen any water in the pools before, but thanks to some rains the week before, most of them were full. There was a trickle of water from a small stream that seemed to be keeping them filled.

I was surprised we weren't the only ones who'd made it here so early in the morning. There was a group of five ladies who seemed to be in some sort of hiking club. They all had on a similar green T-shirt with a picture of a boot with a pair of wings on it. There was a couple with their two children, a boy and a girl. The kids were happily climbing on the low flat rocks surrounding the pool while the parents
~~~~

looked on. On the far side of the pool, near the petroglyphs, was a man who was quietly sitting in a shady spot and appeared to be deep into a book on his Kindle.

Mindy found a flat rock for us to sit on and everyone took off their packs. Although the hike hadn't been hard, my heart was beating at a quick pace and my throat was dry. I pulled out a water bottle and enough of it had already melted for a good drink. I noticed Sophie was doing the same.

"Well, the hike wasn't so bad," Sophie said. "It's nice up here. You know, now that I have these new boots, maybe we should go hiking more often. I bet Snake would like to come up here and walk around in the mountains. It would be good conditioning for football."

After about five minutes, Sophie and I both had our phones out and were walking around taking pictures. We took several of the petroglyphs, which mostly seemed to be in the shapes of animals.

Mindy got up and asked if we were ready. Sophie and I came back to the rock and pulled on our packs. My heart rate had slowed down to normal, but I noticed my pack seemed to have gotten heavier.

~~~~

The wide and well-used trail quickly faded as we continued up the valley. Instead of looking around at the canyon as we walked, I now had to look down at my feet to see where I was stepping. A hundred yards from the petroglyphs, we had to start picking our way around rocks as we walked up the streambed in the middle of the canyon. Not having an easy trail to follow slowed us down, but I was grateful for that. The way had become noticeably steeper and it wasn't long before my heart was again pounding away.

After half a mile of winding through rocks, Mindy stopped and looked back at us. I noticed she wasn't even breathing hard and she still had a look of quiet enthusiasm.

"We're near the spring that's the source of the water for the pools down the canyon. That's where the trail ends. But instead of going up
~~~~

to the spring, we're going off-trail."

You call this a trail?

Mindy opened her pack and pulled out a worn pair of leather gloves. "After we cross over the stream, the going will get slow and steep. We'll be doing some scrambling over boulders, so you might want to put on your gloves."

Sophie and I obediently took our gloves from the packs and put them on. Sophie glanced up the steep mountain, then gave me a look that said she was hoping maybe Mindy was kidding.

Mindy turned to the left, we stepped over the trickle of a stream, and started up a steep and rocky ravine. As she promised, there wasn't any sort of trail and we were mostly scrambling up over large rocks and piles of loose pebbles. The spaces between the rocks were dotted with cacti and creosote bushes, which were just as hard to go around.

"By the way," Mindy said as she took a couple of bouncy steps up the ravine. "You'll often find rattlesnakes here in the canyons. They like to curl up under overhanging rocks. Even though you're wearing gloves, watch where you stick your hands."

What?

I was a few steps ahead of Sophie and I looked back at her. Her eyes had gotten big and she looked a little pale. I had the feeling I probably looked much the same.

~~~~

After twenty minutes of scrambling up the ravine, which Sophie had dubbed the *Gully of Death*, Mindy halted us at a large flat rock.

I took off my pack and pulled out a water bottle. It was mostly melted, and I took several large swallows. My heart was pounding, and my head was spinning. I hadn't exercised this hard in years and I was starting to think I'd feel better if I spent a few minutes throwing up. I looked over at Mindy. She didn't seem to be affected and wasn't
~~~~

even breathing hard.

I looked at Sophie, who was also panting and trying to recover. I pointed to Mindy with my eyes and Sophie also saw the professor wasn't at all tired.

"Why aren't you out of breath?" Sophie gasped at her. "We just climbed up a frickin' mountain. I've got sweat running down into my butt-crack."

"I don't know," Mindy said. "I've been hiking and climbing these mountains for years, usually two or three times a week. I guess you get used to it after a while."

As our hearts began to recover, Sophie and I took in the view. We could see most of the way down the canyon. The pools in front of the petroglyphs were visible, as were the people. The couple with the kids had gone, but it looked like the ladies with the green shirts and the guy with the Kindle had decided to hike up to the spring at the top of the canyon. We could see them slowly snaking their way up the same path we'd used twenty minutes before.

~~~~

After five minutes, Sophie and I had recovered to the point where we were ready to continue. We put our packs on and Mindy began to bounce up the gully while we slowly followed.

At one point, I looked back at Sophie. From the look on her face, I knew she was unhappy she'd volunteered to come along and was becoming more unhappy with each steep step. Honestly, I was feeling much the same way.

After another ten minutes of scrambling over boulders and trying to avoid both cacti and rattlesnakes, we'd made it to within about fifty yards of the top of the gully. Mindy then turned to the left and began to follow the hill in a direction that didn't seem to lead anywhere.

We scrambled along a flat part of the mountain for about a
~~~~

hundred yards, then found our way blocked by a steep cliff.

We approached the cliff from the side, then looked down. The cliff face was a shear drop of at least a hundred feet. Mindy scampered onto a small rock shelf, about four feet wide, which went from one side of the cliff to the other. The shelf was more or less flat, but some parts had eroded away until the shelf was only about three feet wide. It was covered in sand and small pebbles, which made the footing look slippery at best.

"Be especially careful along this part," Mindy called back to us as she quickly walked across the cliff face. "It's easy to lose your footing and it's a long way down. I probably should have mentioned this part of the hike before now. I hope neither of you are afraid of heights."

I looked behind me and noticed Sophie had grown a shade or two paler.

"Oh, hell no," Sophie said as she took a step back. "I didn't think we'd be doing a Spiderman-thing on the side of a frickin' cliff."

"Sophie, you can't stop now. I can't do this alone. Besides, don't you want to see the mine and all the gold?"

"You know, I'm losing interest in the gold pretty quickly. Besides, if it's this much of a pain in the ass to get to, I don't see how great of a mine it could be. I can't see prospectors bringing donkeys and equipment and stuff up to the mine like this."

"I don't either, but you can't stay here. There's no guarantee we'll even come back this way. You'd have to go down all by yourself."

"Fine, but if I fall off this cliff, I want you to promise you'll go down and haul me out before the vultures start to feast on my bloating carcass."

"Fine, I promise."

Keeping as close to the cliff face as possible, Sophie and I inched our way along the narrow rock ledge. Where Mindy had walked across the cliff face in a dozen purposeful strides, Sophie and I kept our backs to the rock wall and walked across with jerky crablike side steps. After what seemed like ten or fifteen minutes of inching along the cliff, we got to the other side, where Mindy was patiently waiting for us.

"The hard part's over," she said. "We'll follow this ravine up to the notch and we'll be at the top." She pointed up to a keyhole shaped cut-out, along a rocky ridge at the end of another cacti filled gully.

Finally, after another ten minutes of hard scrambling, we made it to the notch. It turned out to be a saddle on a ridgeline between peaks, maybe a hundred feet higher on either side. We stopped and again pulled out our water bottles.

As my heart rate slowed, I looked around. The view was incredible. We were overlooking a long canyon running roughly east to west. Like a small version of the Matterhorn, Weaver's Needle could be seen to the northeast, poking over the far wall of the canyon below.

"Wow," Sophie said as she pulled out her phone. "It's beautiful up here."

"That's Hog Valley below us," Mindy said. "There's a direct route up to the cave from there. I'm pretty sure it's the path everyone used to get up to the mine, but honestly, it's more work to go that way."

"You're saying our way was easy?" Sophie asked.

From the top of the ridge, we climbed down a small ravine, which for once didn't have cacti or a lot of loose rock. After only about fifty or sixty yards of scrambling over boulders, there was an overhanging rock on the side of the gully. Mindy headed for it. She stopped and took off her pack. She then extracted a professional looking Nikon and took several pictures of the rocks. It didn't look like anything was there, but she set the camera down and moved a bush and a couple of rocks. Like magic, a hole suddenly appeared, maybe four feet high. She picked up the camera and again took several pictures.

Mindy replaced the camera, then took out a dented green helmet that had a large light attached to it. "Let me go in first," she said.

"The cave is an ideal site for snakes and some of the other desert critters."

She disappeared into the hole, holding her backpack in front of her. Sophie and I took off our packs, took out our water bottles, then looked at each other.

"I'm not having a lot of fun," Sophie said as she took a long drink. "In case you were wondering."

"Hey, you volunteered. I didn't think we'd be doing this either. I still feel like throwing up after climbing up the mountain."

"I can already feel my legs starting to tighten up," Sophie said. "I'm going to feel like crap tomorrow."

Mindy stuck her head out of the hole. "It's all clear. Put on your helmets, turn on your lights, then come on in."

With that, she disappeared back into the cave.

"Well?" Sophie asked.

I opened my backpack, took out the bicycle helmet, and attached the clip-on light to it. Sophie did the same. We both set our packs next to the entrance, then we bent down and crawled into the cave.

For about ten yards, it was a scramble on hands and knees as I tried not to hit my head on the bits of rock hanging out at odd angles. As we continued forward, the walls on either side opened up and the ceiling started to rise. In another twenty feet, I couldn't distinctly see either the walls or the ceiling with the weak light from my headlamp, but I got the sense they were far away.

"Wow," Sophie said behind me. "This place is huge. Not Kartchner Caverns huge, but still pretty damn big."

The floor of the cave was at a slight downhill slant, with the black rocks forming an uneven and broken surface, which disappeared into the darkness. Mindy's light was about thirty yards ahead and we slowly made our way over to her.

"This is amazing," I said.

"You think it's nice now?" Mindy asked. "Give me a second and I'll show you something."

We pointed our lights down to see what she was doing. Apparently, she'd been stringing a long strand of lights out along the floor of the cave. The light string went back as far as the beam from my helmet light would go.

"Get ready," Mindy said.

There was a soft snap as Mindy turned on a switch. The cave was suddenly filled with light.

"Holy crap!" Sophie yelled out.

I sucked in some air and looked around. The cave was bigger than I originally thought. The room we were in was fifty feet wide and at least a hundred feet long. The end of the cave disappeared into darkness, so it could have been much longer. The ceiling had to be thirty feet over our heads. Everything was the same black rock as we'd been seeing all along our hike, but here in the cave it seemed to sparkle.

"This is an old lava tube," Mindy said. "It's similar to the Lava River Cave, up by Flagstaff. It was formed back when this was part of a volcano that covered the entire region. When the lava drained out, it left this tube. It goes back for almost half a mile before it stops. If it had gone on another two-hundred feet or so, it would have gone straight through the mountain and come out the other side."

"You're the geologist," Sophie said. "But I didn't think there's a lot of gold in lava tubes. Aren't they mostly lava and stuff?"

"Basalt," Mindy said, "mixed in with layers of ash as well. You're right about the gold though. From a geological perspective, the Superstition Mountains aren't an area you'd expect to find gold. But what has me excited is this." She motioned us over to one of the walls, about twenty yards from where we were standing. Carved into the rock was a small cross. It was unusual in that each of the four ends of the cross were flared out with three bumps. The carving was maybe twelve inches high by eight inches wide. It looked like it had been there a long time. Mindy had her camera out and was again taking pictures.

"This particular style is a typical Spanish cross of the sixteenth and seventeenth centuries," she said. "I don't think any of the ancient Native American tribes had anything to do with putting that on the wall. I think the cross was carved by Spanish missionaries, probably around the year 1641 or 1642."

"Missionaries?" I asked. "In Arizona? Four hundred years ago?"

"Missionary isn't the right word," Mindy said. "I believe this expedition was sent into the wilderness to get rid of something."

"Your Lost Sister?" I asked.

"Yes. I'll tell you the story after we get back off the mountain."

"Well, there're a few things on the ground," I said as I walked around the cave and pointed things out. "But I've only seen bits of broken wood, some scraps of rope, and a couple of pieces of leather. I don't see anything here that looks like Spanish treasure."

"There's also a rusted kerosene lantern toward the end of the lava tube," Mindy said. "Most of the pieces in here are from the eighteenth and nineteenth centuries. I think people have been coming into the cave ever since the Spanish left and have taken away whatever they could find. It would explain how gold could be found in a region where a geologist would tell you there shouldn't be any."

"Well, I don't see anything in here now," Sophie said. "Unless there's something farther back, this cave is pretty empty."

"It looks like it," Mindy said. "But look at this area of dirt on the floor of the cave." She pointed with her headlamp to a patch of dirt about five feet across.

"You see it now, don't you?"

"See what?" Sophie asked. "It's dirt. There's dirt all over this cave."

"Yes, but don't you see? There shouldn't be dirt in a lava tube. Where would it have come from?"

"I don't know," Sophie said. "Dirt town?"

"I took a sample back with me last time and analyzed it," Mindy said. "It's soil from the bajada, the alluvial plain at the base of Hog Canyon."

Sophie and I looked at her. We both heard the words, but I didn't see what it had to do with the dirt we were looking at.

"This dirt wasn't originally found in the cave," Mindy said. "Somebody hauled it up from the valley floor."

"Why would they do that?" Sophie asked. "It's a frickin' long way to haul dirt."

"Well," Mindy said. "It's what we're here to find out. But looking at the area around the dirt, I think there's likely a pocket in the rock that goes down three or four feet. There's a couple of similar gas pockets toward the end of the lava tube. It doesn't appear the dirt in the pocket's been disturbed since it was first brought up here. Given the probable history of the cave, I'm excited to think what we might find buried in it."

Mindy walked to her pack and dug into it. She brought out three small gardening shovels, each about a foot long.

"I didn't have these the last time I was here. All I had was a small metal geology pick and shovel. These shovels are made from a special plastic. They're strong, but they won't scratch anything they hit. Last time, I turned over a few shovels of dirt and found the nugget I showed you in the office. Today, we're going to dig down and see what else is there."

Mindy took out a clear plastic sheet and laid it on the ground next to the dirt. "Make sure all of the dirt ends up on the plastic," she said. I'll need to come up with some of my students from the university and do a proper survey of the soil we pull up."

We all sat next to the patch of soil and started digging with the tiny shovels. We spent about ten minutes pushing our plastic shovels through the hard dirt before we found anything. Sophie was using the side of her shovel to scrape away the hard dirt, when she uncovered something shiny.

"Damn," she said, excitement rising in her voice. "I found something. I think it's gold!"

Mindy took some pictures, then we all started scraping away with our shovels. We soon pulled out a nugget of what appeared to be solid gold. This one was about the size and shape of a large radish or maybe a small potato. We each took turns holding the nugget, which was surprisingly heavy.

We set it aside on the plastic and kept digging. We'd apparently uncovered the main layer of gold. Each shovel full seemed to pull out something. Most of the chunks were big, but some were small, barely the size of a pea. In the next twenty minutes, we'd found sixty or seventy large nuggets and a big pile of the smaller ones. This had us excited, but then there was nothing.

We eventually scraped down another foot of the hard dirt without finding anything else. From the exasperated sounds Sophie was making, I knew she'd lost interest in going a lot further.

After another ten or fifteen minutes of digging and scraping, my hands were getting sore and I was also losing enthusiasm. I was about to say something, when my shovel scraped against something that wasn't dirt. Mindy and Sophie heard the sound and we all perked up.

"That sounds like wood," Mindy said. She took out a big brush and started brushing away dirt from the wood. After three or four minutes, the outlines of a wooden box had become visible.

"Let's uncover it, but try not to touch the wood with your shovels.

The cave is dry, but this has likely been here for almost four-hundred years."

We spent the next twenty minutes carefully scraping and brushing. Every few minutes, Mindy had us pause while she took pictures with the big Nikon. Eventually all the dirt had been removed from around the chest and we were down to solid rock. Mindy then carefully lifted out the box and set it on the plastic.

The chest was about the size of a large shoe box. It was made of a dark wood with rough metal hinges and an oversized metal padlock. Carved into the top of the chest was a cross, which looked to be an exact duplicate to what had been carved into the wall. Mindy took pictures of it from several angles, then had us roll it over so she could take pictures of the back.

"Look at the patina on the lock and on the hinges," Mindy said with admiration. "From the design of the lock, I'd say the chest is seventeenth century Spanish New World. I believe this is what I've been searching for. It's been almost ten years, but I really think this could be it."

"Your Lost Sister?" I asked.

"Yes," Mindy said, with a huge smile. "At least I'm hopeful it is."

"Um, didn't you say there's a curse on the thing in the box?" Sophie asked, sounding a little uneasy.

"Well, yes. According to the legend, any man who possesses the stolen gold statues will be cursed and suffer a terrible fate at the hands of the gods."

"Okay, that doesn't sound so good. Aren't you worried we've dug it up? Do you think it's a good idea to take it out of the cave? Should we even be touching it? Even touching it sounds like tempting the spirits."

"When it comes to religion, I try not to judge," Mindy said. "Who's to say which religion is the correct one? Maybe they're all true. As far as the religious curses go, I sort of roll with them and so far, I've been alright."

"Well," Sophie said. "Hopefully you'll stay lucky."

"Are we going to open it up?" I asked.

"Yes, but not here," Mindy said, sounding a little shocked at the suggestion. "We'll need to go through a process to remove the lock without damaging it. Before we do anything, I'll need to analyze the chest. We'll need to get an exact age of the wood and take some scans of the interior. We'll also need to get together with Leonard and straighten out the permits on this. I've probably already over-extended what I'm allowed to do here without the necessary paperwork. I'll also need to get the university more involved on the dig permits. But I think we've already made the major discovery from this site. I don't think Professor Babcock will be able to overshadow me on this."

"Okay," I said. "What next?"

"Let's take it outside," Mindy said. "I'd like to get some pictures in the daylight. Then we can come back and pack up. As soon as we get the archeological and treasure-trove permits, I'll come back with some grad students and we can perform a full site survey."

When we got outside, it was so bright I couldn't see for a minute. Mindy had Sophie and I hold the box while she picked up her camera and started snapping pictures. Sophie then took the camera and had Mindy pose in front of the cave opening, holding the chest. The professor had a huge smile as she held the chest over her head.

"Nobody move!" shouted out a deep male voice. "I have a gun and it would be a shame to shoot anyone. Professor, put the chest down, gently."

Scrambling down from the overhanging rock was a man wearing dark shorts, a dark T-shirt, and a broad brimmed khaki hat. I recognized him as the guy from the petroglyphs who had been reading a Kindle. Apparently, he'd followed us all the way up the mountain. With our colorful backpacks sitting next to the cave entrance, it wouldn't have made us hard to find. He was holding what looked like a nine-millimeter semi-automatic pistol.

"Professor," he said, "I'll take the box. I assume the statue's in it? The one you've been looking for? Put it in one of the backpacks sitting there, then step away."

"Who are you?" Mindy asked. "Who sent you? How'd you know I'd be here?"

"That's not important," the man said. "Put the case in one of the backpacks. Right now."

Mindy didn't move. She'd obviously never encountered a man with a gun before, especially one who wanted to take away a newly found treasure.

The man fired off a shot. At close range, the sound was deafening, and everyone jumped. The bullet ricocheted off a rock next to Mindy and left a long white mark on it. The sound of the gunshot echoed back to us several times as it bounced off the canyon walls.

"The next one goes into your knee, Professor. Then, I'll start shooting your friends until I get what I want."

Mindy picked up my pack, pulled out a few loose things, and then slowly slid the chest inside. It was a tight fit, but she even managed to zip it shut. She then took two steps forward and set it on a rock in front of the guy. He waved her back with the pistol and stepped forward. He carefully reached down and picked up the backpack by one of the straps.

"Now," he said. "Everyone go back in the cave and stay there for half an hour. If I see anyone sticking her head out before then, or if I see you trying to follow me, I'll shoot you. No warnings. Just bang and you're dead. Am I clear?"

We all nodded our heads and started back towards the cave. Before we went in, I had a thought and gave Sophie her backpack. We scrambled into the main room and stood there. The lights were still on, but after being outside they seemed rather dull. Mindy had a look on her face that was easy to read. It was a look of being pissed-off along with a deep sadness. I knew her mind must be racing, looking for a way to get back what was stolen.

"Did you recognize the man?" I asked.

"I've never seen him before," Mindy said.

"How did he know about the statue? Who else did you tell about what was up here?"

"I only told a few colleagues about it, but I totally trust them. Unfortunately, I told one friend about it in the university cafeteria, so anybody could have overheard. In fact, there were several people from my department sitting nearby. It was stupid of me."

"I'd like to follow him down and see which vehicle he came in," I said. "If we hurry, maybe we can even follow him back into town."

"But it hasn't even been five minutes," Mindy said. "He said he'd shoot us."

"Yeah," Sophie said. "Losing the box is bad enough but getting shot would really make the day suck. Hey, did you bring your gun? It would really come in handy about now."

"Well, I did," I said. "But, um, it's in the backpack. In the front pocket."

Even in the dim light, I could see Sophie was giving me a look.

"Hey, how was I supposed to know? Look, stay here if you want to, but I'm going after him. I doubt he's waiting around outside. He already has what he wants. I'm sure he's already scrambling down the other side of the mountain as fast as he can."

"You're right," Mindy said. "I'm not thinking straight. We can leave everything here. Let's go after him."

"Um, what about the gold?" Sophie asked. "You know, it's

probably not a good idea to leave a pile of gold sitting out like this. It might not be there the next time you come back."

"I was thinking the same thing," I said. "If one person knows about this, there're likely others."

"You're probably right," Mindy said, looking down at the pile of nuggets. "But we must have pulled out fifty or sixty pounds. There's only two packs left. I can take most of it, but one of you will still need to take ten or fifteen pounds.

Sophie moaned, then started dumping things out of her backpack and scooping in the gold. Mindy was doing the same. We quickly filled the packs and ended up stuffing handfuls of the smaller nuggets into the pockets of our shorts. We then spent several minutes making sure all the zippers and flaps of the various pockets of the packs were shut, so nothing would fall out as we walked back to the Jeep.

After ten minutes, we were done. The cave floor was still littered with equipment, but the gold was safely packed away. Mindy then switched off the lights. The cave again became very dark as the only lights were coming from our helmet clip-ons. It was awkward for Mindy and Sophie, trying to carry the packs, which were now stuffed with gold. We eventually scrambled out to the cave entrance and I had everyone stop.

"I'm pretty sure I'm right about him being gone and not waiting out there to shoot us," I said, "but I'd better go first anyway. You know, um, in case I'm wrong."

Chapter Three

I got to the bright opening and let my eyes get adjusted before I went any further. I then slowly stepped out and looked at the places I would hide if I wanted to ambush someone exiting the cave. I was ready to jump back in at the first sign of movement, but the man wasn't anywhere in sight. I knew he only had a pistol, which would be ineffective at a range greater than about thirty or forty yards.

"It's clear," I called back into the cave.

Sophie and Mindy crawled out and blinked in the bright light for several seconds.

We started to scramble up the gully. Mindy didn't seem to have any trouble with the added weight, but Sophie occasionally staggered under the load. By the time we made it up to the notch, Sophie and I were both again gulping air.

We peeked over the side of the hill, but the thief wasn't in sight.

"Sophie," I said, as we waited for our hearts to slow down. "Let me know when you've had enough of the pack and we can switch off. I know it's heavy."

"You got that right, but I'm okay. Besides, it's all downhill from here."

We started down the other side but had to slow our descent to scramble over the boulders and avoid the cacti. The day was getting warm and I was again starting to feel a little light headed at the exertion.

After only about five minutes, we'd made it to the cliff face. In the excitement of the moment, I'd completely forgotten about the narrow rock ledge. Now that we were here, I stopped thinking about the creep with the gun. My main concern became the dangerous crossing.

Mindy went first and briskly walked onto the ledge.

As she crossed, I looked down the cliff face. As I did, I spotted something bright. "Hey," I yelled out. "There's something on the rocks down there."

Mindy was about halfway across, at the narrowest part of the shelf, when she stopped and looked down. "Come on out. You can see it from here."

Sophie and I slowly walked out onto the ledge and did our sideways crabwalk thing to where Mindy was standing. When we got there, we carefully looked down to where she was pointing.

My backpack was on a rock, about twenty feet directly below where we were standing. It didn't look like it was very stable. In fact, I was surprised it hadn't already slid down the cliff.

"What's your backpack doing down there?" Sophie asked.

I glanced further down the cliff and found the answer. "Look," I said, pointing another twenty yards below the backpack. "I see a hat."

The man's broad brimmed hat was tangled up on a bush sticking out from the side of the cliff. The man was nowhere to be seen.

"Holy crap," Sophie said. "He must have fallen all the way to the bottom."

"How far down does the cliff go?" I asked. "From here it's hard to tell."

"We can see about a hundred feet of it from here," Mindy said. "Past the ridge there's at least another fifty feet. That part isn't exactly sheer, but it's still pretty steep."

"Where does it end up?"

"We're above the Hieroglyphic Valley, so he probably landed somewhere between the petroglyphs and the spring. I don't see how he could have survived."

"That's so gross," Sophie said. "Can you imagine it? You're out for a nice hike with the family, when a guy suddenly falls from the sky and lands on the rocks in front of you. You know, like splat and everything."

We stood there, looking down at the backpack for almost a minute.

"Um, can we get to the other side before we figure out what to do?" Sophie asked, a touch of panic in her voice. "I'm starting to feel a little lightheaded standing here looking down the side of the mountain and the gold in the backpack isn't helping anything."

We inched our way to the safety of the far side of the cliff. Sophie and Mindy stripped off their loads, then we again looked down at the backpack on the cliff.

"I don't think it'll be long before it slides off the rock it's on," I said. "We've got to figure out a way to get it now. You said you always carry climbing gear. Do you still have any of it?"

"Some," Mindy said. "But we took out most of it to make room for the gold."

Sophie found a rock to sit on while Mindy and I sorted through her pack. After about five minutes, we had a small pile of rope and equipment sitting on a flat rock.

"Well," Mindy said. "We left a lot of it back at the cave, but we still have a couple of climbing harnesses, a few carabiners, some pitons, a hammer, several cams, and some rope. Climbing down shouldn't be a problem."

"Do you always carry that much stuff around with you?" Sophie asked.

"Pretty much," Mindy said. "It doesn't weigh a lot and I'm always using it. It sits at the bottom of the pack for whenever I need it."

"Well, great," I said. "You can climb down and get the backpack before it disappears off the side of the cliff. Maybe this will all work out okay after all."

"Um," Mindy said. "About that. I was looking at the cliff. The backpack is only twenty or twenty-five feet down, but there aren't any handholds for climbing. It's a smooth rock face the entire way down. Whoever goes down will need to be pulled back up."

Whoever goes down? Shit.

"I can set it up for a safe climb," Mindy said. "But I'm going to need to stay on the ledge to belay the climber."

Mindy's words seemed to soak in and Sophie's eyes suddenly got big. "Oh, shit no, don't even think about me. I get lightheaded just looking over the side of a cliff. I'm not going to dangle off the side of a freaking mountain like some sort of spider on a web."

With a sinking feeling, I knew what was about to happen. Once I realized it was inevitable, I tried my best to embrace it.

"I'll do it," I said.

Shit.

"Oh, thank God," Sophie said. She quickly realized what she was saying and looked at me. "Um, don't worry. I'm sure you'll do great."

Mindy spent the next fifteen minutes on the ledge, pounding things into the cliff and stringing ropes. She then came back, holding a climbing harness. My heart sank lower as she fastened the straps of the harness around my body.

"You'll do fine," Mindy said. "The area where Sophie and I will be standing is ideal for setting anchors. I've set four lines and they're all supporting each other."

"Um, did you say Sophie and I?" Sophie asked. "You want me to stand out there, on that teeny-tiny ledge, on the side of a shear drop off, and do something safety related?"

"I won't be able to pull Laura up by myself. I have the ropes set up to make it as easy as possible, but I'll need you to be there as well. I have a firm anchor directly behind where you'll be standing and I'll have you attached to the cliff as well. You won't be able to fall."

Mindy took the second harness and started strapping it onto Sophie. From the look on her face, Sophie didn't care how many anchors Mindy had set.

While Sophie was getting ready, I opened her backpack and took out the two helmets. I walked over and handed one to her.

"Don't worry," I said. "I'm sure you'll do great."

"You know, if I fall off that cliff, I'll be so pissed at you," Sophie said. "I could be sitting in the office right now, sipping a peppermint mocha from the shop across the street. Instead, I'm up here on the side of an effing cliff getting strapped up so I don't get pitched off the side as I haul your butt back up. I'm not sure how, but you'll owe me after this."

"Fine, I'll owe you. Get strapped up and lower me down."

Mindy carefully led Sophie out to the center of the ledge. She spent about five minutes attaching her harness to several of the ropes she'd set up. She then came back for me.

"Are you okay?" she asked.

"No, but let's get this over with."

We inched our way to the center of the ledge and Mindy spent several minutes attaching ropes and carabiners to the harness.

"I've rigged it up so you don't have to do anything. Try to keep facing the cliff. I'll lower you alongside of the backpack, so all you'll need to do is reach out for it. You can even keep your eyes closed if you want. All I ask is you don't spin."

"Don't spin?"

"Spinning is bad. It messes up the ropes so we won't be able to pull you back up."

"Right, no spinning. Good safety tip."

"Starting will be the hard part. Sit on the ledge with your legs hanging over, then slowly slide down. Once you're off the ledge, turn around so you're facing the rock. We'll then lower you down, you'll grab the backpack, and we'll pull you back up. Easy peasy lemon squeezy."

With Mindy holding the ropes above my head, I carefully sat on the ledge. I peered over the edge and the backpack looked to be a very long way down. As I looked at the shear rockface of the cliff, it didn't feel so easy peasy to me.

I felt the ropes go taut as both Mindy and Sophie got into position. With a nod from Mindy, I slowly let myself slide off the ledge. There was a moment of panic as I dangled in mid-air, suspended by the ropes.

"Turn and face the cliff," Mindy called out.

It took me a minute to figure out exactly how to turn, but as Mindy lowered me, I was eventually able to use my arms and legs to face the cliff. Foot by foot, they gradually lowered me. It seemed like I was going down a lot farther than twenty feet. Every time they lowered me a foot, I got a small panic attack. I then got another one every time the rope jerked me to a stop.

After what seemed like a long time, I stopped going down.

"Alright," Mindy called out. "Look to your left."

I looked and saw the backpack, about three feet away from me. I carefully stretched out my hand and grabbed one of the shoulder straps. I pulled it toward me, but it seemed to be caught on something.

"It's stuck," I called out.

"See if you can loosen it," Mindy called back.

I pulled and tugged on the strap, but the other shoulder strap was looped around a piece of rock.

"Lift me up a little," I cried out. "I need to get the other strap off a piece of rock."

I felt myself being lifted in short jerky movements.

"Okay," I yelled out. "That should do it."

I again pulled on the strap, but the backpack was still attached to the rock.

Damn it.

With a massive yank, coming mostly from adrenaline and panic, there was the sound of fabric tearing and the backpack came free. Unfortunately, with the release of the backpack, I rebounded out into space and started spinning.

"Don't spin!" I distantly heard Mindy cry out.

With my free hand and my legs, I was able to stop the spinning and again face the cliff. Unfortunately, I'd already gone around two or three times.

"Hold on," Mindy called down. "Let me see how bad it is."

I closed my eyes and waited. I seemed to slightly bounce up and down a couple of times, but I didn't move up at all.

"You're badly tangled," Mindy shouted down. "You're going to need to rotate back around, at least once, maybe twice."

Shit.

"Don't worry," she said, "I'll talk you through it. First, clip the backpack to a carabiner, so you don't drop it."

That part made sense and Mindy's voice was calm and reassuring. I opened my eyes and looked down at the backpack. The zipper was still closed, and it looked like it still had the box inside of it. The pack had a nylon web loop near the top. I used this to clip onto a carabiner on my harness.

"Okay," Mindy called. "Now use your right arm and leg to push hard at the same time. That should do it."

"Easy peasy?" I asked.

"That's right," Mindy replied. "Easy peasy."

I took a breath and pushed with my right arm and leg at the same time. I felt myself launch into space, then the world again started to spin. Within about three or four seconds, I'd crashed back against the side of the cliff.

"You did great," Mindy called out. "Now, do the exact same thing one more time."

You've gotta be kidding me.

Without stopping to think about it, I pushed out again. One more time, the world spun, and I crashed against the side of the mountain. I closed my eyes and waited to see what would happen next.

With a lurch, I felt myself being lifted a foot or so. "It seems alright now," Mindy called out. "We'll have you up in no time."

The rope jerked me up another foot and this process was repeated several times.

"You know," Sophie called down to me as I was jerked up another foot. "You weigh a freaking ton. You could have taken the gold out of your pockets before you went over the side."

When I got to the ledge, both Mindy and Sophie grabbed me by the harness and lifted me onto the ledge. When I realized my feet were on solid rock again, I spent a minute or two breathing hard and shaking.

"See," Mindy said. "You both did great. Let's get you two across to the other side and I'll come back and remove the equipment."

Mindy unclipped the backpack and held it by one of the shoulder straps. The three of us walked to the far side and we again found our rocks to sit on. The day was getting hot, but fortunately the shade of a huge saguaro had moved to the rocks. We positioned ourselves so that we were in the shadow of the massive cactus.

Mindy trotted back to the rock shelf to collect the rope and the other climbing equipment. Sophie and I looked at each other. She looked terrible, but I knew I probably looked worse.

I reached down to my backpack, unzipped the side pocket, and took out the last water bottle. Even after everything, there was still a sliver of ice floating in it. I popped open the lid and was about to take a drink. Sophie's eyes got big and she held out a hand to stop me.

"You're not going to drink from that, are you?"

"That's the plan," I said.

"What if the dead guy drank from it? You'd be drinking dead guy slobber. If I was you, I'd throw it away after you get home. You can't be too careful when it comes to dead guy slobber."

"I don't think he drank from it. It's still full from when I put it in this morning. Besides, at this point, I really need a drink."

"That cliff thing really sucked," Sophie said. "Next time, maybe you should leave me in the office. I like hiking and all, but this isn't a lot of fun."

"You think I enjoyed that? Not so much. Um, thanks for helping back there. I actually felt a little better knowing you were up there with the professor."

"No worries," she said. "It probably won't be the last time I have to haul your butt up a cliff."

~~~~
~~~~

The rest of the trip down the mountain was uneventful. We expected to see a bloody corpse on the trail or vultures circling a spot on the side of the canyon, but there was nothing. We climbed down the gully, crossed back over the stream, and made it to the trail on the valley floor. We all looked, but from there it was hard to tell where the cliff was or where the guy could have landed.

Although there was a silent agreement between us that the guy was dead, I still felt somewhat uneasy when we couldn't find the body. It left me with a strange feeling that maybe he never existed.

~~~~

When we got to the petroglyphs, it was almost noon and it had gotten crowded. There must have been twenty or thirty people climbing on the rocks and taking pictures of the carvings. Kids were bouncing around and couples were sitting on the rocks holding hands. It was a little strange seeing so many happy people.

~~~~

The last mile on the broad dirt path was very easy to walk. After everything we'd gone through, it felt weird not looking down at where our feet were stepping. Unfortunately, the day was becoming even more hot and miserable. The temperature was up into the nineties, and with the sun beating down on us, it seemed to be even hotter.

When we saw the parking lot in the distance, we took a final break under the shade of a mesquite tree. It felt great to take off my pack and Sophie removed hers with a sigh of relief. Mindy didn't seem to be troubled by hers at all, even though it must have weighed fifty pounds.

"Are you ready to switch packs yet?" I asked. "That looks heavy."

"It's not so bad. Honestly, I'd rather be carrying a bunch of gold than a box with a cursed and stolen statue in it."

I finished off the last of my water and we put on our packs for the last push. But, before we took off, Sophie stopped us.

"Um," she said, "what are we going to do about the dead guy?"

"What do you mean?" I asked, although I knew what she was thinking. I'd been thinking the same thing myself.

"Are we going to call the police or anything? I mean, we think a guy pitched himself off a big ass cliff."

"I was thinking about that too," Mindy said. "I'm not sure of the legalities, but I'm not sure if reporting it is the best thing. There'd need to be a search for the body and it would likely show up on the news. We don't exactly have all the paperwork straightened out yet on either the archeological dig site or the treasure-trove claim. The authorities might be a little concerned we're taking items out of a wilderness area without the proper permits."

"Well, don't look at me," Sophie said. "Not calling the police always seems like a good idea. What are we going to tell them anyway? A guy climbed up the mountain to rob us, then fell off a cliff? They'd probably think we pushed him."

They both looked at me. I couldn't think of a good reason to tell anybody about this either.

"Um," I said. "Maybe it didn't happen? Who knows how long it'll be until someone finds the body. Depending on where he landed, they might never find it."

"Yup," Sophie said. "It never happened. I can agree to that."

"It never happened," Mindy said, a look of relief on her face.

~~~~

When we got to the parking lot, it was nearly full. We walked to the Jeep and everyone took off their backpacks with a sense of relief. Mindy started digging around in the piles of equipment in the back of the vehicle, apparently looking for something specific.

When we'd arrived earlier in the day, the only vehicles had been
~~~~

four sedans and a van. Of these, only the van and one of the sedans were still there. I used the lull to walk over and take pictures of the license plates of both. I then texted the pictures to Sophie's phone. She looked at me like I was nuts.

"When we get back," I said. "Could you run the plates? It's likely one of them belongs to our guy. I'd like to know who he was."

"I didn't think he existed anymore."

"Well, he doesn't, but someone sent him after Mindy and that someone will probably try again. I'd like to try to stop that."

"So, he sorta existed, for investigation purposes."

"You could say that."

From the pile of objects in the back of the Jeep, Mindy came up with a sturdy looking five-gallon white plastic bucket. She cleared a space on the floor of the Jeep and set the bucket on it.

"Let's pull out the gold and dump it into this," she said. "It'll be easier to keep track of if we keep it all in one place."

Making sure no one was looking, we spent the next ten minutes unzipping pockets in the backpacks, pulling out chunks of gold and handfuls of smaller nuggets. We then emptied our pockets of the extra loose nuggets. The plastic bucket made a loud thumping noise every time we tossed in another hunk of gold. When we'd finally finished, Mindy snapped a lid on the top of the bucket and locked it into place by pounding on it with a hammer.

We each took a turn trying to pick up the bucket by the handle. We could wiggle and tip the bucket, but no one could lift it.

"How much do you think's in there?" Sophie asked when we were finally done.

"I'm still thinking it weighs about fifty pounds," Mindy said, "Maybe a little more."

"Damn," Sophie said. "It's quite a treasure we've dug up."

~~~~

I had Mindy stop off at an ATM as we were driving through Apache Junction. I pulled out four hundred dollars, then put the cash and card back in my wallet. If Sergio did a record search for Danielle, Apache Junction would hopefully be far enough away to lead him down a false path. Going to an ATM in Dallas or New Orleans would have been even more convincing, but this was as good as I was going to get today.

~~~~

By the time we made it back to Scottsdale Road, it was a little after two. When they saw the In-N-Out Burger, both Mindy and Sophie started saying how hungry they were. Mindy pulled into the parking lot and we all piled out of the Jeep. Mindy took out the backpack with the box and put it on. She then made sure to lock the doors.

Mindy and Sophie each ordered a big lunch. When it was my turn, I only got a chocolate shake. My stomach was still queasy from our adventure in the mountains and I wasn't all that hungry. I was also starting to think about Danielle and how things would be with her living in my apartment.

We found an open table and waited for our orders to be called out. The restaurant sat on the edge of campus and while we were waiting, two groups of students came over and said hello to Mindy. Apparently, she was a popular teacher.

"You were going to tell us why you started looking for the statue," I said.

"Well, about ten years ago, I did my doctoral thesis on an archeological site located in the mountains west of Globe. My thesis advisor, Professor Babcock, originally discovered the site and I was part of his team excavating it. It was dated to the 1640's and there were several graves at the site. The only record I've been able to find of a expedition from that period was the one from the San Miguel chapel in Santa Fe. I thought it was likely they came out here to bury the Seventh Sister, somewhere in the Superstition Mountains. I've always thought it was interesting that the curse on the Seven Sisters and the curse of the Superstition Mountains were so similar. I've been on the lookout for the Lost Sister ever since."

"What are we going to do with, um, our box?" Sophie asked when we had gotten the food, and everyone was munching away.

"I suggest we talk with Lenny," I said. "This gets into an area of the law I can only guess at." I looked at Mindy and she nodded her head in approval.

~~~~

We made it back to the office and fortunately Lenny was in. We went into his office and told him our story, only leaving out the part about the creep with the gun. Mindy then pulled out the box and set it on Lenny's desk. As we gathered around to look at the carvings on the top and at the old brass lock, Gina came in. We gave her the thirty-second thumbnail sketch of what we'd been up to.

"Alright," Lenny said. "If I can summarize what you've told me. You believe there's a pre-Columbian gold figurine in the box called the Lost Sister. You think the Spanish buried it in a cave in the Superstition Mountains in about 1641 because the statue was something they were trying to get rid of. And, they were trying to get rid of it because of a curse that had been placed on it. A curse that only affects men."

"I don't know if it only affects men," Mindy said.

Lenny looked down at his yellow legal pad. "You said when it was originally stolen, the high priestess said, 'Any man who possessed the statues would be cursed.' That seems to let women off the hook."

"Well, that's how the curse was reported," Mindy said, "but I think it was only a way of speaking. I'd think the curse would affect anyone who took the statue."

"I'm not so sure," Lenny said. "Words mean things and the curse
~~~~

seemed pretty specific. Let's figure out what to do next. Sophie, would you make Professor Parker a drink? I'll take another Beam."

Sophie went over to the bar and started making the drinks. I heard her muttering under her breath that Sophia would love a drink too. I was still trying to keep the milkshake down and for once didn't mind when Lenny didn't offer us anything.

Lenny lit up a cigarette as Sophie brought over the drinks. I walked to the window and opened it so we didn't have to sit in the stench of cigarette smoke. Lenny sat back on his chair and stared into space, smoking the cigarette and sipping his bourbon. From experience, I knew this was how he cleared his mind to figure out what to do next. Mindy sipped her drink and had a look of quiet acceptance. She probably assumed this was standard operating procedure for a Scottsdale attorney.

"Okay," Lenny said after he'd stubbed out his cigarette. "Let's start working the current problem. Since the box, and whatever's inside it, came out of a wilderness area, it's still assumed to be government property. It would be best if it were kept at a state university. That'll muddy the jurisdiction enough to keep everyone out of trouble. When the university issues the archeological permits, we can make sure this is grandfathered in, the same with the gold you pulled out. Perform any testing you can to learn what's inside the box, if that's possible. If you could safely remove the statue without destroying the archeological value of the chest, it would be even better. Is there somewhere at the university where you can safely store everything?"

"ASU has a museum of anthropology on campus," Mindy said. "There's a couple of research laboratories in the basement of the building. We have a lot of valuable items stored there and it should be safe."

"Who else would have access to the laboratories?" Lenny asked.

"Only the professors in the archaeology department and the researchers. But each of us has a cage in a separate storage locker where we can keep items. I have a padlock on mine and I have the only key."

"Very good," Lenny said. "But if the item in the box is as valuable as you think it is, not to mention the gold, it's best that you don't go down by yourself. Laura? Sophie? Who wants to go back with the professor?"

Gina looked over at Sophie and me and laughed. "You two look beat. I can't see either of you lifting a fifty-pound bucket of gold. I'll be glad to escort the professor back to campus. We'll make sure everything is somewhere secure, plus I can get a full download of everything that happened today."

Sophie's eyes got big and she made a motion towards Mindy of zipping her lips shut, locking them, then throwing away the key. Maybe it was supposed to be subtle, but we all saw it. When Sophie noticed everyone looking at her, she casually fluffed her hair and glanced around the office, as if nothing had happened.

~~~~

"Your cat threw up all over the kitchen this morning," Danielle said when I walked into my apartment. "I was going to clean it up, but when I looked again, it was gone. I'm not sure, but um, I think he ate it."

"Yeah, I probably should have warned you. Marlowe does that. I usually feed him right before I leave so I don't have to watch him do it."

"It was pretty gross."

"I know. I sometimes think about getting a hamster or something else that won't throw up every time it eats."

Danielle went to the fridge and pulled out two bottles of Corona. She held them up to see if I approved.

"That would be perfect," I said. "It's been sort of a shitty day and a beer would definitely hit the spot."
~~~~

"You look like you're hurting. You're also limping a little."

"I ended up going on a hike from hell and I'm sore everywhere."

As we were talking, I noticed the apartment smelled delicious. I took a few sniffs and looked around. "What's that?" I asked. "It smells great."

"It's cilantro-lime chicken in a green-chili cream sauce. My mama always made it for me if I was upset. There's a Mexican grocery store about half a mile from here and it had everything I needed. I didn't know when you were coming home, but I made plenty for both of us, if you want some. Your timing is perfect. It's coming out of the oven in about ten minutes."

"That would be wonderful. Let me change my clothes and I'll be back out in a few minutes."

Beer in hand, I went into the bedroom and dropped my pack on the floor. I then took a quick shower to wash off the grime that had accumulated during the day.

As I was getting dressed, I looked in the closet and pulled down my jewelry box. Everything was there and nothing seemed to have been disturbed. Looking at the clothes, everything was as I had left it in the morning. This made me feel a little better about having Danielle in the apartment. If this had been some sort of elaborate ploy to rob me, she would have done it already.

I went out to the kitchen as Danielle was dishing up the chicken. As she handed a plate to me, I realized she wasn't wearing makeup and she had on the same outfit as the day before. Seeing this made me realize what a desperate situation she was in. She had no clothes, no car, no money, and would soon be hunted by a gang of ruthless killers.

My heart went out to her and I wanted to do whatever I could to help. While the chicken steamed and started to cool, I went to my purse and pulled out the money and the ATM card.

"I took out four hundred," I said. "Hopefully it'll be enough for a while. We can figure out something if you need more. There's no reason to spend a lot on clothes. I'm pretty sure we're the same size and I have a full closet. Feel free to wear anything you'd like."

I took a bite of the chicken. It was fantastic, and I told Danielle how amazing it was. This wasn't flattery. My idea of home cooking is in the microwave or take-out Thai. Having something like this come out of my kitchen was a pleasant surprise. Danielle saw the look on my face as I popped in another bite and she smiled.

"I also have drawers full of makeup and stuff like that," I said between bites. "Use whatever you'd like. The washer and dryer are stacked up in the hall closet, so you don't even need to leave the apartment to do laundry."

I had a thought and looked down at her feet. "Huh, I even think we're the same shoe size. After dinner, let's head out to a mall and pick up some of the basics. Then you should be set for as long as you're here."

Danielle looked at me. Her face was twisting with emotions and I could see she was searching for the right words. After several seconds, she simply said, "Thank you."

~~~~

After dinner, we got in my Honda and drove to the Superstition Springs mall in Mesa. It wasn't as far east as Apache Junction, but it was on the east side of The Valley. If anyone spotted Danielle, her story of being east of Scottsdale would still hold up.

As we drove east on the Loop-202, I noticed Danielle was acting a little nervous. I thought maybe talking would help.

"Dinner was great," I said. "How'd you learn to cook like that?"

"Growing up in Mexico, we had to move a lot and we always kept a low profile. At first, I thought that maybe mama had done something bad and the police were looking for her. I later found out
~~~~

I was the daughter of Escobar Salazar and the reason we moved so often was to protect me. If someone discovered Escobar had a daughter, I could have been kidnapped and used for leverage. Anyway, we seldom went out, except to the market. I always looked forward to market day, it was my chance to get out of the apartment. My mama was always a wonderful cook, she'd worked in restaurants before she met my father. She taught me to cook to give us something to talk about and do together. I'll always have good memories of that."

~~~

At the mall, we parked in front of Dillard's and went in. My legs were starting to stiffen and ache from the hike. I found a comfortable chair to sit in while Danielle went from department to department, shopping until she had what she needed. On the drive home, we stopped by a Walgreens drugstore. I sat in the car while she picked up a toothbrush and a few of the essentials.

When we were about halfway back to Scottsdale, Sophie called and said she was going out with the cougars. She said they were starting at the Maya Day and Night Club, if I was interested. I let her know I was out but would be going home to sleep. She said she'd see me in the morning.

When we got back, it was a little after ten and I was beat. We each had another Corona while the local news played on the TV. By ten thirty, I called it a night.
~~~

Chapter Four

I woke up early, but when I tried to roll out of bed, I realized I hurt all over. My legs were tight from the climb, my ass hurt from when I'd slid off the rock ledge, and for some reason, both my arms were painfully sore. I didn't think I'd used them a lot, but apparently, I had.

I slowly hobbled into the bathroom and looked at myself in the mirror. Half a dozen places had scrapes and there were several visible bruises. I looked like I'd been in a fight, one I'd lost.

I took a long hot shower and it seemed to help a little with the sore muscles. I got dressed in my normal clothes but found that putting on a tight pair of pants hurt wherever they pressed against me. I stripped off the first set of clothes and tried again with a looser outfit.

I went into the living room where the local news was on the TV. Danielle had again brewed a pot of coffee and she poured me a cup. I noticed Marlowe had made friends with Danielle and was following her every time she went into the kitchen. Danielle's big black bag was again sitting on the coffee table and it was again unzipped. I hoped it wouldn't come to a shoot-out in my apartment. Something like that wouldn't end well for anybody.

As I sipped the coffee, Danielle came back from the kitchen with two plates of chorizo sausage and scrambled eggs.

"I hope you like this sort of thing," she said. "I heard you in the shower, so I timed it for when you'd come out."

"Wow, that's so nice of you. I almost never have time to make myself breakfast. I usually do drive-through at McDonald's."

"You're welcome. I appreciate everything you've done for me the past couple of days."

"What are you going to do today?" I asked as I sipped the coffee and munched on the chorizo.

"I need to get a message to Escobar. It's the only way to stop what's going on."

"Will that be easy to do?"

"No, actually it's sort of a pain in the ass. If I want to get a message to him, I need to leave it in an internet drop box. Depending on what he's up to, it can take up to a week before I hear anything back. I know it's complicated on purpose, so no one can ever trace his location, but it still makes it difficult."

"When do you think Sergio will discover you're missing?"

"Probably today or tomorrow. Before I left on Monday, I told Raul that Escobar had asked me to head down to Nogales to check on our operations there. I didn't return yesterday and that may or may not have caused anyone to notice. When I don't show up again today, it will raise some concerns. By later today or tomorrow, Sergio will realize I've found out about his plans and will send out orders to have me found. Remember, no one other than Sergio knows Escobar is my father. They think I'm only his former admin and my function is to send and receive messages from Escobar, then to pass them along to Sergio. That makes me valuable to the organization, but definitely not in the formal chain of command."

"Do you think he'll still try to have you murdered?"

"It'll be part of his deception. It's likely Sergio will say Tony kidnapped and then killed me. That way, he can shift the blame to Tony, start his war, then have me killed whenever I turn up. When my body is found, he'll simply blame the other side."

"Are you okay getting a message out?"

"I have a card for the Scottsdale Public Library. Actually, I have several cards under different names. I'll walk over to the Civic Center library branch on Drinkwater Boulevard and send the message from one of the terminals there. Then, all I have to do is wait."

"I think I have a date tonight," I said. "I'll probably come by to change, but then might not be back until late."

"Let me know if it doesn't work out and I'll make dinner for two."

~~~~

I got to the office at eight thirty. There wasn't anything else to do with the professor's box and I wouldn't need to do anything with my cheating spouse until the fitness class at eleven.

Sophie was already at her desk, checking out the Southern California Surf Reports and sipping a big gas station coffee. Lenny was nowhere to be seen.

"Hey Sophie," I said, as I plopped down in a chair next to her desk. "How are you feeling today?"

Sophie looked over at me with a look that said she wasn't happy. "I hurt all over. My legs hurt, and my feet are killing me. My new hiking boots ended up giving me a couple of blisters. I think I even pulled a muscle or something in my arm, hauling your butt up that cliff. Let's not do that again anytime soon."

"It wasn't my idea of fun either. I didn't think we'd be going on some sort of alpine survival challenge."

"You know, I was thinking. If there really is a curse on that thing in the treasure chest, maybe you shouldn't be messing with it. If the stories Professor Mindy tells about it are true, people went to a lot of effort to hide it where it couldn't cause trouble for anyone. Maybe you'll start to upset it if you go around X-raying it, opening the box, touching it, and stuff."
~~~~

"I'm not sure if I believe in the curse. Besides, Lenny thinks it only affects men."

"You think Lenny's the final authority on ancient curses? If I was you, I'd be careful. You don't want to piss-off a five-hundred-year-old cursed statue."

"You're probably right, but until we find out more about the Lost Sister, I've got squat. Hey, how are the cougars?"

"Everyone's good and they all say 'Hi'. It was a last-minute thing; Jackie called and let me know they were going out. I thought maybe it would help my aching body to have a few drinks and relax with the ladies. After the Maya Day and Night Club, we went over to Nexxus."

"How was it? Did you meet anyone?"

"Not really. Elle was trying to set me up with this art dealer friend of hers."

"It sounds like he has money. Not your type?"

"No, he was okay…"

"So, what's wrong?"

"When I got home, I passed out. Like I don't even remember getting undressed. I woke up this morning and I had my PJ's on, but I don't remember doing it."

"How much did you drink?"

"Oh jeez, I drank a ton. The guys kept buying me drinks all night. At least I was smart enough to Uber back and forth."

"So, what's the problem? You drank too much and passed out."

Sophie looked around the office to make sure no one could be listening, then leaned forward and quietly spoke. "Um, I've been thinking about the secret software lately. I think I've been using it too much. I think maybe the government's getting wise to me."

"And?"

"And I've been a little worried they might do something to me. I was thinking, what if my passing out last night wasn't only due to the booze. What if it was the government?"

"Why would they do that?"

"Maybe to kidnap me and implant a mind control chip. Maybe that's why I woke up back in my bed without remembering what happened after I got home."

"You think the government drugged you, then took you to some secret medical facility where they performed a complicated brain surgery, and then returned you to your apartment? All within a space of about five or six hours? You're not serious?"

"Well, maybe not when you say it like that. But if you see me acting strange over the next few days, point it out to me, okay?"

"I will, I promise."

"Thanks," she said. "So, what are you going to do with your cheating spouse? Isn't that today? What's his name?"

"Timothy," I said. "He's big, wealthy, handsome, and supposedly a cheating jerk. He works as a financial advisor for the rich people in Paradise Valley. I think the only way I'm going to find out what's going on will be to take the class, then follow the instructor when it's over. Her name's Crystal."

"You? In an aerobics class? Um, you do know what they do in one of those classes, don't you?"

"Hey," I said. "I'm not in bad shape. I bet I could do one of those classes, no problem."

"Well, I know how I feel after yesterday's hike. If I was you, I'd sneak into the back and try to hide for most of the class."

"That's probably a good idea. The class starts at eleven and goes until twelve fifteen. I figured I'd get there early and sign up for the club. I've already taken the tour and they said I can sign up for a month at a time. I'll go to the class, then follow Crystal when it's done. If she's getting together with Timothy, I'll be there with the camera on my phone going. With any luck, Lenny'll have his video today."

"You know, if Lenny's paying for you to have a month of gym membership, maybe I should get one too and we could go together. I still need to work on my ass. If I can drop my ass down a size, I'll have about a dozen pairs of shorts I could wear again. It would be like getting a new wardrobe."

"I'd love the company," I said. "Speaking of wardrobes, I need to go down and get an outfit for the class."

"I'll come with you. Lenny's in court all day and Gina's not coming back until two. The only thing going on here is filing, which I refuse to do. Maybe I'll get an outfit too, that way it'll motivate me to go to classes with you."

"You took fitness classes about a year ago, didn't you? Don't you still have the outfit from that?"

"Well, sure, but that's an old outfit. If I'm going to be motivated, I'll need a new outfit, new shoes too. That old outfit wouldn't motivate me to do jack shit."

As Sophie was talking, I looked around the office. The stacks of unfiled folders had been steadily growing over the last month. Most of the flat surfaces in reception now had a thick stack of file folders on them. "Speaking of filing, how do you keep track of everything?"

"Until Lenny hires a new admin, I've developed my own system. If I think I'm going to need a file relatively soon, I keep it here on my desk or behind me on the bookshelf. If I'll need it within a week or two, I'll put it on one of the stacks here in reception. And, if I won't need it for a while, I toss the file on one of the stacks in the conference room. That way, if Lenny has a meeting in there and moves the stacks around, it won't mess up my system too much."

"We do have an office with file cabinets," I said. "Why don't you put some of them in there?"

"That would make it look too much like I was filing. I need to keep the pressure up on Lenny or else he'll never hire another admin."

~~~~

Sophie forwarded the desk phone to her cell and locked up the office. She put a little sign on the inside of the front window with a picture of a clock, saying the office would be open at one o'clock.

We went out the back door and got into my Honda. As we drove over to Dick's Sporting Goods, I hit a bump. This made my trunk lid slam down against my car as the bungee cord strained to keep it in place. Sophie shook her head as she listened to the noise. "You know, after having that hot convertible, this car doesn't suit you anymore. When are you going to get something new?"

"I can't afford a new car and I don't think Tony will give me another one after the last one blew up."

"What about the insurance?"

"What insurance?"

"The insurance on your convertible. You did have insurance on it, didn't you?"

Thinking about the insurance brought a wave of depression. "Sure," I said. "I had insurance. Unfortunately, the book value on a twenty-year-old Mercedes SL convertible is only about six thousand dollars."

"But Tony totally redid the car. It was as good as new. How could they only give you six thousand dollars?"

"It wasn't even six thousand. I had a five-hundred-dollar deductible and I had to pay to have it towed. It was so badly burnt, even the salvage company didn't want it."

"Well, that sucks."
~~~~

"When I added that to what we got from Digga, I ended up with enough to pay off most of my credit cards, but that was it."

"Well, that's something," Sophie said. "Even with Digga's check, I still have a couple of credit cards with balances on them. Of course, it's really not my fault. Ever since we started going out with the cougars, it's like I have an excuse to buy shoes and purses and stuff."

~~~~

We pulled into the Scottsdale Fashion Square parking lot and made our way over to Dick's. When we walked in, I was a little overwhelmed at the size of the place, but Sophie seemed to know her way around. She led me to the fitness section and we each spent several minutes pulling clothes off the racks and holding them up to see how'd they'd look on us. While Sophie was standing in front of the mirror, she kept looking at her head. At one point, she lifted the hair behind her ear.

"What are you doing?" I asked.

"Just checking."

"For what?"

"Scars. If they implanted a mind control chip, there'd be a scar, wouldn't there?"

"I'd think you'd notice if the government planted a mind control chip in your brain."

"I'm not so sure. I think they'd program you not to notice."

After several more minutes in front of the mirror, I'd narrowed it down to three outfits; black stretchy pants with either a teal, a salmon, or a pink stripe, along with a matching fitness top. Sophie was having a harder time deciding and could only narrow it down to six outfits, mostly bright florals and neon geometric patterns.

We went into the dressing rooms and came out a few minutes later. I'd chosen the black and pink outfit. It fit alright and looked
~~~~

reasonably good on me. Sophie took longer and when she came out she looked a little disgusted with herself.

"What's wrong?" I asked.

"I was trying on outfits in front of the mirror and saw I'm starting to get back fat. I've never had back fat before and it's so gross."

"You don't have back fat," I said.

"It's only starting, but I can see it forming, right around the straps."

"So, get looser outfits. That way you won't notice."

"That would be admitting defeat. Now I'll have to go to that stupid fitness class with you today. My legs feel like crap and my head's still fuzzy from the booze last night, but I've gotta do something or else my back fat will only get worse."

~~~~

We drove down to the gym and both signed up for a month. Sophie said since it was for an assignment, we should probably put everything on Lenny's credit card.

We went into the locker room and I put on my outfit. I'd brought my old cross trainers and the outfit looked okay. Sophie ended up buying three outfits and two pairs of shoes. She'd brought everything into the locker room and was busy making fashion decisions, finally going with a pair of black pants, a red top with black geometric patterns, and red Nikes. She then went to the mirror, touched up her makeup and put her long dark hair in a ponytail.

"I'm ready," she said. "Let's go and exercise the crap out of this place."

~~~~

We walked into the fitness studio and looked around. It was a spacious room with a high ceiling and a bouncy wooden floor. Several ceiling fans were going and they made a swirling breeze throughout the room. Against one wall was a selection of huge rubber balls, hand weights, and stretchy fitness bands.

There were already ten or twelve women in the room, with more trickling in by ones and twos. Some were standing around in small groups and some were stretching on soft mats on the floor. Some of the women had already grabbed hand weights, as if the class wasn't going to be hard enough without pumping a little extra iron. Timothy came in and started talking with the women in one of the groups.

"Which way's the back?" Sophie asked. "Now that we're in here, I'm thinking my legs still don't feel so good. We should probably ease into this exercise thing gradually and only half-ass the class today. Maybe next time we can get more into it."

I had to look back at the door and remember the class layout from my tour two days before. "I think the back's this way," I said, pointing to a wall covered in floor to ceiling mirrors."

"Well, let's get back there and hide before anyone else decides to take our spot."

We positioned ourselves in front of the mirrors as people started to drift towards the center of the room. I looked toward the door and Crystal came in. I'd seen her before, but this was my first time seeing her up close. She had a toned body, a pretty face, and long red hair, which was pulled back into a big ponytail.

"Is that Crystal?" Sophie asked. "She seems alright. Maybe this won't be so bad after all."

Crystal said hello to some of the women, then went to an expensive-looking audio system and grabbed a wireless microphone headset. She switched it on and said a few words to test it. She then hit a button and loud military marching music blasted through speakers hung all around the room.

Crystal's face went through a weird transformation. The pleasant-looking woman of a few moments ago was replaced with a sadistic-looking, snarling beast. The transformation on its own was a little disturbing, but what suddenly had me more alarmed was that she was walking towards the back of the class, directly towards Sophie and me. She stepped between us, took another two steps, and stopped at the wall of mirrors. I looked around the room and every person in class was now facing in the direction of Sophie and me.

Shit.

"Ladies and Gentlemen!" Crystal yelled out as she turned to face the class, her amplified voice booming out of the speakers. "Are you ready to suffer to get that hard body we all want?"

"Yes!" yelled everyone in the room. They had also transformed into snarling beasts and everyone started marching in place.

"Well then," Crystal shouted, "welcome to Guerilla Bootcamp!"

As the military music grew louder and the beat quickened, I looked over at Sophie. Her eyes were wide with panic.

"Shit," she said. "We're in the middle of the frickin' front row. You said this was the back. I'm outta here."

"You can't go now. We can't do anything to draw attention to ourselves."

"Do you really want to stay here and do frickin' Guerilla Bootcamp?"

"It's too late to go now," I said. "We're going to have to tough it out."

I looked up and Crystal was staring at both of us. I glanced around the room and saw everyone else was also looking at us. I slowly turned to the front and started marching in place. Reluctantly, Sophie did the same.

"You're soft and weak," Crystal yelled out to the class as the marching music continued. "Well people, for the next hour and fifteen minutes, your body belongs to me. I'll transform that soft marshmallow of a body into a lean muscular body you'll be proud to show off. Are you ready?"

Everyone in the room yelled out, "Yes!" The music swelled, and I got a feeling close to desperation in the pit of my stomach. After a moment, the music switched to a new piece and everyone started to exercise.

Shit.

The next hour and fifteen minutes was a twisted swirl of pain and exhaustion. The class started out with moves that were mostly designed to stretch the muscles and warm the body. This wasn't so bad and I was thinking maybe I could survive the class. But the second song was a little faster and Crystal was having us kick out with our legs and swing our arms. By the time the two warm-up songs were over, my heart was pounding and I was gulping air.

It was then that the real pain started. For the next hour, one song after another came pounding out of the speakers. With each song came a new arm-swinging and leg-kicking move that ensured I couldn't breathe and my heart could only pump faster.

After every three or four songs, the class briefly halted for what Crystal called a pulse-check. Everyone grabbed a water bottle and walked around for ten or fifteen seconds, holding two fingers to their necks. I also tried the two-finger neck-pulse thing. All I could tell was my heart was still pumping, but at a speed that said it would likely give out at any moment. I looked over at Sophie and I could see her mouthing the words, "I hate you."

Crystal gathered us back together and the torture began again. As with the day before, my head started to swim, and my stomach knotted up. At one point, she made everyone go to a rack and get two stretchy bands, like big rubber bands, but each about three feet long. She then used the bands in devious new ways to inflict pain. With each song, Crystal found a muscle that hadn't been totally wiped out and gave us a move to ensure it was quickly burning.

Finally, after what seemed like two or three hours, Crystal let us put away the bands and a slow song came on, which she called the cool-down. My heart gradually started to slow down, but my stomach was getting worse. I knew this wasn't a good sign. The song ended and everyone in the room clapped. I bolted for the door, ran to the locker room, and went into the first bathroom stall I could find. I closed the door and sat as the world spun.

I heard the other women gradually filter into the locker room and Sophie knocked on the stall door. "Hey, Laura, are you alright?"

"Yeah, I'm okay. Where's Crystal."

"She's here in the locker room, back by the showers somewhere."

"Okay, stay near the exit and if she leaves, see where she goes. Have your phone with you and take a video if anything happens."

After about ten minutes, the room stopped spinning and I felt much better. I came out and found Sophie sitting on a bench in front of a wall full of lockers.

"Did Crystal leave yet?"

"Nope, I've been here the whole time. She must still be taking a shower or something back there."

We walked back to the showers but didn't see Crystal anywhere. We then searched the entire locker room, but with no luck.

"Let's see if Timothy's still here," I said.

We walked out of the locker room and to the glass wall in the front of the gym that overlooked the parking lot.

"Which car is his?" Sophie asked.

"It's a red Audi A5 convertible."

"You mean that one?" she said as she pointed to a red Audi driving across the far end of the parking lot.

"Yup, that's the one."

"So, where's Crystal?"

We looked around the club and Crystal was standing at the front desk, casually chatting with a couple of guys. She still had on her fitness outfit.

"Okay," Sophie said. "That doesn't make a whole lot of sense. I know she didn't walk past me."

We walked back to the locker room and got dressed. After we'd fixed everything in front of the mirror, we again looked around the room. There was the main locker area, some private changing stalls, and a back section that had the shower stalls, the steam room, and the sauna. There was a door next to the sauna that led to a maintenance and janitorial hallway.

We walked down this new and somewhat grimy hall. We opened one door and found a room full of tools and spare parts. Behind a second door was a room with janitorial supplies, a pallet of clean towels, and a hotel-sized rolling hamper full of dirty towels. Sophie was about to open a third door, when I pointed out the sign on it that read, *Men's Locker Room.*

"Oops," Sophie said. "I almost found myself in a room full of muscular naked men. That would've been a damn shame."

We followed the hallway to the end, but it only ended up going back into the weight-room.

"You're right," I said. "It doesn't make any sense. Next time, we're going to need to stick to Crystal and see where she goes and what she does."

"Next time?" Sophie asked. "You do know I almost passed out in there today. Why don't you sit in the locker room and wait for Crystal to come in after class? Or better yet, ask Gina. You know how much she loves this exercise shit. Hey, why'd you run out of class when it was over today? You said not to call attention to ourselves."

"I thought I was going to throw up. I figured if that happened, it would cause a scene."

"Didn't you say you felt like throwing up yesterday too?"

"Well, sure. We were trying to follow Mindy-the-mountain-goat up that hill."

"Yeah, it was exhausting, but I never felt sick. Same with today. You know, I wouldn't tell a lot of people how you keep feeling like throwing up. Everyone will think you're pregnant. Remember that lame-ass rumor you started about me last summer?"

Sophie started laughing, then stopped. I must have had a weird look on my face. "What?" she asked. "Oh my God, you aren't, are you?"

I was doing a quick calculation in my head. "Um, I don't think so."

"You don't think so? Well, think back. Was the last time before or after you were with Max?"

"Um, I really never keep track. My body tends to have its own schedule when it comes to that and I've given up trying to predict. Before, maybe?"

"So, you could be, and it could be Reno's, or it could be Max's?"

"Look, I don't think I am, so let's drop it. If I find out differently, I'll let you know."

~~~~

We drove back to the office, but when we tried to get out of the car, we both found our legs had stiffened to the point that it was hard to move.

"Between the frickin' mountain yesterday and that frickin' fitness class today, I don't think I'll be able to walk for two or three days," Sophie said as she slowly climbed out of the car. I was feeling much the same, but didn't say anything, mostly because it was my fault Sophie had come along both times.
~~~~

We made it up to reception. Sophie sat at her desk and I flopped down on one of the red leather chairs. We both sat without moving for several minutes. The only sound we made was an occasional groan.

Gina came up from the back holding a folder, which she dropped on Sophie's desk. "I'm finished with this one," she said. "I wish more people would sign a pre-nup so we wouldn't need to take pictures of spouses having sex with other people. I'm starting to lose faith in humanity."

Sophie started laughing.

"What?" Gina asked.

"Laura said exactly the same thing, like two days ago. But, it's probably a good thing people get tired of each other. Otherwise none of us would have a job."

"True," Gina said. "But it sometimes seems like taking pictures of naked people having sex is all we do. Back on the force, we at least had some variety." Gina got a faraway look in her eyes and sighed. "People get killed in all sorts of interesting ways." She then looked down at us with concern. "What's wrong with you two? You both don't look so good."

"We just went through Guerrilla Bootcamp," Sophie said. "Both of my legs have gone numb. I probably won't be able to walk for another two or three hours. I may even have some nerve damage. I don't ever want to have to do that again."

Gina looked at me for an explanation.

"I've been following a guy named Timothy for a week," I said. "The only time he and his presumed mistress, Crystal, get to within a mile of each other is when he's at the fitness center, where she works as an aerobics instructor. It somehow has to be either before or after class. I've followed Timothy from his house to his office, then from his office to the fitness center, four times now. I don't see how it can be before class. They aren't in the same room until class starts and then they're surrounded by fifteen or twenty people. But, after class, he goes straight to the locker room, changes his clothes, and is back out within ten or fifteen minutes. He then goes directly back to his office and doesn't see Crystal again until the next fitness class."

"Well, when's the next class?" Gina asked.

"Friday at eleven. I'll go back and see what I can find out."

"Would you like some company?" Gina asked. "No guarantees, but I should be free Friday morning."

"Yes!" Sophie said as she clapped her hands together. "See, I told you Gina loves to exercise. I knew she'd be perfect for this."

"Well, now that the snowbirds have started to come back, it's getting busy here," Gina said. "The money from the extra work always comes in handy, but I haven't gotten a lot of chances to exercise lately."

"What'd you do with the money we got from Digga?" Sophie asked Gina.

"I put it into my house fund. Unless I can find a rich man, who'll throw himself at my feet, I'll need to come up with the down payment myself."

"What about the guy from your gym, Brandon? Didn't you go out with him again over the weekend?"

"Well, yes, and he is throwing himself at my feet, but he's hardly rich."

"You'll need to plan better with the next one," Sophie said.

My phone started ringing with an unknown local number. Sophie looked at me and I shrugged my shoulders. I then pressed the accept button.

"Laura, it's Mindy."

From the tone of her voice, I could tell something had happened.

"Mindy, what's wrong," I asked.

"I went down to the lab to get the box. I wanted to do some preliminary analysis on it. But when I got to my storage cage, it had been ripped open and the box was gone. They left the bucket with the gold but took the statue."

I quickly relayed to Sophie and Gina what had happened. I then turned on the speakerphone.

"Are you okay?" I asked.

"I'm fine, just in a panic about the box."

"What about the main door to the lab?" Gina asked. "Did it look like someone also broke into that?"

"No, only my personal cage. It looks like they took a crowbar and pried the lock off."

"Who else has access to the lab?" Gina asked.

"All of the professors in the department, along with some of the grad students."

"Where are you?" I asked.

"In my office, Matthews Center room two-ten. It's on the second floor of the old Matthews Library on main campus, next to University Avenue."

"I'll be right down," I said. "Make a list of everyone you can think of who has access to the lab and I'll start looking into it."

~~~~

I went to the ASU main campus in Tempe and drove around until I found a visitor's parking spot. I was about to get out of my Honda, when my phone buzzed. I looked down and it was a text from Max wanting to know if dinner was still on for tonight. I texted back that I was still good and for him to name the place. He wrote back to meet in the lobby of the Scottsdale Tropical Paradise around six o'clock
~~~~

and he'd have something set up.

It felt a little weird to be back at my alma mater. Even though I lived less than five miles away, I hadn't been back to main campus in several years. The first thing I noticed was that the students seemed to have gotten a lot younger. They looked more like they should be in high school, rather than on a university campus.

I walked to a campus directory and found the Matthews Center building. Fortunately, the walk wasn't too far. My legs were still aching from the class and, if anything, they seemed to be getting worse. I made it to the building but didn't find an elevator for the second floor and had to take the stairs. I took the steps one at a time but, even at that, I had to stop halfway up and rest.

Mindy's office was at the end of a long hallway full of similar offices. Her door was open, so I went in.

Mindy was at her desk, typing on a laptop. I expected her office to look like an archaeological museum exhibit, with dinosaur bones everywhere. Instead, every surface was covered in rocks. Some were mounted on pedestals, some were cut open and polished, but most were laying in piles wherever there was some shelf space. Mindy looked up as I walked in.

"Hey," I said. "I'm sorry to hear about the box. Tell me about it. Where was it stored? What happened today?"

"There isn't a lot to tell. Gina and I put the box and the bucket of gold in my storage locker in a lab in the basement of the School of Human Evolution and Social Change last night. That's the building that houses the Museum of Anthropology."

"And today?"

"I went down to get the box. I wanted to take it in for a CT scan, some X-rays, and to pull out a small core sample of the wood for radiocarbon dating. Everything looked normal until I got to my cage. The lock had been pried away from the metal frame. Nothing else but the wooden box was taken, so they seemed to know exactly what they were looking for."

"Can you show me?"

"Sure, the School of Human Evolution is next door. We can head over and I'll show you the damage."

We walked over to the school, then marched down the stairway to the basement. The research lab was in a brightly lit hallway and the door seemed very sturdy. I looked up and there was a security camera facing the door. Unfortunately, the camera was at the far end of the hallway. I wasn't sure how great the video quality would be of anyone going into or out of the lab.

"Do you know where the camera feed goes?" I asked, pointing to the ceiling.

"No, but I can find out."

Mindy entered a combination on a keypad lock, the door opened, and we went into the laboratory. There were a dozen lab benches, all covered in instruments of every sort. Some of the instruments seemed to be chemistry related, with test tubes and glass beakers, while some appeared to be more geology related. Most I couldn't guess what they were for. There were dozens of storage shelves, all full of large cardboard boxes. The lab also had three separate storage rooms, all with sturdy looking doors.

"My locker's in here," Mindy said.

She used a key and we went into one of the storage rooms. I noticed the lock on this door seemed to be intact.

Inside the room were a dozen lockers, each about four feet high and three feet wide. Each locker had a sturdy wire mesh door and a solid looking padlock. Mindy's locker was easy to spot, the lock was hanging useless off the end of a twisted metal latch.

"This is how I found it an hour ago," Mindy said. "Nothing else was touched and some of the other items are valuable on their own. The bucket of gold's still there. Of course, it's not marked and there's no way for anyone to tell what's in it."

I looked around the area, but the only security camera I could find was back in the lab itself, facing out toward the main door. There wasn't anything in this room to record who'd jimmied the lock and took the box.

"You said all the professors have access to the lab," I said. "Who would have a key to this storage room? The lock didn't appear to have been forced."

"Well, everyone who has a locker, so that's a dozen right there. Plus, I imagine some of the museum staff would need to come down here, so probably twenty-five or thirty people all together."

I sighed with frustration. Finding a thief among thirty people would likely take several days, if not a week or two.

"I think we should talk to the department director about this," Mindy said. "After what happened yesterday, this seems to be going beyond a simple theft. They can alert campus security."

"That's a good idea. We'll probably need their authorization to get the security tapes. Although, I'd stick with this theft and not talk a lot about what happened on the mountain yesterday. When was the last time you saw the box?"

"It was last night when I came here with Gina. I spent most of the morning trying to wrap up my other projects. I'd like to be able to devote myself full time to this."

"So, that gives us about eighteen hours from when you put the box in your locker until you found it was missing. That means anyone who walked out of the lab last night or this morning carrying anything bigger than your box will be a suspect. You'll need to help me review the security tapes."

"Let's go back to my office," Mindy said. "I'll start the letter to the department director."

Chapter Five

We walked out of the school building and noticed several people clustered in groups on the sidewalk in front of the Matthews Center. A police car was on the pedestrian sidewalk with its lights flashing and another one had pulled up to the side of the building. A campus patrol officer was guiding an ambulance to the front entrance of the building. The ambulance also had its lights flashing.

We watched as the EMS crew was led into the building with a gurney full of equipment and instruments.

"What's going on?" Mindy asked one of the students who'd been watching the events.

"Professor, they said somebody had a heart attack. Someone in our department."

We stood around and watched the scene for another few minutes. As always, the calmness and professionalism of the police and EMS fascinated me. Somebody may be having a serious health issue, but to them, it was business as usual.

We drifted into the building and I slowly walked up the stairs. My legs were still throbbing from the class and all of the walking wasn't helping. Four doors down from Mindy's, several people were clustered around an office. The sounds of beeping instruments and the indistinct chatter of walkie-talkies filled the air.

"Oh my God," Mindy said. "That's Professor Babcock's office."

"Professor Babcock? Why does that name sound familiar?"

"I told you about him. He's a full professor in the department and my thesis advisor. He seems to be in line to make department director in a few years."

To get to Mindy's, we needed to slide past the knot of people gathered at the door to Professor Babcock's office. As we did, we both glanced inside.

EMS was busy attending to a middle-aged man who was stretched out on the floor. They had him wired up to a couple of monitoring machines and it looked like they were about to roll him onto a gurney.

In addition to the man on the floor, I spotted Mindy's wooden box. It was sitting in the middle of the man's desk. Next to it were a couple of screwdrivers, a hacksaw, a pair of pliers, and a hammer.

"Did you see that?" Mindy whispered to me as we took a few steps down the hall. "My box was sitting on Professor Babcock's desk."

"I saw it," I said.

An older woman with a dazed look on her face was sitting in a chair in the hallway writing out a statement on a police clipboard. Mindy seemed to recognize her. She went to the woman and asked what had happened.

"Oh, Professor Parker," the woman said. "It was terrible. I came in after lunch and had a stack of folders to deliver to Professor Babcock. I knocked several times, but no one answered. I didn't want to leave everything out in the hallway, so I used my key to unlock his office. When I went in, he was pitched back on his chair with the most horrible look frozen on his face. I thought he was dead, but when I picked up the phone to call 911, he moaned. It almost scared me to death. I told the operator to send an ambulance and they showed up about ten minutes ago."

Mindy and I went down to her office and I closed the door so we could talk.

"We've got to get that box," I said. "Let's go back and see if you can grab it. I'll create a distraction if I need to."

We walked back to Professor Babcock's office. The professor had already been wheeled out, but there was still a campus police officer and an EMT, who was quickly packing up the rest of the equipment. The floor was littered with an assortment of wrappers from the various medical devices that had been used. The woman, who Mindy had talked to previously, had finished up her statement and was giving it to the officer. After a moment, the EMT scampered out the door. The campus officer placed the statement in a folder and also left.

"Rebecca," Mindy said to the woman. "We'll straighten up the office if you'd like to take off."

"Are you sure?" the woman asked. She still had a dazed expression on her face.

"It's not a problem," Mindy assured her. "I know you've had a long day."

The woman gave us a grateful look as she took off. This left Mindy and I alone in the office.

"Close the door," I said. "Let's pick up the trash, then see what we can find."

We quickly cleaned up the mess, which wasn't as bad as it looked, then turned our attention to the box on the desk.

"Oh my God," Mindy said as she examined the box. "Look what he did."

I looked at where she was pointing. It looked like the professor had been using a hacksaw and a pair of pliers on the lock. It was deeply gouged and bright copper-colored metal was shining through the scratches.

"He's a full professor of archaeology," Mindy said. "He knows there're ways of removing these old locks without damaging them. Why would he purposefully try to destroy something so beautiful? This goes against everything we do."

"Well, he didn't get very far on it. Tell me about Professor Babcock."

"He was my thesis advisor and I was one of the grad students with him on the original dig out by Globe. Honestly, I've never liked him. His research is spotty and crude, but he's published several books on archaeology and he thinks he's a celebrity. Plus, when he drinks, he thinks he's a ladies' man and he starts to get handsy. I've seen it more than once at department parties."

"Now that you have the box back, you should probably find out what's actually in it. It seems like a lot of people are willing to steal it with hopes of what might be inside."

"I still need to run my tests to determine the age and do the scans to get a look at the contents of the box. Nothing will be definitive until we make an observation with our own eyes, but the tests should give us a pretty good idea of what's inside."

"Good. With that information we can figure out what to do next."

"Okay, that's a plan," Mindy said. "But what are we going to do with the box until then? It's obvious the lab isn't secure. I also probably shouldn't keep it in my office. That's the first place they'll look."

"I wonder, did someone already break into your office? Have you noticed anything missing or messed up?"

Mindy thought for a moment. "When I walked in this morning, I did notice two of my drawers hadn't been pushed all the way in. I assumed I'd left them that way, although I'm usually pretty good about closing them."

"What about your file cabinets?"

"I don't know, I don't lock them or anything. I keep my office locked, but as you saw, lots of people have keys to the offices. Rebecca is our department admin and has a key for most of the doors in the building. I imagine maintenance and the janitorial staff have keys as well. If Professor Babcock wanted an office key, it wouldn't have been hard for him to get one."

"According to Lenny, the box needs to be stored on the grounds of the university. But at least two people already know about your statue and have tried to steal it. It's possible there're others. Do you know of anywhere on campus it would be safe?"

Mindy thought for a moment. "Well, speaking of safe, one thing comes to mind. A few years ago, one of the professors brought down a safe that had been discovered under the floor in an old bank in Jerome. We hired a professional to open it up, but there wasn't anything inside except for a few insurance documents. The safe's still in the basement of this building and I kept the combination."

"Do you think anyone else will be able to get into it?"

"I doubt it. Once people found out the safe was empty, they lost interest. I thought it was an interesting artifact from the late nineteenth century, so I asked the safecracker for the combination. I have it in one of my notebooks. As far as I know, I'm the only one on campus who still has it."

Mindy pulled a notebook from a shelf and started flipping through the pages. When she found the combination, she copied it onto a piece of paper and shoved it into her pocket. I couldn't think of a reason not to put the box in the safe, in fact, it seemed like a pretty good idea.

"How long will it take to run your tests?"

Mindy looked at the clock, it was a quarter after four. "Everything's about to close for the day, so we'll need to do this tomorrow morning. We'll go to the radiocarbon lab to pull a micro-core sample of the wood, but that will only take a few minutes. I'll submit the sample to the tech and we should get the results back in a day or two. Not a lot of people use the campus X-ray lab anymore, so that should be quick. I'll also call over to the CT lab and see if they have an opening in the morning. If all goes well, we should have the tests completed by noon tomorrow."

"Let's get the box into your safe. We should probably put the gold in there as well. I'll come back in the morning and we can get started. What time?"

"Nothing on campus opens until eight. Let's meet here at seven forty-five."

Mindy found a reusable Bashas grocery bag and we used it to carry the box down to the basement. The old bank safe was sitting in the corner of an office that had been converted to storage. The safe was green, about five feet high and three feet across, with flecks of white paint all over the front. Stenciled across the door, in faded gold lettering, were the words: *Sheffield Safe Co., London.* Several boxes had been stacked in front of it and there was an old wire birdcage sitting on top.

Looking around the dusty room, I had to agree with Mindy. Not a lot of people would know about the safe and I'd be surprised if anyone else had the combination.

On the front of the safe was a large brass dial and a steel handle. Mindy pulled the piece of paper from her pocket, looked at the combination, then started spinning the dial. It took her a couple of tries, but in about five minutes she had the door open and the box was safely inside.

Mindy closed and locked the safe, then we went back for the gold. Mindy said she and Gina had used a wooden pole and an old belt to jointly carry the bucket and it had worked well.

When we got back to Mindy's cage, I was relieved the gold was still there. Mindy slid the short wooden pole under the bucket handle, then tied it into place with the belt. We both bent down and lifted on the pole. The bucket moved, but it was heavier than I thought it would be.

The two of us struggled as we half slid, half carried the bucket out of the lab, then to the stairs. Looking up the flight of stairs made me wince a little. We started by heaving the bucket up a step, pausing to reposition ourselves, then lifting the bucket up to the next step. By about the sixth or seventh step, my arms and legs had started to burn. Fortunately, Mindy didn't seem to be affected and we eventually got the bucket to the top of the stairs. We then slid the gold out the front door, then down to the main campus walkway. The Matthews Building was only about fifty yards away, but wrestling with the bucket made the distance seem much farther.

We'd made it about halfway there, dragging the bucket along the sidewalk, when someone came up behind us. "Hey, Professor Parker, do you need some help?"

We turned to see a large, but good-natured student. "That looks heavy," he said. "Where's it going?"

"I need to get it down to the basement of the Matthews Center," Mindy said. "Thanks Xavier, I'd appreciate the help."

The student bent down and grabbed both sides of the handle. He lifted it, but you could tell, even for him, it was an effort. He walked it down the sidewalk and almost made it to the Matthews Center, but then tripped on a step. He lost his balance and the bucket fell. It hit the sidewalk hard and I had visions of fifty or sixty pounds of gold nuggets spilling down the walkway. Fortunately, the lid held and nothing came out.

"Sorry Professor," the student said.

"Don't worry about it," Mindy said. "The bucket's full of mineral samples. You can't hurt them."

The student carried the bucket into the building and Mindy had him put it on the floor at the bottom of the basement stairs. She then thanked him and he took off.

Inwardly moaning with despair, I bent down as Mindy and I grabbed the wooden handle and dragged the bucket down the hall to the storage room.

Mindy quickly opened the safe, but it took us several tries to get the bucket inside. There wasn't room in the safe for the handle to be used, so we had to pick up the bucket by the sides. By the time we'd muscled the bucket into the safe, our arms were burning and we were both panting.

"Next time you find a treasure," I said, "try to find one that doesn't weigh as much."

~~~~

I drove back to my apartment house and took the elevator up to my floor. I then slowly walked to my apartment. My legs had gone from being merely tight to actively aching. When I walked into my apartment, Danielle was in the kitchen, stirring a pot of something that smelled delicious. I collapsed on the couch and tried to relax. As usual, the local news was on the TV.

"Are you okay?" Danielle asked as she walked into the living room. "You still don't look so good. Still hurting from your hike?"

"I went to a gym today and took a group fitness class. My legs can barely move. Everything hurts."

"You took a fitness class the day after your hike? You're very ambitious."

"It was for work."

"In that case, I don't think they pay you enough."

"You got that right."

"I spent an hour with Grandma Peckham today. It was nice. She made me drinks with Diet Pepsi and Appleton Rum."

"She calls them Jamaican Jerks. There's a story behind it, but I've never been able to get it out of her."
~~~~

"Grandma wanted to know all about me, so I had to embellish on your story a little. I'm a cousin on your mother's side. I'm from Albuquerque and I've come to Scottsdale to look for a job. Anything that's office-related."

"That seems reasonable."

"I also told her I'm moving to Scottsdale partly to get away from an abusive ex-boyfriend, so if anyone comes asking around, she's never heard of me."

"That's good thinking, but I doubt anyone would think you'd be over here."

"You never know."

"Did you have any luck sending the message to Escobar?"

"Well, I sent it, but it usually takes a few days to hear back. Sometimes it takes up to a week."

"What do you think he'll do?"

"I'm not sure. Escobar wants everything to run smoothly. I've told him we could coexist with Tony and his group. Sergio's always wanted confrontation. So far, I've been able to persuade Escobar to see things my way, but who knows how this new turn of events will play out. Do you still have a date tonight?"

"Yes, I came home to change."

"I heard you aren't dating Max anymore. I won't pry into your personal life, but I was sorry to hear that. You seemed to like him a lot."

How could she know if I was dating Max or not? Maybe she still has spies in Tony's organization?

"Um, well, you know how it is. With Tony laid up, Max really doesn't have a lot of time to date."

"I hear Tony's starting to walk again. Maybe he'll take back the group sometime soon?"

"Um, maybe. I don't know a lot of details on what's going on over there."

I went back to my bedroom and changed into something more appropriate for dinner with Max. I then spent a few minutes in front of the mirror, trying to make it look like I hadn't been through exercise hell over the past couple of days.

~~~~

I drove to the main lobby at the Tropical Paradise and used valet. I hated to pay for parking, but I could barely walk and the idea of climbing up the hill from the visitor's lot was giving me flashbacks of the hike up the mountain the day before.

I looked around the lush tropical oasis that is the lobby of the hotel, but instead of finding Max, Johnny Scarpazzi walked up to me.

"Good evening, Miss Black," he said. "It's good to see you again."

"Johnny, it's great to see you too."

"I'm here to escort you up to dinner. I've already told Max you're here and he'll meet us up there."

Johnny led me through the lobby and up the wide curving stairs that led to the mezzanine level. I tried my best to keep up with him, even though each step was a burning agony in my ass and thighs. We went past the security station and through the double glass doors that led into the offices of Scottsdale Land and Resort Management. Even though it was late in the day, a surprising number of people were still working.

As we walked through the offices, I thought I'd try to get some information out of Johnny.

"Are the police still watching Max here at the resort?"

"Off and on. But they consider it to be a low-level assignment, as you'd expect. To help keep them occupied, we let them order room
~~~~

service at cost and we always have two of the girls bring the dinners up to them. We've encouraged the girls to chat with them for several minutes before they leave. We'll time it so if we need to do anything important, the cops are distracted with the girls."

Johnny led me to an elevator I hadn't noticed before. We went in and he used a keycard to allow him to activate the top button, which was labeled *Terrace*. As soon as the elevator doors closed, I felt Johnny relax, if only slightly.

"I'd like to thank you again for what you did for me," he said as we rode up. "I think about what happened and I know it could have easily gone the other way."

"No problem," I said. "Anything for a friend. How's Suzi? I haven't seen her in a few weeks. Is everything still alright with you and her?"

Johnny smiled. "Everything with Mistress is better than it's ever been. The whole thing seemed to bring us closer."

"I'm glad. You both seem good together."

When the door slid open, we found ourselves in a short hallway that only had one door, located at the far end. Gabriella was standing next to the door at a small security station, her black Farucci bag was sitting on a podium next to her. When she saw Johnny and I come out of the elevator, she took a keycard from her pocket and buzzed open the door.

I walked out to a large alcove, maybe thirty feet by forty. The space was open to the sky, but wasn't exactly on the roof, since there were walls on three sides. The forth side was open and facing west, with only a low wall and railing. The view of Camelback Mountain and Piestewa Peak was beautiful. The sun had dipped below the mountains and there were several light fluffy clouds in the sky to the west, already glowing yellow. I knew we were in for a gorgeous sunset.

A small round table, with place settings for two, sat by the railing.

Next to the table, the neck of a champagne bottle was poking out of a silver cooler. The rest of the space was filled with comfortable furniture and tropical plants, but I only had eyes for Max. He was standing at the railing, looking over the city.

I walked over to Max as he turned to meet me. My last few steps were more of a limping run and I threw my arms around him. It felt great to have him against me. I gave him a kiss, then started to feel somewhat awkward. Although I knew many of his secrets, I was still a little uncomfortable kissing Max in front of Johnny. But, when I turned, we were alone.

Yes!

It was like somebody had given me permission to be naughty. I began to kiss Max in a way that let him know I really missed him. He smelled great, all man with a hint of some sort of expensive cologne. As our kissing became more passionate, one of my hands began to travel up and down his body, stopping at every interesting place it could find.

After two or three minutes of this, it was pretty obvious we'd need to decide if we were going to have dinner on the terrace or sex. I was sorta hoping for sex and was secretly happy I'd chosen my black sparkly skirt for the evening. I was more than a little disappointed when Max stopped our kissing to pop open the champagne.

Okay, dinner now, sex later.

He poured out two glasses and handed one to me. He then held up his glass in a toast.

"It's damn good to see you," he said.

"Yes it is," I said, still a little out of breath from kissing.

I clinked my glass against his and we sat next to each other at the table, looking at the mountains and sky as we sipped our champagne. The clouds to the west had started to take on the iridescent orange glow of an Arizona sunset.

"This is a great view," I said, as my heart started to slow down. "I didn't know the hotel had a place like this."

"It's Tony's private retreat. He put it together when they were first building the resort. He said I could use it while he was recovering. I know he sometimes comes up here when he needs to think out a particularly difficult problem. This view can't help but relax you."

We slowly sipped our way through the first glass, then started on a second. As we drank, the clouds in the west went from orange to red and lights began to come on all over Scottsdale.

"It's so beautiful here. I love the way the city sparkles. Did you know the Paradise Park song, *Golden City,* is about the nighttime view of Scottsdale? Christine Johns told me the city at night was so beautiful, she had to write a song about it."

"You've mentioned you met Cristine Johns before. When was that?"

"It was on an assignment a few weeks ago. The same one with Stig Stevens."

"You do get around."

"Are you still keeping our relationship a secret? It's okay if you are, I just wanted to know."

"It seems to be for the best, at least while I'm leading the group."

"You're probably right, I suppose. Who knows about us so far?"

"Well, Johnny and Gabriella. They're too close to hide anything from either of them. Tony knows, of course. I tell him everything I do. I also decided to let Milo know. I figured with him dating Sophie, he'd know sooner or later anyway."

As if on cue, the door to the terrace opened and Milo came out wheeling a waiter's tray covered in stainless steel domes. As always, he had a broad grin that showed off his gold tooth.

Good thing we didn't decide on sex.

As Milo played waiter and set down our dinners, it struck me as a little surreal that I'd had breakfast with the head of the Black Death in the morning and was having dinner with the head of the largest crime family in Arizona that same night. It wasn't like I'd planned on becoming close to both Max and Danielle, but it sort of seemed to work out that way.

"Sorry to talk business," Max said, as we started on the delicious appetizers. "We'll have another proposal ready for Sergio in a few days. It seems like we're getting closer to an agreement. If you wouldn't mind having another meeting with your contact over there to give her the outlines, we'd appreciate it."

"Um, sure. Do you know when you'd like me to do it? I'm glad to have a meeting, but work's starting to get busy, especially with the snowbirds starting to come back into town."

That, and Sergio's trying to murder Danielle, so she really won't be in the mood for a negotiation meeting anytime soon.

"I'll let you know. Do you need to rush out of here tonight?"

"No, I'm okay," I said. "What's up?"

"Well, I have a couple of hours and I happen to know of a room that will be free for the evening. It's a nice suite with a splendid view."

Yes!

"It sounds perfect. Maybe you could show it to me after dinner?"

"I'd be glad to."

We chatted and flirted for almost an hour. After we'd finished up the entrees, Milo brought up dessert and another bottle of champagne.

I only picked at the dessert, but gladly had another glass of champagne. I could feel how painfully tight and sore my legs were getting and I was dreading how I would feel when it was time to stand.

Max got up, then walked around to pull back my chair. As I stood, I gasped in pain. After sitting for so long, everything had stiffened up. As I tried to stand, every muscle I had screamed out in pain.

"Are you okay?" he asked.

"Yes, but I've exercised more in the past two days than I've done all year. I'm a little stiff."

We started walking toward the exit, but my body was in agony. Each step was becoming more painful and difficult. I finally had to stop. Beads of sweat had broken out on my forehead and I was becoming dizzy. Max helped me to one of the chairs and I slowly sat.

"I'm okay," I said, trying to sound cheery. "Give me a minute to get the circulation going."

I sat and stretched for several minutes, desperately willing my legs to work.

"I think I'm okay now," I said. "Let's try this again."

Max helped me up and I tried to walk. It was slightly better. As I clung to his arm, I was able to shuffle along in painful jerky steps.

We'd almost made it to the door leading off the terrace, when I had Max stop again. My right leg was starting to twitch. It started deep in the muscle of my thigh, but I could feel it getting worse with each step.

"You'd better help me sit down," I said. "Maybe for a minute or two."

Max led me to a couch at the back wall. As I sat, I watched as my leg began to twitch and shake, like a dog when you rub its tummy.

No. Why now?

"Perhaps we should make some adjustments to our evening," Max said.

I started to protest that I was fine, but realized he was right and hung my head in defeat.

Max picked up his phone and punched a button. He murmured half a dozen sentences into the phone and hung up. He then took my glass from the table, filled it with champagne, and handed it to me.

"I'm so sorry," I said. "I had to climb a mountain yesterday and take a Guerilla Bootcamp fitness class today. I'm not used to that much healthy living."

Max grinned and softly chuckled, more to himself than to me. We sipped our drinks and, in about five minutes, the terrace door opened. Milo came gliding out, sitting on a purple mobility scooter. I'd often seen seniors in the mall riding them but had never been on one before. Milo was so big, he hung over the sides of the padded seat.

"The resort is pretty big," Max said. "We have several of these scooters for our guests who are uncomfortable walking long distances."

"Um, thanks. Alright, help me up."

Max reached down and effortlessly picked me up. I took the opportunity to wrap my arms around him. I felt a little sad when he sat me on the scooter. I had visions of him carrying me through the hotel to our room, like a groom carrying his bride across the threshold.

We then formed a little parade. Max and I led, with Gabriella and Johnny following at a respectable distance. We ended up taking the elevator down to the offices, snaked our way through several long corridors, then took a separate service elevator to a group of rooms attached to the conference center. Max led me to a room and used a keycard to open the door. As he led me in, I had to laugh.

"Do to your, um, condition," he said, "I switched out the room. This one doesn't have the same great view, but it does have this."

Sitting in the corner of the beautiful room was a hot tub, sized for two. The water was swirling and I couldn't wait to crawl in. Next to the tub was a cooler with another bottle of champagne.

"How long do you have tonight?" I asked.

"Only about two hours, I have a teleconference at nine. But you can stay here all night if you want to."

"No, sitting naked with you in a hot tub for two hours sounds just about right. Why don't you open the champagne?"

~~~~

By the time Max had to go to his meeting, I felt much better. Between the champagne and the hot tub, I felt good for the first time in days. Getting dressed was still a slow process, but not as painful as I feared it would be.

"Thank you so much for the hot tub. I'm not sure how long the effects will last, but I feel great now. I hope I didn't mess up your plans too much tonight."

"Not at all. Spending time with you was the goal and it doesn't really matter what we do. I'm still scheduling next weekend off. That's nine days from now. I hope you're also able to free up your calendar."

"That's the plan."

"Good, it'll give me something sexy to think about as I sit in meetings all day."

Max picked up the phone and gave some orders. A minute later, Johnny knocked on the door.

"I'll have Johnny drive you home," Max said. "Milo will take your car and follow."

Max helped me onto the scooter and I gave him the final hug for the evening.
~~~~

~~~~

Johnny led me down to the lobby and out to a back entrance. A black Town Car was idling and Milo was waiting next to the open rear door. I slid in and latched the seatbelt, which for once was easily accessible.

As I sat in the back of the big black sedan, being driven down Scottsdale Road, I had a vague feeling of being important and special. I could see how people got used to this sort of lifestyle.

This thought was shattered when we were about a block from our destination. I had a sudden fear Johnny might want to check my apartment before he let me in. From the way Milo talked the last time he'd driven me home, it was considered standard operating procedure. I didn't think it would be a good idea if everyone knew Danielle and I were roommates, even if the situation was only temporary.

We pulled into the parking lot of my apartment house. Johnny opened my door and Milo parked my car. He locked the doors, then walked over and handed me the key.

Johnny helped me out of the back seat and I leaned against the side of the car. After being out of the hot tub for half an hour, my legs had started to stiffen up again. Standing was a challenge.

"We'll escort you in, then say goodnight," Johnny said.

Shit.

"No, I'm fine," I said, trying to add as much authority to my voice as I could.

"The boss won't be too happy with us if a bad guy was in your apartment and we let you go in without checking it first," Johnny said.

"Look, I'm a big girl and I go into my apartment every day all by myself. I'll be fine."
~~~~

Johnny looked at me as if he were having some sort of inner debate.

"I'll be fine," I said again.

"Very well," he said. "In that case, we'll wish you a pleasant good evening."

I took a couple of shaky steps, then felt Johnny prop me up.

"Alright, help me to the elevator. Then, I'll be fine."

~~~~

The door to the elevator opened and I began the long walk down to my apartment. I'd almost made it, when the door to Grandma's opened and she stuck her head out.

"Well, Laura. Land's sakes, what are you doing, shuffling down the hallway at this time of night? Are you alright? Did someone tie you to a bed again?"

"What are you still doing up? No, I'm fine. I over-exerted myself the past couple of days. I was in a hot tub earlier and it was great, but now I'm stiff and sore to the point I can hardly move."

"Well, come on in. I have just the thing for you."

I shuffled into her apartment and collapsed on the couch. A few moments later, Grandma walked over, holding a caffeine free Diet Pepsi and a big blue pill.

"I take these whenever my arthritis starts acting up. Two of these babies and I'm able to walk down to the store and bring back a couple of sacks of groceries."

"What are they?"

"I don't know what they're called. They're generics that replaced a name brand a while ago. Honestly, I take so many pills, I don't even try to keep track of the names anymore. All I know is the blue ones work. I take two, but you should probably start out with one. They
~~~~

take some getting used to."

"At this point, it's take something or sit on the couch for the next couple of days."

I took the pill and washed it down with the Diet Pepsi. "How long until they take effect?"

"You'll start to feel it in about ten minutes, but they really kick in about fifteen minutes after that."

"What's going on with you and Grandpa Bob? Did you give him an answer yet?"

"No. We're going out on Saturday and I promised I'd tell him then. I still don't know what I'm going to do. Your cousin says I should follow my heart, but at my age it's more about being practical."

"What do you mean?"

"Well, take where we're going to live. I have an apartment full of furniture and so does he. When I sold my house to move here, I had to give away so many beautiful things, I hate to get rid of anything else. I think Bob feels the same way about the things at his place."

"You could always get a bigger place, or maybe even go back to a house."

"I've thought about getting one of those no-maintenance houses out in Mesa, the kind with cacti and crushed green rocks instead of a real lawn, but honestly, even at that, having a house is a lot of work. Then there's the kids, the grandkids, and now the great-grandkids."

Grandma pointed over to her shelves full of family pictures.

"I can barely remember everyone's name. It makes my head spin trying to keep up with birthdays, graduations, anniversaries, and weddings. If I marry Bob, that problem only doubles."

"You've told me you get along well with him. It would probably be nice to have someone to keep you company."

"I'm not saying being with Bob would be a bad thing, he's a good man, and he still has what it takes in the sack. But I'm not sure if I'm ready to give back my independence quite yet."

As Grandma was talking, a feeling of peace and happiness began to descend on me. I started feeling like things weren't so bad in my life after all.

"Well, let me know what happens," I said. "Marlowe and I would hate to lose you as a neighbor, but we only want you to be happy."

"Thank you, dear," Grandma said. She then looked at me and smiled. "How are you doing? Can you start to feel it yet?"

"Maybe, does it put you in a good mood?"

"That's the first thing it does. I've never been sure if it's because of something they put in the pill or because you're not hurting as much. How are you feeling?"

I gave one of my legs an experimental stretch. It still hurt, but it wasn't as bad as it had been.

"I think it's taking effect."

"Give it another ten minutes and you'll be right as rain. If it's still not enough, you can toss a Jamaican Jerk on top of it. It'll make you pass out after a few minutes, but your entire body will go numb. No pain at all."

As we sat and chatted, I felt the tension in my shoulders ease up. I hadn't realized they'd been so tight. It was like a minor miracle, as one muscle after another loosened and relaxed. It was like being back in the hot tub.

I then felt something weird happening with my leg. I looked down at my right thigh. Even as the pain receded, it had begun to twitch. It was the same thing that had happened when I was with Max, only this time it was worse. I became a little concerned as I stared down at it.

"I'm afraid the pills won't stop the twitches," Grandma said. "But you should be able to move again."

"How long do they last?"

"The main effects last for seven or eight hours, but it'll probably take the edge off for a day or so. Come on back if you need another. You know, in your line of work, you should probably get a prescription for them. I bet they'd come in pretty handy."

~~~~

Fifteen minutes later, I was back in my apartment. As Grandma predicted, I could walk again and the pain had receded to a simple annoyance. Danielle was on the couch watching the late news on TV. Marlowe was curled up in a ball next to her.

"How was your date?" she asked.

"Well, it was different. My legs were too bad for anything but dinner and some time in a hot tub."

"You look better now. Hopefully by tomorrow you'll feel okay again."

"It's only because I stopped by Grandma Peckham's. She gave me one of her arthritis pills."

"That'll do it. My mama used to take those. I tried one once and it made me loopy all day."

"Have you heard back from Escobar yet?"

"I'll check tomorrow, but I don't expect to hear anything for at least a couple of days. Security around him is tight and even his email is handled discreetly."

"Did you do anything else today?"

"After the library, I started to get a little buggy sitting around the apartment. I put on one of your scarves and a big pair of plastic sunglasses as a disguise. I then walked over to Old Town. I didn't
~~~~

know there were so many tourist shops there. I stopped by the Rusty Spur Saloon and listened to a singer playing acoustic guitar while I had a couple of beers. It was nice. I then went down the street to a place called The Grapevine. I'd never been there before, but it was beautiful on the inside."

"I haven't been to The Grapevine for a couple of years. Did you go upstairs?"

"No, it was closed off, but the downstairs was nice. I had a glass of wine and it was like all my troubles melted away."

"I love that place. We should go there sometime when we get a chance to hang out."

It was getting late and I was starting to feel a little spacey from Grandma's arthritis pill. I said my goodnights, went into the bedroom, and quickly crawled into bed.

Before I went to sleep, I texted Max to thank him again for the wonderful dinner. I also changed Mindy's ringtone to the theme from *Raiders of the Lost Ark*. This made me smile as I drifted off to sleep.

Chapter Six

When the alarm went off at six o'clock, I decided I was still too tired to get up. I hit the snooze three times before I even tried to get out of bed. My entire body was still stiff, but I didn't hurt as much as I'd expected. Maybe Grandma was right and the pill had some sort of residual effect. I only hoped it would be enough to get me through the day.

I took a shower, put on my big pink robe, then headed out to the kitchen. I'd gotten used to Danielle making the coffee and I was a little surprised to see her still snoozing away on the couch. I put on a pot to brew, then went back to the bedroom and got dressed.

By the time I'd made it back out to the living room, Danielle was sitting on the couch, watching the local news, and sipping a cup of coffee. Her hair was going in all directions and her eyes had a sleepy and unfocused look. Marlowe was curled up in a ball on her lap.

"Good morning," she said in a sleepy voice. "Thanks for putting the coffee on. I had a hard time getting to sleep last night."

"Thinking about Sergio?"

"Sergio, Escobar, and what I'm doing here in Arizona. It's hard to relax knowing there're people trying to murder you."

"What are you doing today?"

"I'll stop by the library and check messages. I'm also thinking about getting a disposable cell phone. At some point I'm going to need to be able to talk directly with someone without Sergio being able to trace it."

"That's a good idea, but pay cash and remember, after you give out the number, they'll be able to trace your new phone's location whenever it's on."

"I was thinking I'd make something for dinner, if you think you'll be home."

"I'm not sure what my schedule will be tonight. If you get a disposable, call me and we can coordinate schedules."

~~~~

I drove over to ASU and it was early enough for me to find a good parking spot. Campus was a hurried buzz of students going to classes as I walked to the Matthews Center building. Going up the stairs wasn't as painful as it had been the day before, but my legs still ached with each step.

Mindy was in her office with the door open. I knocked on the frame and she looked up from her laptop.

"Are you ready?" I asked.

"I'm like a kid at Christmas," she said. "It's finally sinking in and I'm starting to get excited about this. Let's go find out what's in the box."

~~~~

For the next three and a half hours, I followed Mindy around campus and the East Valley. She was carrying the box in a small backpack, so she looked like any of the thousands of college students normally out and about. We went to the ASU radiocarbon lab, then to the X-ray lab, and then to a medical lab in a building next to Desert Samaritan Hospital for the CT scans.

"When will you have the results?" I asked as we drove back to campus.

"I'll have the age of the wood tomorrow morning when they finish running the tests. I already have the raw data from the CT scan, but I'll need to analyze it before I can say anything for sure. I should have the results later this afternoon. The X-rays show the object in the box is about the right size and shape, assuming this statue is similar to the other six sisters."

"That's encouraging," I said. "I'd hate to go through all of this for an empty box."

~~~~

We parked and walked back to Mindy's office. She unlocked it and we went in. Mindy took two steps into the room, then stopped and looked down at her desk.

"What's wrong?" I asked.

"My desk. Everything's been moved. Someone's been in here again. This time they weren't as subtle."

"Let's look around and see what they took. I'm sure they were only here for the statue, but you never know."

I closed the door and began to look around the office. As Mindy opened drawers and looked on her shelves, I became aware of a strange noise in the hallway. I realized I'd been hearing it ever since we walked into the office. It was a sort of metallic clanking noise, followed by a hard scraping sound. For some reason, it reminded me of a ghost pirate dragging his chains in a *Pirates of the Caribbean* movie.

Clank-Scrape. Clank-Scrape. Clank-Scrape.

The sounds gradually grew louder as whoever was making them walked down the hall. Mindy finally heard the sounds and she glanced up at me with a puzzled look. I shook my head and shrugged my shoulders.

The sounds were so unusual, I didn't see how they could pose a danger. But when they stopped in front of Mindy's door, I became concerned. I walked back to the desk where my bag was sitting. I
~~~~

wanted my Baby Glock to be close at hand in case there was trouble. But, before I could get it, the door swung open and a man was standing there. He had a gun in his hand.

The man in the doorway was leaning on a metal crutch and looked like a refugee from an intensive care ward. His left foot had a hard plaster cast that went up to his knee. His right arm had a cast from his hand up to his elbow. A big bandage was wrapped around his head and his face was an angry mass of purple and red bruises. At first, we didn't know who he was, our attention was drawn to the gun in his good hand. Recognition came to Mindy and me at the same time.

That's impossible.

"Oh my God," Mindy said. "How are you even standing here? You fell off the ledge on the cliff and went down a couple of hundred feet. You shouldn't be alive."

"Fell?" the man sneered. "More like I was pushed off that ledge. No, I can't explain it either, but I was pushed. As I fell, I managed to grab onto a bush. It cut up my hand, but it slowed me down some. I slid rather than fell the rest of the way, that's what saved me. When I finally landed, I broke my ankle, my wrist, and cracked about half of my ribs. It took me a couple of hours to crawl back down to the trail. Lucky for me, two college guys came by soon after. They gave me some water then helped me back to the parking lot where they called an ambulance. I noticed none of you came to see if I was alive or not."

"Um, you robbed us at gunpoint," I said. "Did you forget that part? Besides, I also don't see how you survived. We assumed you were dead."

As I was talking, I studied the gun in his hand. It was different than the one he had on the mountain. That one was a dull black and this one was shiny chrome. The black one must still be at the bottom of the cliff.

"Well, I'm not dead," he said. "Give me the fucking box and I'm out of here."

"Why are you doing this?" Mindy asked.

"I thought that'd be obvious. There's a man who's willing to pay a lot for this. Babcock failed, so it's up to me. That's alright, this way I won't have to split the finder's fee."

"You mean the 'stealing it' fee," Mindy said.

"You have no right to talk. It's not like this is yours any more than it's mine. You only want to put it in a freaking museum, but I happen to know someone who'll pay a lot of money for it."

"Who is it?" I asked, not really expecting an answer.

"He's a billionaire out of California. I bet you'd know his name if I told you. He runs an internet company and he's been buying anything unusual that comes onto the market." He looked at Mindy. "After you started blabbing all over campus you'd found the Lost Sister, it didn't take him long to find out about it."

An internet billionaire from California?

"I'll need that box now," he continued. "I assume it's in the backpack on your desk and I'm not in the mood for a long discussion. Hand it over, now."

Mindy walked to the desk, unzipped the backpack, and took out the box. I could tell she was thinking about how she could stop this from happening again. The man must have seen it too.

"I know what you're thinking," he said. "So, this will be your one warning. Since I'm not able to properly defend myself at the moment, I'll shoot at the first sign either of you are trying anything. Are we clear? You stole the box from a wilderness area, so I know you can't call the police. But, if either of you follow me, or try to stop me, you'll die. I'm giving you this warning because I don't want your deaths on my conscience in case somebody tries to be a hero."

Mindy decided that now was not the time to make a stand. She held out the box and the man grabbed it. He then awkwardly held it against his body. He backed up a few steps into the hallway.

"Close the door," he said. "If you open it before twenty minutes go by, you'll die. Again, no warning. I'll shoot the first person who sticks her pretty head out of the office."

Mindy closed the door and we heard the *clank-scrape* sounds of the man going down the hallway.

"We'll need to follow him," I said. "He's moving slowly, so it should be easy, at least until he gets to a car. Maybe he drove himself or he might have a cab waiting somewhere. We'll let him get out of the building, then I'll follow. You go and get your car. I'll call you and tell you where to meet me."

From down the hallway, the man cried out in surprise. There was a loud crashing sound and we heard the quick *thump-thump-thump* of something falling down the stairs. There was silence for a moment, then we heard two people talking in loud panicked voices.

We ran out of the office and down the hallway. When we got to the stairs, we could see the man was sprawled out at the bottom. From the items scattered over the staircase, it appeared he fell the entire way down. Two students, a man and a woman, were standing over the body, waving their arms, clearly not knowing what to do. When they looked up and saw Mindy, relief spread on their faces, knowing that someone in authority was here to take charge of the situation.

As Mindy hurried down, I noticed the man's gun on the third step from the top. As I descended, I casually bent down and slipped it into my bag. I then gathered his crutch and a large chunk of his leg cast that had broken off and was lying on the stairs. I also saw the box. It was a short distance from the man at the bottom of the stairs and appeared to be undamaged.

"There's an Emergency Call Box on the sidewalk about halfway to the Anthropology Building," Mindy said to the students. "It has a big blue light on top of it. You two go together. Call the police and let them know EMS is needed here in the Matthews Center right away."

The students quickly obeyed and took off to call for help. We both went and stood over the body.

"Maybe he's dead?" Mindy asked hopefully, as she poked at the man's ribs with her foot. The pain from her prodding seemed to be enough to have the man briefly regain consciousness and he let out a low moan.

"Great," Mindy said. "He's not dead. What are we going to do with him?"

"He's still breathing, so there's nothing we can do. If we tell the police about what happened upstairs, the entire story of the cave and the statue will need to come out. Fortunately, they'll take him to a hospital and I'm guessing he'll be out of our way for at least a week, hopefully more."

I bent down and pulled the man's wallet out of his back pocket. It only took me a second to find his driver's license. "Thaddeus Murphy," I said. "He lives on Fig Springs Road in New River."

I put the license and the wallet back, then turned to Mindy. "Take the box and put it back in the safe. I'll stay here until the students come back. We'll let EMS figure out what to do with him."

~~~~

Mindy was still gone when the ambulance and the campus police came. The two students told the police they were there when it happened and that it seemed to be an accident. I hung out in the crowd of bystanders until they loaded the man into an ambulance. I asked one of the EMT's where they were taking him and she said Desert Samaritan, the same hospital in Mesa we'd been to earlier in the morning.

Mindy came back as the ambulance took off. I asked her to keep
~~~~

her office door locked and to let me know when she learned the test results.

~~~~

I drove back to the office and walked up front to reception. Sophie was looking at herself in her compact mirror. I sat down on the chair next to her desk.

"Are you alright?" she asked. "You don't look so good."

"I've had sort of a shitty morning."

"Really?" she asked, her interest now up. "What happened this time? Did somebody shoot up your car again? Not that you'd notice so much nowadays."

"Shut up. But no, no shootings…"

"Did somebody lock you in the back of a semi-trailer again and leave you to die in the middle of the desert?"

"No, nothing like that…"

"Well, that's good. Remember what your hair looked like after that? You didn't get near an exploding wedding cake again, did you? You were a real mess after that happened."

"Are you going to let me tell it or not?"

"Sorry, go ahead. Whenever you have a shitty day, I get a new story to tell Gina."

"You don't tell Gina everything that happens to me, do you?"

"Um, no, of course not. What happened this time?"

"Remember the dead guy on the mountain? The guy who robbed us then fell off the cliff?"

"You mean the guy who never existed and none of that ever happened?"

"Yeah, that guy. He showed up in Mindy's office this morning and
~~~~

stole the box again."

Sophie stared at me as the color drained out of her face. She absent-mindedly crossed herself.

"Sophie? Are you okay?"

"There's no freaking way he could be alive after falling down that cliff. You saw it. It was like a hundred feet straight down, then there was another drop-off that disappeared into the canyon."

"I know. He had a broken ankle, a broken wrist, and a bunch of cracked ribs."

"No, that's not what I mean. I don't know what you saw today, but there was no way he could still be alive."

"What? You don't think he was alive, even though he was talking and threatening us with a gun?"

"He might have looked alive, but I don't see how he could have been. You might have been dealing with a zombie. You know, the walking dead."

"I don't think he was a zombie. I'm pretty sure he was alive. He told us the story about what happened after he fell down the cliff. The weird part was he said he was pushed off the ledge. I really can't explain that at all."

"It was the curse."

"You think the spirit in the box pushed him off the cliff?"

"I don't see why not. And, if it could push him off the cliff, it could probably bring him back from the dead. What happened after zombie man stole the box?"

"Um, he fell down the stairs. He's back in the hospital and Professor Mindy has the box again."

"Ha! See, I told you. It's the curse. That statue doesn't like men."

"His name's Thaddeus Murphy. I checked his ID before EMS got there."

"Yeah, I know. He lives in New River."

"How'd you know that?"

"I ran the plates from the vehicles in the parking lot. Remember, you asked me to? His was the white van."

"You ran the plates even though he was dead?"

"You said you wanted to know who he was, so you could trace him back to whoever sent him. Besides, I know our luck. Whoever he was, I figured he'd somehow be back."

"What'd you find out about him?"

"Does this mean he exists again and we can talk about him?"

"Sure. What do you know?"

"Not a lot. He goes by Tad; I guess he doesn't like Thaddeus. He's been busted a few times for armed robbery and breaking and entering. His credit is crap. He's had a string of shitty jobs and always seems to get fired after a few months. From what I saw up on the mountain, I'd say he probably has some anger and aggression issues too."

"Anything that ties him in with the statue? He said the buyer was an internet billionaire from California."

"Wasn't the guy who wanted to buy *The Child* an internet billionaire out of California too?"

"Yeah, but until I learn more, I'm not going to assume it's the same guy. There're a lot of internet billionaires in California."

"Okay, but how many of them show up in Scottsdale? I bet Digga knew who he was. Any way to get ahold of him, so you can ask?"

"No, other than his name and his profession, I never learned anything about Digga."

"Well, in that case, would you look at my scar?"

"What scar?"

"The one on my forehead." She picked up her compact and stared at it. "It looks different."

"Are you still worried the government implanted a brain control chip?"

"Well, maybe."

I bent down and looked at it. "Isn't that the scar you got when you were surfing? You said you crashed into Huntington Pier back in high school."

"Yeah, but does it look different? Like maybe that's where they went in to plant the chip the other night."

I looked closer at it. "Nope, it's still so faint you can hardly see it. If somebody opened your skull, you'd think there'd be a bigger scar."

Sophie looked at the scar in her compact again. "Well, maybe. But I still get the feeling something's not right."

~~~~

By the time Sophie had convinced herself that the government didn't cause the scar, it was past lunchtime and we were getting hungry. Sophie suggested a new Mexican place she'd heard of, up by the Scottsdale Fashion Square. We took her car and made it to the restaurant a little after one o'clock.

We'd each ordered a margarita and were munching on a basket of chips and green salsa, when, across the room, I saw Reno come into the restaurant. Unfortunately, he wasn't alone.

Damn.

"Sophie," I said, bending forward and talking low.

"What?" she said, also talking low.
~~~~

"Reno just came in. He's with a tall blonde."

"No shit? Your ex showed up with another woman? Tell me about her. Is she pretty? How old is she?"

"I can't tell. They're walking through a crowd. She looks vaguely familiar, but I can't place her. You should be able to see them in a second."

"Yup, they just sat down. Reno's back is towards me, but I can see her."

"Well?"

"Um."

"Um, what?"

"Um, she's pretty."

"How pretty?"

"Well, she has nice hair. It's long and blonde, lots of big curls."

"How old?"

"About as old as you. It's hard to tell. Maybe a couple of years younger."

Ouch.

"Do you have any idea who she is? She sorta looked familiar."

"Nope."

"Wearing a ring?"

"Nope. If it's a date, she's not married."

Sophie could tell by the look on my face I wasn't happy. "So why are you getting all bent out of shape over Reno dating someone else? You knew it was going to happen."

"I know, but I didn't think I'd have to watch him doing it."

"See, you should have taken my advice. You could have kept Reno and still dated Max on the side. For as few dates as you've had with Max so far, Reno never would've noticed."

"I would've noticed. One man at a time's the only way I can do it. You know how much guilt and anxiety I've had over the five times I kissed Max while I was with Reno."

"You kept a count?"

"Well, yeah. I felt guilty each time I did it."

"But now you feel less guilty because you're only kissing Max?"

"Of course, I feel much better about that. One at a time. That's my motto."

"But now you're sad and frustrated because Max doesn't have any time to see you and the guy you dumped has already moved on?"

"What does that have to do with it?"

"The way I look at it, if you're going to be unhappy in either case, you should be unhappy because you have too many men in your life. It's more fun that way."

Sophie stopped talking and got the faraway look she gets when she's thinking.

"What?" I asked.

"I know who she is."

"Who?"

"Remember when you had a busted leg and we went over to Reno's that night, so you could make up with him. But instead of making up, he showed up with a blonde?"

"Oh my God. The foot fetish woman? Really?"

"I bet you. Didn't Reno say when he woke up she'd crammed half her foot in his mouth? Didn't she make him suck her toes?"

"Cynthia Redburn," I said, suddenly remembering. "That was her name."

"Eeeewww, thinking about that foot thing is so gross. Didn't Reno use her for a rebound the last time you dumped him?"

"But that was almost two years ago."

"I guess she's still on the market. Must be hard to find a guy who likes to suck toes."

The waiter brought our lunches and we ate quickly without saying a lot. The food was okay, but I'd lost my appetite. The waiter brought the bills and we left.

~~~~

We climbed into Sophie's Volkswagen and started driving back to the office.

"Did Reno ever ask to suck your toes?" Sophie asked.

"No, shut up."

"Hey, I was only asking. Maybe he's had some secret foot fetish desires all along. I'm thinking maybe you two would have gotten along better if you sometimes stuck your foot in his mouth and made him suck your toes."

"Shut up. That's so gross. You know why Reno and I broke up and it didn't have anything to do with what he sucked on."

~~~~

We got to the office and I went straight to my cube. After seeing Reno and the foot fetish woman, I wasn't feeling very social. After wasting ten or fifteen minutes on the internet, I started entering notes, but I was too distracted to have them make any sense. I went back up front where Sophie was entering information into her computer.

"I'm too preoccupied to work," I said. "I think I'm going home. Maybe I'll have better luck working from there."

"Don't let the Reno thing bum you out. Call up Max and talk with him. That will make you feel better about things."

My phone rang with the *Raiders of the Lost Ark* theme. When I answered, Mindy sounded excited.

"I've finished analyzing the CT scans. The statue does appear to be in the box. It's size and shape conform to the other six sisters. It appears to be wrapped in several layers of something organic, linen or maybe muslin. There's also a small cross laying on top of it. It appears to be similar in shape to the cross on the lid of the box and carved into the wall of the cave. It was only a light shadow on the X-ray, so I assume it's also made of wood."

"Great," I said. "What's next?"

"I need to get the lock off, hopefully without damaging it."

"It's not simply a matter of finding a locksmith?"

"Not exactly. A lock this old wouldn't open, even if you had the original key. All the brass parts are covered with a thick layer of patina. That's a natural tarnish produced by oxidation or other chemical processes. You can sort of think of it as rust."

"Okay, so how do you go about opening it?"

"They have mildly caustic solutions designed to target oxidized brass. From the X-rays we took of the lock, it's a standard design of the early seventeenth century. It's ornate, but not designed to be pick-proof. If I inject the cleaning solution into the body of the lock, especially in the area around the clasp, it should free the mechanism enough to open it. I might also need to free the shackle from the case of the lock. But if the interior components haven't been compromised, I should be able to open it without damage."

"How long will that take?"

"An hour or two, once I can start on it. The cleaning solution will be delivered tomorrow morning. We'll need to find somewhere secure to do it. I'd planned on using the campus archaeology lab, but that clearly isn't going to work.

"Alright," I said. "Let me know if you come up with any ideas about where we can go to do it. Hopefully on a campus that big we can find somewhere away from prying eyes."

"Um," Mindy said. "There's one other thing. I think there's a woman following me."

Shit, it figures.

"What does she look like?"

"She's dressed like a student, but older. Maybe in her forties. Short blonde hair."

"And she's following you?"

"Well, maybe. I had lunch on campus after you left. When I walked out of the Matthews Center, I happened to notice her sitting on one of the benches along the walkway. I didn't think anything about it, but she showed up at the same cafeteria. When I returned to the office, I looked out the window and she was back on the bench."

"Is she still there?"

"Yes."

"Alright, I'll come right down and see what I can find out about her. Do you still have your Nikon with you? Would you be able to take any clear pictures of her?"

"I don't have my telephoto lens, but I can try."

~~~~

I quickly drove down to ASU, but it took several minutes to find somewhere to park. When I found a space, it was halfway across campus and it took me another ten minutes to walk over to the Matthews Center. Class must have just gotten out for the day and the pedestrian paths were busier than normal. Groups of students walked by me as I wound my way through campus.
~~~~

I decided to change things up by approaching Mindy's building from the south, when my normal route would have me come in from the north. Whoever was there might be expecting me to come in from my usual direction and perhaps they wouldn't spot me as readily.

As I got near Mindy's office, I slowed and stayed to the side of the walkway. The first thing I noticed was every bench was filled with people of all types, from college students to mothers and their children. On the benches along the path outside Mindy's office, there were two women who could have fit the description.

I felt my phone vibrating. I looked down and it was Mindy.

"Are you anywhere nearby?" Mindy asked. "She sat there for almost half an hour and didn't move. She then got a call about a minute ago and took off."

"Which way did she go? North or south?"

"South. As soon as she got up I lost her in a big crowd of students, but she can't be too far."

"Can you describe her?"

"Medium height and medium build. Short blonde hair. Dark pants, light shirt, with big black sunglasses."

"Damn, she probably passed me on the sidewalk. Did you get a picture?"

"Yes, but the resolution isn't the best. Come up and look."

I slowly climbed the stairs and walked down to Mindy's office. My legs were still painfully sore and climbing a flight of stairs wasn't helping them feel any better.

I knocked and Mindy came to her door and unlocked it. I went in and she showed me an image on her laptop. It was a wide shot of the pedestrian walkway outside of her office. Two benches were visible and several people were on each bench.

"This is the woman I think was following me," Mindy said, pointing to a woman with a non-descript outfit of dark pants and a light button-down blouse. Her hair was relatively short and parted to the side. She had big sunglasses that covered much of her face.

"How far can you zoom in on this?" I asked.

Mindy adjusted the computer and the woman on the bench grew to take up the entire screen. Unfortunately, about the time the picture was zoomed in enough to be able to make out her features, it became pixelated to the point where all detail was lost.

"If I'd had my telephoto lens, it would have been much clearer. I tried to take a picture with my phone, but the resolution was a lot worse, even at full zoom."

"I was hoping your Professor Babcock and the creep with the gun would be the only two involved with this. But it's likely you've been followed for a day or two. Keep an eye open for the woman or anyone else. She might be working with a partner."

"It figures. I'm thrilled to find the Lost Sister, but I should've known something so valuable would attract attention. It's my own fault. I should have kept quiet when I suspected what was in the cave. It's no wonder people are following me."

"How valuable is something like that?"

"In terms of history, it's priceless. The other six Sisters have been in museums for over a hundred and fifty years. The existence of the seventh Sister has been well documented and is widely known. It's been sort of a holy grail for archeologists in this part of the world for the last hundred years or so."

"And if it went up at an auction house?"

"Hard to say, I'm not on that side of museum acquisitions. Several hundred thousand dollars, at least. Maybe a million, maybe more."

Damn.

~~~~

I got back to my building about six thirty and met Grandpa Bob waiting for the elevator.

"Well, if it isn't Phillip Marlowe," he said. "What's buzzin' cousin? Nab any more bad guys lately?"

"Hey you," I said. "I heard you and Grandma are thinking about getting married."

"Well, I asked," he said as we stepped into the elevator. "But I'm not so sure she's keen on the idea. Geeze Louise, she's been thinking about it for a week now. How long does it take you gals to make up your minds?"

"I'm sure she'll come around. She worries about her independence and she'd hate to start throwing her things away if you both moved into one place."

We got out of the elevator and slowly walked down the hall.

"Do you really think that's her beef with the whole idea? I could care less about the stuff at my place. My kids picked out most of it to be practical in an apartment. I could toss the lot and be just as happy. And to be honest, I worry about getting tied down as well. I'm not a wet blanket, but I've been on my own ever since my wife passed, sixteen years ago. I like doing things my own way, but I think I could come around."

We finally stopped in front of Grandma's door.

"You should let her know," I said. "It might help her make up her mind."

"Thanks for the advice, chickee."

"Let me know how it works out."
~~~~

Chapter Seven

I went into my apartment and found Danielle sitting on the couch. There was an old science fiction movie on TV and there were half a dozen empty Corona bottles on the coffee table. Danielle was holding another half-empty beer in her hand. I couldn't put my finger on it, but she looked terrible. Not because she must be halfway to getting hammered, but it was something else. She had the distant look of a woman who'd somehow been traumatized.

"Danielle, are you alright?" I asked. "What happened?"

She looked up at me and I could see she'd been crying. "Get yourself a Corona. I've got some unwelcome news."

I went to the fridge and pulled out a beer. I opened it and sat next to Danielle.

"I heard back from Escobar," she quietly said. "Apparently, he has some spies in the group who report to him independently of what Sergio and I tell him. I don't know who these people are, but they seem to write an overall summary every day and send it off to Escobar as a matter of course. From what they've reported, my disappearance didn't fool Sergio for as long as I'd hoped. Sergio reported to the group on Tuesday morning that I'd turned traitor, left the group, and was now working for Tony DiCenzo. Sergio has the entire organization looking for me, with orders to kill me on sight. He's justifying this by saying I know too many secrets to be allowed to be used by Tony. Of course, these spies have no way of knowing

Escobar is my father. They're only reporting what they've heard."

"But your father can't believe that."

"I've told him my side of the story. How Sergio wants to take over the Black Death and how he issued orders on Monday to have me assassinated, on the pretext of me being a traitor. I let Escobar know I'm in hiding and waiting for instructions."

"So, that should settle it. Your father now knows what's going on and he'll do something to fix it, right?"

"Unfortunately, I know Escobar too well. I know what's going through his mind. He knows there's a problem with the group in Arizona. So far, he's gotten two versions of what the problem is, not including what Sergio's told him directly. So, I guess he now has three versions. My father never acts rashly or without reason. In his mind, he'll want to know the facts before doing anything that would cause a major change to the organization."

"Well, that's good, isn't it?"

"No. Escobar's note today said he's sending his brother, Tio Francisco, to Scottsdale to learn what's going on."

"But that still sounds good. He wouldn't send his brother unless he wanted to get the facts. Don't you see that as a positive?"

"Yes, but the note also said that my uncle is bringing Largo."

"Largo?"

"Señor Largo's a man who's both violent and sadistic. I suppose every one of the cartels has a man like him. Someone who'll eliminate any threats to the organization, usually through brutal methods. My uncle is the power behind my father and Largo is how he enforces his decisions. I love and respect my uncle, but I fear Señor Largo. I know when he shows up there'll be carnage."

"You're making him sound a little bit like Carlos."

"Carlos for a time worked directly under Largo. They went on several operations together. After one of those operations, the men started calling him Carlos the Butcher. You can only imagine why."

"How long will it take your uncle to come up here? What if they have trouble getting over the border?"

At that, Danielle started laughing. It was the genuine laugh of someone who's heard something ridiculous.

"Oh, Laura, I don't think you grasp the concept of how this works. My uncle and Largo aren't going to sneak over the border fence in the middle of the night, then be picked up by a coyote who'll smuggle them to Scottsdale in the trunk of his car. My uncle's an executive in a large multinational corporation that has legitimate operations in a dozen countries. Same with Largo. I imagine they'll take the corporate jet from Guadalajara and land at the Scottsdale Airpark."

"Um, okay. When do you think they'll get here?"

"The note said to expect them within two days."

~~~~

We ordered in a pizza, then sat and watched TV for a couple of hours. We each had a few beers and by nine o'clock I was ready to call it a night.

I went into my bedroom and put on a big T-shirt. After everything that had happened today, I needed to hear a friendly voice. I called Max and he picked up almost at once.

"Hello, beautiful," he said. As always, his deep and powerful voice made me melt. "I hope you're feeling better."

"I'm slowly getting over it. Grandma Peckham gave me one of her arthritis pills last night and it took most of the soreness away."

"I'm glad to hear that. How's your day been?"

"Oh, the usual."

He started laughing. "The usual for you would be a day from hell
~~~~

for most people."

"It's sort of been the day from hell for me as well. I still feel terrible that I messed up our date last night. When do you think we can try it again? I don't want to wait until next weekend to see you."

"I was thinking about that," he said. "I have a video conference set up tomorrow night at nine, but I should be free for a couple of hours before that. Come over and I'll have a dinner set up for us somewhere."

"I'd love that. What time can you make it?"

"Let's plan for six, assuming nothing comes up on your side."

"I'll shoot anyone who tries to delay me."

"Aggressive," he laughed. "I like that."

~~~~

I woke to the alarm and crawled out of bed. My legs and arms had finally started to calm down, but I knew by the end of the day I'd feel like crap again.

I put on my robe and walked out to the living room. As usual, Danielle was watching the local news and the room smelled like coffee. I went to the kitchen and poured myself a cup.

I realized I was starting to get used to having her in my apartment and having a pot of coffee waiting for me in the morning seemed kind of nice. Marlowe also seemed okay with the situation. He was asleep next to Danielle with all four feet in the air.

"Good morning," I said, as I sipped the hot coffee. "What's up today?"

"I drank too much last night. I had to raid your medicine cabinet this morning for some Advil. After a while, I'll go down and check messages at the library. I've been going to the branch on Drinkwater Boulevard, so I might go to a different one today. There's the Mustang Branch Library up on 90th Street, but I'll need to take a cab
~~~~

for that one."

"Are you expecting another email back today?"

"Not really. My uncle will contact me with instructions on where to meet once he gets into Scottsdale, but that probably won't be until tomorrow, maybe Sunday if there's a delay. But I'll need to check messages in case something else has come up."

Something about her tone had me concerned. "Are you doing alright?"

"Not really. By now, Sergio knows Tio Francisco and Largo are coming to Arizona to investigate what's going on. Sergio knows if he's caught in a lie, he'll be punished. His desire to lead is well known and I don't think his story will sound believable. But he's stayed alive this long by being resourceful. I'm sure he's coming up with a story my uncle will believe. Sergio's other option will be to find me and kill me before my uncle can question me directly. If I'm not there to present my side of the story, Sergio will probably be able to get away with it."

"Maybe you should stay in today?"

"No, I'll just need to be careful."

~~~~

I drove down to the office. There was nothing specific I had to do before I went back on Timothy's trail, but it was always nice to check in with Sophie and see if anything new was happening. When I got there, her yellow Volkswagen was the only car in the carport.

When I walked up front to reception, Sophie was sipping a coffee and flipping through pages on her tablet.

"Hey, Sophie, where's everyone?" I asked, looking around the office.

"Lenny's at the District Attorney's office. He's trying to work out a plea deal for somebody. Gina has some paperwork to catch up on.
~~~~

She said she'd do it at home and drop it off about nine-thirty or ten."

"Did you find out anything more about Professor Babcock or Tad Murphy?"

"Some. I got the standard six or seven pages I get on everyone. Where they grew up, where they went to school, military service, parking tickets, scrapes with the law. But nothing too unusual with either of them. Thaddeus Murphy is a small-time crook and Dr. Clifton Babcock is a respected university professor."

"Nothing that ties either one of them to a California internet billionaire?"

"Nope. Babcock grew up in Vermont and Murphy's an Arizona native. Other than the fact that the professor has been Mindy's college advisor for several years, there's nothing obvious that ties them in with this at all."

"Let me know if you can find out anything else. This whole thing is messed up. Mindy now has a stalker. A woman in her forties."

"At least it's not cheating spouses."

"That's true. I did ask for something different."

"Are you sure you have to go back to that fitness class today? The last time almost killed you."

"I really don't have a choice. Somehow, Timothy and Crystal are getting together at the fitness center. I need to stay close to her the entire time. It won't look as suspicious if I'm a student in her class."

"Is Gina still going in with you?

"That's the plan. She said she'll be at the fitness center when Timothy arrives. We'll tag-team them and hopefully come away with the evidence."

"How are your legs? I know mine are still sore."

"Grandma Peckham gave me one of her arthritis pills two nights ago. It helped for a while, but I'm back to being sore again. Dragging the bucket of gold across campus the day before yesterday didn't help either. I'm not looking forward to the class."

"That class almost killed me. I hope you don't barf all over the fitness studio today. Did you ever find out if you're pregnant or not?"

"I still don't think I am. I think I'm getting queasy because I don't exercise a lot."

"But you still don't know for sure? You still could be? You know, you could take one of those drug store pregnancy tests."

"I tell you what. If I go another week, I'll take a test. Until then, you can stop talking about it. I never know who can overhear us and I don't want another rumor to go around."

"Well, okay, but let me know how it works out."

~~~~

I left the office and drove over to Paradise Valley. Timothy's office was in a group of high-rent buildings on Lincoln Drive. When I got there, his Audi was parked in his designated spot. Since it wasn't even nine o'clock, I knew I'd have almost two hours before he left, but I wanted to make sure he wasn't somehow getting together with Crystal before class.

While I was waiting for something to happen, I called Mindy. When she answered, I asked if she'd figured out where she was going to take the box to get the lock off.

"They should be delivering the cleaning solution to my office by ten thirty or eleven. I know the anthropology lab is off-limits to us, but I have a friend over in chemical engineering. They have a lab over there that'll be perfect. It's certainly big enough and they have the facilities to properly dispose of the chemicals when we're through with them."

"I'll be on another assignment until one thirty or two," I said. "But after that, I'll come over and escort both you and the box over to the
~~~~

engineering lab."

"Perfect. There's one last project I'm finishing this morning, then I'll be able to devote myself full time to the Lost Sister."

~~~~

At about ten twenty, Timothy appeared at the door to his office and walked to his car. He drove to the fitness center on Scottsdale Road and made it with about twenty minutes to spare before class started at eleven.

I followed him into the club and watched as he walked straight into the men's locker room. Gina was at a weight machine doing some exercise involving her arms. The machine was positioned so she could have an unobstructed view of the entire weight room and the entrances to both locker rooms.

"Is Crystal here yet?" I asked Gina.

"She went into the ladies locker room about a minute ago. You get dressed and keep an eye on her. I'll watch and see if he comes out."

I went into the dressing room and saw Crystal in the back corner getting into her fitness outfit. I changed clothes while Crystal spent several minutes at the mirror, brushing out her long red hair and putting it into a pony tail. Watching her go through her routine, she didn't look like a sadistic drill sergeant or a slut determined to break up a marriage. She looked like any nice woman you'd meet on the street.

With about five minutes to go before class, Crystal left the locker room and went up to talk to one of the guys at the front desk. Gina was now at a different weight machine, this one focused on her legs.

"Timothy left the locker room and walked into the fitness studio about two minutes ago," Gina said. "After class, let's stick close to them and discover what they're up to."

We drifted into the fitness studio, where Timothy and a dozen women were stretching on the floor or talking in small groups. We
~~~~

positioned ourselves in what I now knew was the back corner. From here, we could easily see everything in the room. The women in the class began to organize and Timothy ended up two rows ahead of us.

Crystal came in and started up the music. The class began to march in place as Crystal yelled out how soft and weak we were. As with the last time, the pleasant looking woman from the locker room had transformed herself into a snarling beast, intent on inflicting as much torture on us as possible. She started us out with an easy stretching song, but again quickly transitioned to a more intense workout.

The pain and exhaustion were almost as bad as the first day. The only thing that saved me was that we were now more or less hidden in the back and I didn't need to do the moves as enthusiastically as when Sophie and I had been in the middle of the front row.

By the third pulse-check, I was starting to get lightheaded and my stomach was again a twisted knot. Gina calmly took a sip from a water bottle and looked at me.

"I'm up to one fifty," she said with a big smile. "This is a great class. It's usually hard for me to get my pulse above one forty. Hey, are you alright?"

"I'm good," I said, gulping air like a fish who's been tossed on a river bank. "The class is more than halfway over. I can make it through."

The music started pounding away again and we continued to exercise, now with the stretchy fitness bands. This new form of punishment pushed me toward a wall of exhaustion. My efforts became weaker and more feeble with each passing minute. I tried to balance how much I was exercising with how fast the world spun and how queasy my stomach was feeling. By the last song, I was barely moving at all.

With a sense of relief, the cool-down song finally began to play and everything started to slow down. With the end of the song, everyone again clapped and I knew I'd made it through the class.

Unfortunately, my head and stomach had reached a tipping point.

As the class filed out, I went down to a knee and waited for the world to stop spinning. My stomach was still making up its mind what to do and I was glancing around to see if there was a handy trash can, in case things didn't work out.

As the room emptied, Gina bent over me with concern. "Are you going to be okay?"

"Yeah, I'm alright," I said, even as the room continued to spin. "Give me a second. You follow Timothy, I'll follow Crystal."

I got up and stumbled out of the room. From across the fitness center, I saw Crystal would beat me to the ladies locker room by a dozen steps. I made it there after a long and unsteady walk across the weight room, but Crystal wasn't anywhere. I went to my locker, fumbled open the lock, and grabbed my phone.

I did a quick search, but didn't see her in the showers, the sauna, or the steam room. I went out the back door of the locker room and down the dim maintenance hallway. I got back to the weight room, where Gina was standing, without seeing either Crystal or Timothy.

"Nothing?" I asked, leaning against a weight machine so I wouldn't fall over.

Gina shook her head. "He went into the locker room and hasn't come out yet."

With a flash of insight, I suddenly knew where they had to be. I mentally thumped my head that I hadn't realized it before now. I set my phone to video and led Gina back down the dim hallway to the door of the janitorial room. I held my finger to my lips, then slowly pushed open the door.

Crystal was bent over the pallet of towels with her fitness pants lying next to her. Timothy was behind her with his shorts around his ankles. He was holding Crystal's long ponytail with one hand, like he was holding the reins on a horse. He was using his other hand to smack her bare ass. They were both actively involved in an aerobic activity and didn't hear the door opening. Maybe they didn't hear us because Crystal was loudly moaning, "I'm a bad girl, such a bad girl," over and over.

Gina and I stood there for two or three minutes, with me recording video the entire time. I found if I leaned against the doorframe, the room didn't spin quite as badly.

When they finished and had started to untangle from each other, Crystal noticed we were standing there watching. She pushed Timothy away, grabbed her pants, and quickly put them on. Timothy looked at us as he pulled up his shorts.

"Who the hell are you?" he barked out at us. He then looked at the phone in my hands, which was still recording the video. "What the fuck are you doing?"

"We're investigators with Halftown, Oeding, Shapiro, and Hopkins," Gina said. "It's the law firm representing your wife in the divorce."

Timothy suddenly understood why we were there and what would happen because of the video. "Like hell you will. I'll take that phone, bitch," he said as he took three quick steps towards me, his powerful arm outstretched.

Gina stepped forward, grabbed the man's hand, then casually spun her body around in a circle. It was so smooth, it really didn't look like she was doing anything. But when she stopped, Timothy's face was smashed against the cinderblock wall and his arm was locked behind his back in what must have been a very painful position. Gina was using her other hand to bend back a finger to an angle that must have been agonizing. Timothy was breathing hard and standing on tippy-toes to help relieve the pressure on his arm, but even at that, I was surprised tendons weren't already snapping.

"Don't worry, bitch," Gina said. "Your attorney will get a copy of the video. It's likely the judge will get a copy too."

~~~~

I drove over to campus, found a place to park, and slowly walked to the Matthews Center. I again came up from the south but didn't see anyone who matched the description of the woman who'd been following Mindy. I took a good look at everyone sitting on the benches in front of the professor's office, in case there were multiple people involved in the surveillance.

I climbed the long staircase to the second floor and walked down to Mindy's office. I knocked and she unlocked her door and let me in.

"Are you ready?" I asked as I walked into her office.

"Why are you limping? You look like you hurt all over."

"Long story, but I had to take a fitness class today called Guerilla Bootcamp. You're right, every muscle in my body hurts."

"You had to take a fitness class, for your job? That sounds like fun."

I couldn't help but notice Mindy had a big smile on her face.

"What?" I asked.

"The test results came back on the wood."

"And? How old is the box?"

"They dated the wood to between 1610 and 1615. It's perfect."

"But didn't you say the box was buried in like 1641?"

"That's when the box was buried. But for something like this, I imagine they made the box out of wood that had already been put to a holy or religious use, like maybe it had been an important part of a church or something like that. That would likely account for the difference."

"Seems reasonable to me. Did you get your lock opening solutions?"
~~~~

"Yes," she said, picking up a cardboard box from her desk. "I also got a set of generic padlock keys for the common Spanish locks of the era, along with some general cleaning supplies. If we can dissolve away the oxidation to the point the internal mechanisms free up, I should be able to use one of the keys and open it like any other lock."

"Where'd you get keys that would fit locks from the sixteen hundreds?"

"The internet. You'd be surprised what you can find on the archaeology supply sites. Let's go open the lock."

We walked down to the basement and then to the storage room. I stood outside in the hallway while the professor retrieved the box from the safe. As I stood alone in the empty corridor, I felt a little vulnerable. I started to think about Gabriella, Danielle, and the arsenals they kept in their bags. Although I have my Baby Glock, and I knew it could help get me out of a lot of jams, the thought of having Gabriella's Uzi suddenly seemed like a really good idea.

Mindy came out with the box, again in her backpack, and we walked across campus to the Fulton Engineering Center. I kept a lookout, but I never did see the woman from the day before or anyone else who looked familiar from the benches outside of Mindy's office.

I'd never paid a lot of attention to this area of campus when I was going to school here, but the Engineering Center turned out to be a series of large buildings numbered 'A' through 'G', all lined up against each other like a row of books on a shelf.

Mindy went in a main entrance, then we made our way through a dozen hallways and a couple sets of stairs. Like a rat in a maze, I quickly lost all track of where we were.

At least we won't be followed.

We ended up in front of a door on a lower level in a hallway that seemed rather empty. We entered what turned out to be a small laboratory. There were half a dozen black laboratory benches with sinks and various pieces of equipment and glassware scattered across each of them.

Mindy started arranging things in a large opening in one of the walls. It had a glass front, which Mindy had raised up to expose a flat working surface and a sink.

"This is called a fume hood," she said pointing to the opening. "There's a lot of room to do work, but more importantly, it's connected to the building's vapor collection system. It will draw away the caustic vapors as they come off the lock."

While Mindy set up her chemicals and cleaning supplies, I looked around the lab and stuck my head back into the hallway. Even though I knew nobody could have followed us, I went back into the lab and locked the door.

Mindy removed the wooden box from her backpack, then took a roll of plastic food-wrap and rolled it around the box, again and again, until everything but the lock was wrapped with several layers of the plastic film. The professor put on a pair of chemical-proof gloves, then worked for an hour and a half on the lock. She took syringes and squirted three or four different chemicals into the lock. She put chemicals on long wooden sticks, with cotton swabs at the ends, and dabbed all around the shackle. She then took some sort of penetrating lock oil and used a syringe to squirt it into the lock.

"Okay," she said at last. "The interior parts should have been freed from each other. Wish me luck that one of these keys work."

Mindy had a set of six generic keys and she got to the fifth one before anything happened. With the fifth, the key turned slightly and there was a subtle metallic grinding noise from inside the lock. When the lock didn't open, Mindy took some more of the lock oil and used the syringe to squirt it up into the mechanism. She tried the key again and this time it turned. There was a subtle metallic clicking noise and the lock opened.

"Oh my God," she said. "It's open." She was panting with

excitement and starting to giggle from being nervous.

"The box is still wrapped up in the plastic," I said. "Do you want to open it here or somewhere a little grander than a basement lab in the Engineering Center?"

"I can't wait. Let me document what we've done so far, then let's open it. Right here."

She pulled the Nikon from her backpack and started snapping photos of the lab, the fume hood, the chemicals, and the box wrapped in plastic.

She went to one of the big lab benches, cleared off a space, and took out a large piece of thick white cloth from her backpack. She spread it out, then carefully placed the box and the now open lock on it. She also took out a metal ruler and set it next to the box. She then took several pictures of the box and the lock from the front, the sides, and the back.

"Okay," she said, in a quivering voice as she handed me the camera. "Would you take pictures as I do this?"

Slipping on a pair of white cloth gloves, she reached out to the box. Her hands were shaking to the point where it took her a couple of tries to get hold of the end of the plastic.

I took pictures as she slowly unwrapped the layers of film. After about a minute, the plastic was off and the box was ready to be opened.

"I put penetrating oil on the hinges when Gina and I brought the box back with us to the lab on Tuesday night. I'm hoping it will be enough to open the lid without damaging the wood."

I lifted the camera to my eye and took pictures as she took hold of the lid and slowly lifted. The hinges made metallic creaking and popping noises, but the top opened smoothly.

Sitting on what appeared to be a bundle wrapped in yellowed cloth was a small wooden cross. As Mindy had speculated, it looked to be a match to both the crosses carved into the cave wall and on the top of the box.

Mindy carefully lifted the cross and set it on the white cloth. I took several pictures of it, then Mindy turned it over while I took pictures of the back.

"Alright," she said. "Are you ready?"

She carefully reached into the box and took out the cloth-wrapped bundle.

"I didn't realize it would be so heavy," she said as she felt the weight of it. "It must be ten or twelve pounds."

Gently setting it down on the bench, she slowly peeled off six or seven large rectangles of ancient fabric from around the central object.

"This should be the last layer," Mindy said. Her voice was now stammering so bad I could barely understand her words.

Mindy unwrapped the final layer to reveal a shining gold statue, about eleven or twelve inches high. It was of a young woman, maybe fifteen or twenty years old, naked from the waist up, who was in a kneeling position. She had an elaborately carved headpiece and an exquisitely detailed necklace.

But more than either the gold or the intricate carvings, the thing that immediately drew my attention was her face. The woman looked both compassionate and wise. It was the same look I'd sometimes seen on statues of the Buddha or on Jesus.

"She's beautiful," I whispered.

"She's amazing," Mindy whispered back. "You can see why the ancients worshiped her and her sisters. Don't forget to take pictures and be sure to include the ruler in some of them for scale. My hands are shaking too much to hold the camera."

I took the big Nikon and snapped a dozen pictures. I

photographed the statue from the top, the front, and the back. I then had Mindy pick up the Lost Sister while I took pictures of the bottom of the figurine. Having a bit of an inspiration, I had Mindy stand while I took several pictures of her holding her treasure.

"Look down at it," I said. "Really look at the figurine and think about the ten years you've spent looking for her."

Mindy looked down at her statue and, for a brief moment, her face shone with a look of happiness and wisdom, matching the face of the statue in her hand. As I tripped the shutter and heard the camera click, I knew the picture would be a keeper.

~~~~

We spent another fifteen or twenty minutes looking at the Sister and taking pictures. There was a digital scale in the lab and Mindy spent several minutes weighing the figurine and measuring its dimensions. As she got the numbers, she wrote everything down in a battered laboratory notebook she'd pulled out of her backpack.

While Mindy was working, I pulled out my phone and took pictures of the statue, the box, the lab, and of the professor, who was busily working at her trade. I knew these types of pictures could often tell a story the formally posed pictures could not.

At last, Mindy decided to return the statue to its case. She had me put on a pair of the white cloth gloves and we carefully rewrapped the sculpture in the yellowed cloth and placed it in the box. We set the cross on top of the Sister and everything fitted perfectly, as if we'd never taken it out. Mindy closed the lid, then picked up the lock.

"In theory, we should be able to use the key to open the lock whenever we want without damaging it. This box has kept the Sister safe for the last four hundred years, we might as well use it until we figure out what to do with it. She fastened the lock back onto the hinge and snapped it shut. It locked with a soft metallic click.

"Alright," she said. "Now I'm nervous. I'd love to put out a press release, but without the permits it would be premature, maybe even
~~~~

disastrous. I'm going to write a paper on the discovery, but even if one of the journals accepts the manuscript right away, they still wouldn't publish it for four or five months."

"Why don't we get it back to the safe," I said. "It's the most secure place we've found on campus. I doubt anyone could figure out how to get it out, even if they did know where it was."

~~~~

It was almost four thirty and I needed to drive back to my apartment to change for my date with Max. On the way over, I called Sophie.

"Hey," she said when she answered. "Gina says you caught Timothy balls-deep in Crystal today and were able to get a video of the whole thing. At least you won't have to take the fitness class again. How are you feeling?"

"My legs are killing me. I might need to ask Grandma Peckham for another arthritis pill."

"Gina says you almost threw up again after class. Are you sure you aren't pregnant?"

"No, shut up."

"I'm just sayin'. You should probably go somewhere and find out for sure."

"I'm probably not, so stop bugging me about it. Did you forget what we talked about this morning? I called to tell you we opened the box this afternoon."

"Well, was her Lost Sister in it?"

"Yes. And it's a beautiful piece of art. I'll send you a picture of it."

"What's Mindy going to do with it?"

"Nothing until the paperwork gets sorted out. The Lost Sister's in a safe and Mindy's going to spend the next couple of weeks writing a
~~~~

paper on it so she can publish it in an archeological journal."

"So, you've got the cheating spouse video and are pretty much done with the Lost Sister. It sounds like you might get the weekend off."

"I could use it. It's been a shitty week. What are you doing tonight?"

"Meeting up with Snake. He said he wanted to go somewhere quiet for dinner, then I think we're going out with some of his friends."

"That sounds like fun. I'll give you a call tomorrow if anything new comes up."

"Okay, but don't call until nine thirty or ten. I imagine I'll be out sorta late tonight."

~~~~

I made it to my apartment house and took the elevator. My legs were too sore to even think of climbing up the stairs. When the door to the elevator opened onto my floor, Marlowe was sitting in the middle of the hallway, looking up at me.

"What are you doing out here?" I asked.

I picked up my cat and listened to him purr as he went limp in my arms. I think he was as confused as I was. I started going over scenarios for how he got into the hallway and none of them were good.

I was getting a bad feeling as I walked down to my apartment. My door was closed, but some instinct made me try it without a key. The door was unlocked and it swung open without a sound. With my heart rate rising, I sat Marlowe down and quietly slid the Baby Glock out of my purse.

No one was visible in the apartment as we walked in. Marlowe hopped up on the couch and followed me with his eyes as I started the room-to-room search.
~~~~

The living room was alright. A couple of things were on the floor, but there didn't seem to be signs of a struggle. Danielle's bag wasn't on the coffee table, but her sunglasses were. I walked into the kitchen, where there was an open Corona on the counter that only had a few sips out of it.

I walked towards the back of my apartment, where the hallway closet was standing open. The washer and dryer weren't being used and I'd never known Danielle to not close the doors. The bathroom door was open and a quick glance told me no one was hiding in the shower.

More confused than ever, I walked towards the bedroom. Again, the door was open and I knew it had been closed when I'd left.

Another quick glance showed no one was in the room, but the closet door was closed. This struck me as odd after everything else had been left open.

If someone was hiding inside the closet, they'd wait until I started to open the door, then fling themselves against it to knock me over. I instead stood next to the door and put my back against the wall. I then reached out to turn the handle with my left hand. The idea being, if they crashed against the door, they'd find no resistance and go sprawling on the floor. At least that was the idea.

I turned the handle and swung the door open a foot. I kept telling myself to look who it was before I shot, but my stomach was a knot and I wasn't making any promises to myself.

The room was silent as I waited for a response. When nothing happened, I took my foot and shoved the door open the rest of the way. When this was also met with silence, I stepped out to investigate the closet. Although it was crammed full of my shirts, pants, dresses, and shoes, there were no legs visible underneath the rack of clothes. A further glance showed my jewelry box hadn't been moved from its place on the top shelf.

I looked around the room to see what else had been disturbed. The door to the balcony was ajar, when I'd specifically checked it before I'd left. I walked over and looked outside, but no one was lurking there either.

I stood in the middle of my bedroom to assess what I'd seen. It was obvious my apartment had been searched, but it hadn't been ransacked. Danielle had either been taken or wasn't at home when they'd been here.

"Well shit," I said out loud.

"Laura?"

I froze and my heart sped back up. It sounded like Danielle was in the bedroom, but she wasn't anywhere visible. It was a weird feeling, hearing a voice come from an empty room.

"Danielle? Where are you?"

I saw an arm come out from under my bed.

"Help me?" she said. "I'm stuck under here."

I pulled on her arm, but she was tightly wedged. I eventually had to slide the mattress off the bed so I could lift the box-spring and the frame off her.

Danielle crawled out from her hiding place and she was a mess. Her hair was at all angles and she was covered in dust, hair, and lint. I'd been in the apartment for over three years and had never vacuumed under the bed. All the accumulated grime was clinging to Danielle like she'd been a dust mop.

She looked down at herself and shook her head. I knew what she was feeling since I'd been there myself a few times.

"Maybe go on out to the balcony and brush yourself off?"

"Good idea," she said.

I went back into the living room and locked the door. I again looked around but didn't find anything missing.

Danielle walked into the kitchen and grabbed the beer that had been sitting on the counter.

"That one's probably warm," I said.

"Doesn't matter, I've been laying under your bed for almost an hour thinking about how much I wanted it."

"What happened in here?"

"Let me get cleaned up and I'll tell you all about it." She went into the bathroom and didn't come out for almost twenty-five minutes. When she did, she'd washed her hair and had on a clean outfit. She opened another beer and sat on the couch next to Marlowe.

"I was in the living room, when someone knocked on the door. I didn't answer and fortunately I didn't have the TV on. After a minute, I heard someone doing something with the lock, like they were trying to pick it. I took my bag and quietly went into your bedroom. I pulled out a gun and thought about going out onto the balcony, but I knew Grandma Peckham was out for the day and she probably keeps her balcony door locked. I knew I didn't have a lot of time, so I slid under the bed and pulled the bag in next to me."

"I haven't been under a bed since I was a kid. I'm surprised you fit. I didn't think there was a lot of clearance down there."

"It was a tight fit, but I think adrenaline helped me do it. Once I was there, all I could see was the bottom of the door to the living room from a gap between your comforter and the floor."

"What happened?"

"About five minutes later, I heard the sound of men in the living room. There was quiet talking and the sounds of a few things being knocked over."

"I saw the mess in the living room. But it wasn't as bad as it could have been."

"It didn't take them long to come into the bedroom. They were still talking in low voices, but I recognized them. They're both soldiers in the Black Death. The funny thing is, I like them both. They do what they're told and neither one is needlessly violent. I heard one of them say, 'She could be hiding in here.' I didn't know where he was talking about, so I tightened my grip on my gun and got ready to shoot out both of their legs. I guess they were talking about the closet, because I heard the sounds of them opening the door and searching through the clothes."

"I can't imagine how scared you must have been."

"After they looked through the closet, I assumed their next place would be under the bed. But instead, they opened the door and looked out on the balcony. After that, they went back into the living room. The place has been quiet for about twenty minutes, but I didn't know if they had left or were still in the living room, waiting for me to come out. I heard noises again and thought they were still here. But then, I heard you talking and I knew they'd gone. That's when I called out."

"They can't know you're living here, otherwise they'd have knocked down the door. I'm probably only one name on a long list of possibilities. It'll probably take them a day or two to come back and look again. But we've got to find you a better place to hide while we sort this out."

"I was thinking the same thing, but where would I go?"

"Let me work something out. Tonight probably won't matter so much, but we need to find somewhere for you to go by tomorrow night. Have you found out anything new about your uncle?"

"He's coming in tomorrow. He told me to keep my disposable phone on and he'll call me when he's ready to see me."

"Do you trust him not to reveal your location to Sergio?"

"Yes, it's never my uncle's way to act sneaky or to go behind someone's back. If he holds judgement against someone, it's always to their face."

"Alright. If your uncle needs you to be somewhere and I'm not here, give me a call and I'll come back and drive you."

"Thanks. I know this is a big imposition on you. But I really do appreciate it."

I looked at the clock and it was already five-fifteen. I quickly put on a clean outfit and fixed my makeup.

"Keep the door locked," I said as I headed back into the hallway. "I'll probably be back by nine-thirty or ten."

Chapter Eight

The drive to the Tropical Paradise was uneventful, except for a rising sense of excitement. Dating Max was turning out to be more complicated than I'd imagined it would be, but when we were able to be together, it was wonderful.

I pulled into the huge guest parking lot a little after six. On the drive up to the hotel, Max had sent me a text with a room number. I walked over to a big map of the resort and found where the room was located. Normally, I would walk, but my legs had already started to stiffen up and I didn't want to risk another problem like I'd had the last time. I went back to my car and drove to a cluster of rooms overlooking the fairway of the first hole on the Kokopelli course.

I parked and started walking to the room. It was on the second floor and I wasn't looking forward to the climb. I'd almost reached the bottom of the wide staircase when I saw Gabriella sitting on a bench, overlooking the block of rooms. I walked over and asked how she was doing.

"I am good. No cracked ribs, no broken bones. No problems."

"Thanks for watching over us. I always feel better knowing you're out here."

"I protect Max and now I protect you. It is good."

I said goodbye and slowly walked up the long staircase to the room on the second floor. I knocked and Max opened the door. He was dressed in his work clothes and looked like he'd just gotten here. I wrapped my arms around him and he had to reach out to get the door closed. The smell of his cologne was wonderful. Although it had only been two days since we'd been together, it seemed much longer.

"Damn, I've missed you," I said. "I'm glad you could work this out. Especially after I messed up Wednesday night."

"Don't worry about Wednesday. It was nice. How are you feeling?"

"Not a lot better. I took another fitness class for work today. Fortunately, we were in the back and I didn't have to exercise as hard as last time. I'm sore, but I think I'll be okay."

"Good. Champagne?"

"That would be great."

Max walked over to a table that had place settings for two and a large shrimp cocktail set next to a silver wine cooler. He poured two glasses and handed one to me. The room had a balcony overlooking the fairway and I walked out onto it. It was a beautiful day and the course looked very peaceful. I took a sip and could feel Max behind me.

"It's nice to be able to come out to a room like this," I said. "It's a great perk of you being the boss."

"Taking over for Tony is keeping me busy, but you're right. It does have some nice benefits."

"You put in so many hours. Isn't it starting to wear you down?"

"The long hours are mostly my fault. There's a lot to learn with a job like this. But I think I'm finally starting to get the flow of it. As I go on, I think I'll be able to work a more normal schedule. Tony's been great. We talk almost every day and he always gives me good advice."

"It sounds like you're enjoying the job."

"Honestly, I am. I've been able to do some good things with our group. I'm hoping I can do some more before Tony comes back."

"I'm glad. I got the feeling you were a little apprehensive when you first started."

"Well, the challenges of running a company as large and diverse as ours was a little overwhelming at first. But now, I know I can do it and can be successful at it."

"Will you be disappointed when Tony comes back?"

"No, not disappointed. I know I'm only the stand-in while he recovers. In fact, being one of the guys in the background will have some advantages."

"Like having a girlfriend you can be seen with in public?"

He kissed the back of my neck. "Speaking of that," he said, "we should probably go in. Too many prying eyes out here."

He slipped an arm around my waist and gently pulled me back into the room. I turned and looked into his eyes. I'd seen the look before and knew what was on his mind. I got a sudden rush of excitement, since I'd been thinking the same thing since I'd first stepped in the room. I felt my face flush, thinking about being with Max.

"Are you in the mood for dinner?" he asked.

"There's a shrimp cocktail. That should be enough. I'd rather not be interrupted tonight."

He pulled me towards him. As with every time Max kissed me, I felt a warm excitement spread through my body. But now, I didn't have the guilt of being with Reno holding me back. I kissed him in a way that told him I wasn't thinking about food.

After several minutes, he let me go and walked over to a phone. He dialed a number and quietly talked into it.

"Alright," he said after he hung up. "We won't be disturbed."

"When's your meeting?"

"It's at nine. I'll need to leave here about fifteen minutes before that."

"That's just enough time for what you'll need to do to me."

"Do to *you*? What about what you'll need to do to *me*?"

"Well, we might be able to work that in too."

~~~~

I was lying in bed, trying to ignore Marlowe's demands for food. "It's Saturday," I said, as I blindly reached out to push the purring cat away from my face. "Go talk to Danielle."

I was pushing him away for the third or fourth time, when my phone rang with the theme to *Raiders of the Lost Ark*. I groped around on the nightstand to pick it up.

What now?

"Hi, Mindy," I said, trying not to sound like I'd just woken up.

"Laura, I'm sorry. I know it's early. I got a call from a woman who wants to talk to me about the Lost Sister. I think it's the woman from the bench who's been following me."

This woke me right up. "When and where does she want to meet?"

"She said as soon as possible and she's leaving the where up to us."

I looked over at the clock. "Okay," I said. "It's seven twenty. I can be somewhere by about nine. How about you?"

"I've already been up for a couple of hours. I'm working on the journal article on the discovery."

"Do you have a way of getting hold of her?"

"She gave me a cell phone number. I looked it up on Google. It's
~~~~

registered to Caroline Holiday of Los Gatos, California. I looked up Los Gatos and it's a suburb of San Jose. So, we're talking Silicon Valley."

"Alright. Do you know where the Morning Squeeze is on Scottsdale Road? Let's meet there. At least this way we can get a good breakfast out of it."

I hung up and took a quick shower. I was thankful my legs weren't any worse. In fact, they seemed to be a little bit better. After exercising for a week, they might even be getting used to it. I briefly thought about starting a regular exercise routine to not lose what I'd started.

Who am I kidding?

I went to the closet and got dressed in the first thing that caught my eye. One of the nice things about October is eighty percent of the clothes in my closet will work.

Danielle was eating cereal on the couch with the volume on the television turned low. "You're up early," she said. "After everything that happened last night, I couldn't sleep. I've been listening for the sounds of someone trying to pick the lock. I hope the TV didn't wake you. I keep looking for signs of trouble between Sergio and Tony. I don't know if it would show up on the local news, but I don't know where else to look."

"I haven't heard of anything, but I'll let you know if I do. Is your uncle still due in today?"

"As far as I know. He has my new phone number and said he'd call when he comes in."

"You already know I can't be directly involved in any of this but let me know if you need a ride or anything like that. I'll be working on an assignment this morning. No guarantees, but I'll possibly have the afternoon free."

"Thanks. I'm freaking out a little over this."

I looked out the peep hole before I opened the apartment door. No one was in the hallway, but when the elevator doors opened, Grandma Peckham stepped out.

"Hi, Grandma," I said. "You're out early."

"Well Laura. It's not that early, it's already eight thirty. I've been up since four. How are you feeling today? I know the other night you weren't doing so well."

"I'm much better. Thank you for the pill. You were right, the effects seemed to last a couple of days. What's going on with you? Have you decided what you're going to do with Bob yet?"

"Well, we had a long talk the other night. I told him my concerns and he talked about his. When we were done, there didn't seem like there was a reason not to do it."

"So? Are you engaged?"

"Not yet. He's taking me to the J&G Steakhouse at the Phoenician Resort tonight. We've been there before and it's very romantic with that wonderful view they have of the city. He'll probably give me the ring then. Tomorrow we're going over to his daughter's house so I can meet the family."

"I hope that goes well. Let me know if I can help out."

"I will," Grandma said. "Oh, before I forget. I know your cousin was having a problem with her old boyfriend in Albuquerque. I think he might have showed up yesterday afternoon. When I left to go to the store, two men were hanging out by your door. They said they were looking for Danielle Ortega and they described your cousin. I told them that there wasn't anyone like that around here and I would know because I'm old and nosy. They left, but I could tell they might want to come back."

"What did they look like?"

"Neither one was very tall, but they were both broad. They both had short black hair and mustaches. The man I talked to had a

Spanish accent."

"Thanks, Grandma. I'll keep an eye out for them."

~~~~

It was a quarter to nine when I pulled into a space down the street from the Morning Squeeze. I hadn't been here in a couple of months and as I walked up to it, I realized coming here was a mistake. Floods of memories of Reno and the times we'd been here washed over me as I went through the doors.

Mindy had beaten me to the restaurant and was sipping coffee in one of the bright yellow and turquoise booths along the back wall. Fortunately, she wasn't in one of the ones Reno and I usually sat in.

"When did she say she'd be here?" I asked as I slid in.

"Nine o'clock. I should tell you, this is way outside my comfort zone and I'm a little freaked out about this."

That makes two freaked out friends and it's not even nine yet.

Mindy must have already alerted the waitress to my coffee needs, because a hot mug was brought over as soon as I sat down.

"Look," I said. "She gave us her cell phone number, we know who she is, and she let us pick a public place. I think she's interested in talking rather than shooting. We don't have the Sister with us in either case and I don't think she'll try to force us out of the restaurant at gunpoint to get it."

~~~~

The woman came in about five minutes later. She was pretty much as Mindy had described her. Shorter blonde hair that was nicely styled, medium height, and a medium build. Her age was somewhere in the early to mid-forties.

Two days before, she'd looked like any other college student, but today she looked like any of the women you'd see at the Scottsdale Fashion Square. She was dressed in a beautiful red silk top and a skinny navy skirt. Her shoes and purse were Farucci.

The woman walked directly to our booth. "I'm Caroline Holiday," she said in a businesslike voice. "May I sit down? I'd like to discuss the Lost Sister."

"Go ahead," I said. "I'm Laura Black and I assume you already know Professor Parker."

"Yes," the woman said. "We've been following Professor Parker's work for many years." She then looked at Mindy. "Congratulations on finding the Lost Sister, Professor. It's a remarkable achievement. It will likely be the highlight of a very productive career. People who know nothing about archaeology will soon know your name."

"Thank you," Mindy said. "That's very kind of you to say. But what do you want with me?"

"I'm the Director of the Charles and Susan Barton Foundation. Mr. Barton is a very wealthy man and I'm head of the group that spends part of his fortune on various worthy endeavors. I'm here because I'd like to purchase control of the Seventh Sister. We're willing to pay a large sum of money to the university and give you a finder's fee. We know where you found the statue and the legal issues that it has brought up. However, we have several lawyers who are ready to step in and clear that up. We'll also pay for the legal fees you've already incurred. As finder of the artifact, we'll give you full credit and you can publish your discovery in whatever scientific journals you wish. In fact, we'd encourage it, to add to the legitimacy of the piece."

"The only place the statue belongs is in a museum," Mindy said.

"Of course it does. The only question is, which one? Since the Lost Sister was discovered in a wilderness area, the government will ultimately control it. We'd only like to help make sure it's placed in the correct museum."

"We have a nice museum on campus," Mindy said. "I think it would look good there."

"No doubt it would. But if my foundation would give your college, say, a million dollars for control of the statue, would that help? We could give it in your name, as the discoverer of the artifact, and you could donate that to your campus museum. For that much, I imagine they might even change the name to *The Professor Mindy Parker Museum*."

Mindy's face went a little pale. "A million dollars? Why would anyone spend that much just to control which museum the statue goes to?"

"There's the history of the piece to consider and the story of how it was found. That alone makes it an interesting piece."

"Still, a million dollars."

"As you know, six of the seven statues have been recovered and are in museums around the world. Three of the seven are in the National Museum of Anthropology in Mexico City, two are in a museum in Madrid, and one's in the Natural History Museum in London. Several years ago, our organization gained a seat on the board for the museum in Mexico. That's where Mr. Barton first became acquainted with the story of the Seven Sisters. Over the course of the last several years, our foundation has gained seats on the national boards of the other two museums as well."

"Why would you go to so much trouble to be on the museum boards?" Mindy asked. "It's not like anything in the collections are personally yours."

"That's true," Caroline said. "However, Mr. Barton collects a lot of things. He's primarily known as a collector of antique jewelry and gemstones, but many years ago, he fell in love with the Seven Sisters and their unique history. He believes it's a story the world needs to know about. He's within a few months of putting together a traveling exhibition of the six known Sisters. The mystery of what happened to the Lost Sister would have added some romance and intrigue to the show. But now that you've found the remaining Sister, he's hoping all seven of them can tour together. To do that, he needs to make sure he can direct the figurine to a museum that is willing to let it travel. He's often said if he can show them all together, he can make them as famous as King Tut."

"Do these tours make a lot of money?" I asked.

"Oh yes, millions. When you're able to sell tickets to people for them to merely look at something, it's a great business model. All of the institutions involved should make out quite well."

"You said he's been doing research and working to obtain the Lost Sister?" Mindy asked.

"In looking for the Seventh Sister, Mr. Barton came upon the story of how it was sent away to the San Miguel chapel in Santa Fe, back in 1610. He's even recovered an original document that describes how it was sent west into the wilderness in 1640. We'd be glad to send you a copy of the document, for your records. When you published your thesis on the Spanish encampment, almost ten years ago, he thought the two events were likely connected. A little over nine years ago, he contacted Professor Babcock to take up the search for the Seventh Sister. My employer has covertly funded him and provided all needed research assistance."

"Why Professor Babcock?" I asked. "Why not work with Mindy?"

"It was originally Professor Babcock's dig," Mindy said. "I was only one of his graduate students. I guess that explains why he's been pestering me for information on my search for the Lost Sister all these years."

"Professor Babcock called us a few days ago and said he believed you'd found it, which is why I'm here. Unfortunately, it seems others have heard about it as well."

"I think these others have recruited your Professor Babcock," I said. "He tried to steal the box and was in the process of tearing it open when he had a heart attack."

"Yes," Caroline said. "Mr. Barton was rather disappointed to hear the professor had switched sides. We'd invested a good deal over the years into his research on the Lost Sister."

"I'd never heard of the statue until a few days ago," I said. "I'm surprised so many people know about it."

"It's no secret the Lost Sister is something Mr. Barton has wanted for many years, so it's no surprise there'd be other interested parties who've shown up to get it. They'd either sell it to our foundation at a high price or sell it on the open market, whichever way they thought would bring a higher amount."

"I didn't think it was something you could sell," I said. "It belongs to the government."

"I didn't say they would do it legally. Would you happen to have any pictures of the Seventh Sister?"

"I can't release any information on the statue to the public until the wilderness area paperwork is complete," Mindy said.

"Of course," Caroline said. "Quite right. But could I see a picture? If I'm going to begin the process of transferring a million dollars, I'd like to see what you were able to find."

I looked at Mindy and she shrugged her shoulders. I took out my phone and flipped to the pictures I'd taken in the basement of the chemical engineering building. I found a picture of the statue sitting on the white cloth and showed it to Caroline.

She looked at the picture for almost a full minute. Zooming in to see the details of the Sister's headdress, necklace, and particularly her face. Then zooming back out to see the entire statue. As she looked at it, she became rather emotional and a tear rolled down her face. For some reason, seeing the tear made me feel better about her intentions toward the little figurine.

"Do you have any others?" she asked.

I took the phone and showed her what I had. She seemed especially interested in the pictures of the box that were next to the ruler. She copied down several notes into her phone.

"There's one thing I don't understand," I said. "These others you're talking about. Do you know who they are?"

"That would likely be Mr. Barton's former business partner, Derrick Root. You see, they had a falling out several years ago. When Derrick found out about Mr. Barton acquiring control of the six statues, he decided it would be fun to prevent us from getting the last one. I believe he's the one who's been actively trying to steal the one you found. He's spent the last several years doing things to purposefully annoy Mr. Barton. I think he's still a little bitter about the way the original company worked out."

"So, you aren't working with Thaddeus Murphy?"

"Never heard of him, but it's predictable local thugs would be the first ones given a shot at recovering the statue. Derrick Root is extremely wealthy, but he's also very cheap when it comes to parting with any of his fortune. Unfortunately, since both the local thugs and Professor Babcock have failed, you can expect a higher level of criminal to come for it. It's likely they'll be more direct and more violent to get what they want."

"Charles Barton, does he know about the curse?" I asked. "Does he know he can't ever touch it? I'm not sure how, but this statue doesn't like men."

"He's mentioned something like that to me. I suppose it's one of the reasons he sent me, rather than someone else. But a curse would explain much about its history."

"I guess Derrick Root hasn't heard about the curse. All he's sent are guys."

"I doubt he cares all that much about curses. From my experience in dealing with him, he's not too bright."

~~~

I left the restaurant, got back in my car, then headed back to my
~~~

apartment. As I was driving, I called Sophie. It was after ten thirty, but I think I woke her up.

"Hey Sophie. How was your date with Snake?"

"We had fun last night," she said through a sleepy yawn. "He's been there long enough to have some friends with the career players. We met a bunch of them and hung out at Nexxus all night."

"How was being with a group of football players?"

"It was different. Their game isn't until Monday this week, so they weren't under their typical Friday night drinking restrictions. I swear, they spend money faster than the cougars. They were having the servers bring out Cristal champagne three bottles at a time."

"When you're up to it, I'll need information on Caroline Holiday of Los Gatos, California. Mainly, I need to verify who she's working for. I also need to know what you can find out about Charles Barton and Derrick Root, the internet billionaires. They're both public figures so it should be easy."

"Do you need a deep dive on any of them?" she asked, still with a half focused sleepy voice."

"Depending on what you find, I may need one on Derrick Root. He seems to be the one causing the problems."

"Alright, but this one will cost you lunch. I hadn't planned on even getting dressed today."

"Eeeewww."

"I mean dressed in clothes. I've got on some soft pajamas. I was thinking about binge-watching all fourteen episodes of Firefly today and tomorrow, then topping it off with the Serenity movie."

"Sorry for messing up your plans."

"You haven't messed them up, just delayed them a few hours."

"Good, meet me at the office and we can go somewhere for lunch.

Maybe twelve or twelve fifteen?"

"I'll see you then."

~~~~

I drove down to the office and parked in the back. The entire way over I was having an inner debate on how I wanted to handle things with Danielle. I didn't want to get pulled any deeper into her troubles, but I also didn't want to get anyone else involved. I finally decided to confide what I could to Sophie and maybe together we could find a way to do something for Danielle, without getting tangled up in the Black Death.

Sophie was at her desk typing into her computer. She looked up and smiled when I walked in."

"Old Town Tortilla Factory," she said.

"What?"

"That's where you're taking me for lunch."

"I thought you said that place was all snowbirds this time of year."

"Well, sure, it'll be full of tourists. But I was thinking a Millionaire's Margarita would hit the spot. They make the best ones in Scottsdale."

"Okay, actually that sounds really good. But before we go, there's something I need to talk over with you. I'm having a problem figuring out what to do with something."

"Uh oh."

"Why, uh oh?"

"You've got that crease thing in the middle of your forehead, the one you get when you're about to give me bad news."

"I don't have a crease thing."

"Yes, you do. And you're about to give me bad news, aren't you?"

"Well, sorta. Do you remember the day of the big shoot-out
~~~~

between Tough Tony and Carlos the Butcher?"

"Hard to forget that one. When we found you, you were hanging from the ceiling like a piñata."

"Well, right before everything went to hell, I found out Danielle is the daughter of Escobar Salazar, the head of the entire Black Death. She's secretly leading the group here in Arizona. Carlos was taking his orders from her."

"No shit? Our Danielle? The head of the Black Death? And you've known about it since the big shoot-out with Carlos? Well, I guess that explains why you've been so pissy around her lately."

"Um, it gets worse. Now that Sergio has taken over from Carlos as the figurehead of the group, he's decided to kill Danielle and make it look like Tony did it. It's his intention to use her death as an excuse to fully take charge and start a war. She's been hiding in my apartment for almost a week."

"Why didn't you tell me all of this sooner?"

"Danielle said she'd kill you and Gina if I said a word about it."

"Well sure, she'd have to say something like that. She wouldn't want you to blab that to just anyone. We have to help her."

"What do you mean help her? She's head of the group that's caused mayhem and destruction, not only to Tony and Max, but all through Scottsdale. I'm only trying to figure out a way of having her go somewhere else."

"I mean help her with Sergio."

I gave Sophie a look like she was nuts.

"Look," Sophie said. "She's our friend and she's up here all alone. If we don't help her, how long do you think she'll last on the street?"

I sighed. I knew Sophie was right. But instead of backing away from a dangerous situation, this would only pull us further in.

"Alright, but you realize this'll put us in the middle between the Black Death and Tony. I'm not so sure that's a great place to be."

"Oh, you forgot the police and maybe the other drug cartels. We'd be in the middle of them too."

"Great. Oh, there's one more thing. It looks like her uncle, someone named Tio Francisco is coming up to Arizona to investigate the situation and pass judgement. According to Danielle, the guilty party could face execution. The muscle Tio Francisco is bringing is a man named Largo. We need to find out everything we can about them."

"You're not talking about using the secret software again, are you? I just started a search on your Derrick billionaire guy. You know how I'm starting to feel about tapping into their database. The government might have already planted a mind control chip in my head for using it so much. I really don't want to see what else they'll do to me."

"Well, look at it this way. If they did put a chip in your brain, you wouldn't be able to use the software unless the government allowed it, right?"

"I suppose so."

"So, go and try to run the search. See if you can make your fingers type out the instructions. If you can do it, then either you don't have a mind control chip, or else you do have a chip, but the government doesn't care if you use their software. What do you think?"

"Well, I'll try it one more time, for Danielle. But if the chip explodes inside my head and scrambles my brain, you'll have to promise to wheel me around and feed me and stuff. I'm talking for the rest of my life."

"Fine, I promise. Type in the search, let's do lunch, then we'll go to my place and talk with Danielle. Maybe together we can figure out what to do."

~~~~

After lunch at the Old Town Tortilla Factory, where we each had a Millionaire Margarita, Sophie and I went to my apartment. When I opened the door, Danielle was sitting on the couch reading one of my books. There were three empty Corona bottles on the coffee table. As always, her black bag was unzipped and within easy reach.

When she heard someone else coming into the apartment, Danielle's hand smoothly reached into the bag and came out with a pistol. She started to lift the gun but stopped when she saw it was Sophie. She at first looked surprised, but quickly became upset.

"Laura," Danielle said in an angry tone as she stood up. "Why did you bring her here? Don't you remember your promise to me?"

Sophie walked up to her and softly spoke a few sentences in Spanish. At first, Danielle simply stood there, glaring between Sophie and me. But as Sophie continued to talk, Danielle's mood began to soften. Her face went from angry to sad, and then from sad to worried. Finally, she spoke a few quiet sentences to Sophie in Spanish.

Sophie started laughing. "You're worried about *my* safety? You think something bad will happen to me if I know your secrets? Trust me, if you knew how many secrets I have floating around in my head you'd be amazed. One more won't hurt anything. You're our friend and we're here to help."

Sophie opened her arms and Danielle took two steps forward and gave her a hug. When Danielle stepped back, you could see most of the tension had flowed out of her.

"You have any more of those Coronas?" Sophie asked as she walked to the fridge and came back with three fresh ones. "I don't see limes in your empties. You know, if you live in Arizona, you've got to learn to fruit your beer."

We all sat on the couch and Danielle looked over at me.
~~~~

"Is Sophie the only one you've told? Did you also tell Gina?"

"Oh no," Sophie said. "Gina likes rules far too much to tell her something like this. Let's keep it to the three of us."

After everyone had a few sips, we got down to the business of planning out what to do.

"The first thing," I said to Sophie, "is to figure out a place for Danielle to stay until everything calms down. She's been staying here, but I'm apparently on a list of known associates. Two men came over last night and searched the apartment. It's likely they'll be over here every few days until things are settled."

"That one's easy," Sophie said to Danielle, "you'll come and live with me."

"Sophie, thank you for your kindness," Danielle said. "But you would be in as much danger as Laura."

"She's right," I said. "I thought about having her move in with you. But if I'm on a list as a known associate, you'll be on the same list. If Danielle stays with you, she'd be in the same danger, only in a different apartment."

"No, they won't find me. At least not very easily."

"Why not?"

"Um, I'm off-the-grid."

"What do you mean, off-the-grid?"

"It was about two weeks ago," Sophie said in a quiet voice. "You know how it always takes a day or two for us to get results from a secret search? Well, I was messing around with the software, trying to make it give me results faster."

"What'd you do?"

"Um, I found a new function. It's called 'purge'. I wasn't sure what it would do, so I typed my name in. After that, it wanted my social security number and birthday."

"What happened?"

"I've been removed from the internet."

"You've been removed?"

"I'm not anywhere on the internet anymore. My name and address are gone, references to me in Facebook, Twitter, and Instagram are gone. I looked and I'm not even listed as having graduated from my high school in California. You can now look up Sophia Rodriguez on the internet and find twenty of us in and around Scottsdale, but I'm not listed with them."

"If you've disappeared, won't that affect your credit rating?"

"No, I checked and I'm still an eight-twenty."

"How do you have an eight-twenty?"

"Um, I gave myself an eight-twenty about six months ago. The software has some really cool functions. But honestly, I think I might have gone a little too far this time. As soon as I found out what I'd done with the purge function, I tried to reverse it. I don't think I can. I'm worried all of my messing around with the software might have triggered some sort of alarm with the government."

"Is that why you think they've installed a mind control chip in your brain?"

"Well, yeah. They might have labeled me a security threat and decided to make me a mind-controlled zombie slave."

"I guess we'll need to keep an eye on you then," I said. "We'll also need to get Danielle some cash. We can't use her ATM card now that Sergio's searching for her."

Sophie thought for a minute, then looked over at Danielle.

"You're in charge of an office, so you know how to file. How would you like to earn some money filing a few stacks of file folders?

I know the work's a little beneath what you currently do, but I've been trying to get Lenny to hire a full-time admin for months. Until I get someone, I need the files in reception put away. I'll tell Lennie I hired you as casual labor and we'll pay you daily, in cash."

"Sure," Danielle said. "I like filing. It's relaxing and I'm sure we'd have fun together. I'll need to head to a library occasionally to check my messages, but it would be great to not sit around an apartment all day."

"We'll need to come up with a plausible story for Gina," I said. "It wouldn't be good to have her dig too deeply into why Danielle isn't working in her office anymore."

"If she asks," Sophie said. "Let's tell her there was a layoff at the truck company. They said it would only be for a few weeks, but Danielle's looking for something new, in case it doesn't work out."

"That sounds believable."

"I'll need to go home and get my place ready. Why don't you two come over later tonight. I'll have some Coronas and some limes."

"What's to get ready?" I asked. "You have guys over there all the time."

"That's different. The guys just see my bedroom, with maybe a few minutes on the couch first."

"Eeeewww. Is that the same couch I'll be sleeping on?" Danielle asked, a look of disgust on her face.

"Like I said, I need to get my place ready for a guest."

~~~~

Sophie took off and I was sitting at the kitchen table, going over my notes. Danielle was on the couch, flipping channels, when her disposable phone started to ring. The ringtone was a cheap sounding electronic tune that reminded me of a kid's birthday card.

"If it's not your uncle," I said, "hang up right away and we'll get rid
~~~~

of the phone."

Danielle answered and got a look of relief on her face. She smiled and gave me a thumbs-up. She then talked for almost fifteen minutes in rapid-fire Spanish. Even after taking two years of Spanish in high school and living in Arizona my entire life, I still didn't catch more than an occasional word or two.

From the look on Danielle's face, she was concerned, but not in a bad way. More like she'd been given a difficult work assignment. Finally, she hung up and powered down the phone.

"It was Tio Francisco. He's in town and wants to meet with me right away up at his house in North Scottsdale. I didn't want to get you involved by having someone come to your apartment, so would you mind driving me?"

"No problem, and thanks for trying to keep me out of this. I know enough secrets as it is."

Chapter Nine

We looked out the window but didn't see anyone lurking around in the parking lot. We went down to my car and fortunately no one came at us. Danielle gave me the address, which I then punched into my phone.

We got on Scottsdale Road and drove north. We drove past the Loop-101, past Greyhawk, past Pinnacle Peak, and finally turned right on Dynamite Boulevard. This put us in the middle of the estates of far northern Scottsdale. The houses in this part of town are big and beautiful, each sitting on several acres of rolling land, all with natural desert landscaping. We went east about half a mile, then turned north onto a dirt road. We drove by half a dozen estates, but I could tell we were coming up to Tio Francisco's house. It was the only one with a ten-foot-high white adobe wall.

I stopped the car in front of a massive iron gate. Danielle hopped out to push a button on an intercom system built into the wall. After a few seconds of speaking to the person on the other side of the intercom, she got back into the car and the black gate slowly swung open.

"Um," I said. "Do you want to go in by yourself? I could wait out here on the road."

"I didn't think this part out very well. They won't allow someone to sit in a car outside the gate. One of the reasons my uncle chose this house was it's very secluded. People don't happen to stop by."

She pointed to a security camera mounted on a pole by the road. "They've already seen you drive up and they know who I am. I didn't tell them who was driving me, and they'd become suspicious of you almost at once."

"Fine," I said as I put the Honda in gear and slowly drove through the gate.

The house was on a low hill, surrounded by about ten acres of virgin desert landscaping. It was a beautiful three-story Spanish-style white stucco, with wide arched balconies surrounding the upper floors. I could see the estate was built with defense in mind.

Two men were standing on the third-floor balcony, watching us drive in, not trying to hide their assault rifles. I pulled up in front of the house and was about to get out.

"Hold on a minute," Danielle said. "We'll need to go through a process to get into the house."

A minute later two men with black rifles stepped out the front door and stood on either side of the porch. A second later, a thin athletic man came out and stood next to the door. Where the two men on either side of him were clearly goons, this man was different. He was slightly older than a typical gangster, maybe in his fifties. He had a handlebar mustache, a lean weathered face, and piercing blue eyes. His dark blond hair was cut in a short military style.

After briefly glancing at us, he stood on the porch and scanned the entire courtyard. I tried to place where I'd seen something like that before and at once thought of Gabriella. Once I'd made the association, I couldn't get it out of my mind. It was then that I noticed the man had a brown leather satchel hanging over his shoulder with the bag resting on his hip. The bag looked big enough to carry a compact machine gun, along with several high capacity clips of ammunition.

"That's Largo," Danielle quietly said. "Be very polite to him. He's always been nice to me, but he doesn't know you and his temper can easily flash."

At a word from Largo, another man came out. He was much smaller than the two goons, but he looked more intelligent. He was carrying a notebook and he briskly walked down the stairs of the porch and then to my car.

"That's José Luis, my uncle's secretary. He's nice and very efficient."

The man came out to the car and we rolled down the windows. He looked at Danielle and gave her a few polite words of greeting in Spanish. She responded with similar friendly words. He then smoothly switched to flawless English.

"Who is your driver?" he asked, still with the pleasant voice.

"This is Laura Black. She's a *friend*." Something about the way she said "friend" seemed to imply some deeper meaning that I didn't get.

"Very well," he said. "Please come in and wait in the front parlor while I let him know you're here."

We walked up the stairs, past the goons, and into the house. I was surprised when only Largo followed us in. It seemed the other two men were going to stand guard while we were in the house.

José Luis led us about twenty feet down a wide hallway, then opened a massive wooden door into what I assumed was the parlor. The room wasn't large, but it was comfortably furnished and even had a wet bar. There were several coffee table books and knickknacks scattered around, most of them having something to do with Mexico.

"Wait here," he said. "I'll return when he can see you. Feel free to make yourselves a drink. The door in the corner leads to a powder room. Largo has men patrolling the corridors. Don't go out there unless invited. Knock on the door to the hallway if you need anything."

José Luis left and gently closed the door. I could see how nervous Danielle was as she sat on a chair, looking out the window to the courtyard. Honestly, I was feeling a little uneasy myself. I hadn't been too bad as we'd driven up here, but being trapped in a room, surrounded by goons with guns, was more than a little uncomfortable.

I walked over to the wet bar and went through the mini-fridge. Finding some Diet Pepsi, I pulled one out and asked Danielle if she wanted anything.

"I'll take a water. I'm getting nervous and my throat's a little dry."

Ten minutes later, José Luis returned and told Danielle: "He'll see you now." He told me to wait in the parlor while Danielle was away.

~~~~

For the next half hour, I sat in the room looking at people come and go in the courtyard. After about twenty minutes, a pattern emerged where a two-man team was walking the inner perimeter and another two-man team would circle the outside of the wall. When they were done with their sweeps, they'd trade places and perform the rounds again. I'd already seen two men on the third-floor balcony and there were two others guarding the front door. It made me wonder if either the police or the DEA knew about the house, or who occasionally used it.

Half an hour later, I heard footsteps coming down the hall. When the door opened, I was relieved to see both José Luis and Danielle.

"I'm glad you're back," I said. "Are we ready to go?"

"Um, not yet," Danielle said. "Tio Francisco wants to talk with you."

"With me? What about?"

"I don't know. Maybe he wants you to corroborate my story."

Shit.

"Alright. But we never talked about me doing this. I hope I don't say anything to mess things up."
~~~~

I stepped into the hallway and followed José Luis. Largo was about twenty feet down the corridor, stalking behind us as we walked through the house.

I was led into a room that appeared to be a combination office and library. It was a large space with Spanish tile flooring, floor-to-ceiling bookshelves, and small alcoves along the walls with white statues on pedestals. It was like a smaller version of the library at Elizabeth's house.

A man, who I assumed was Tio Francisco, was seated behind a massive wooden desk. There was an open laptop and several small piles of paper. He was tall and broad, maybe sixty-five years old. He was wearing a navy-blue sports coat and a white button-down shirt, open at the collar. If I didn't know better, I would have assumed he was a banker or sold real estate, rather than being the number two in an international drug cartel.

He looked up when I came in. He had on black glasses, which he removed as he motioned for me to have a seat in one of the wooden chairs in front of the desk. José Luis took a seat off to the side of the office, where he could hear and take notes, but it was obvious he wasn't going to take part in the meeting. Largo took up a position in a back corner of the room. He seemed to disappear so completely, he again reminded me of Gabriella.

"You're Laura Black?" the man behind the desk asked.

"Yes."

"My name is Francisco Salazar. How's your Spanish?"

"I can order beers and ask where the bathroom is when I'm on vacation, but that's about it."

"Okay, we'll do it in English. It's always good for me to practice and we try to use English as much as possible when we conduct business in America. It helps us blend in, no? I've heard some things about you over the past few months, Laura Black. Carlos blamed you for always being nearby whenever something he did went wrong. I also heard you where there when he died. I tend to discount individual reports, since by the time they reach me they've been filtered too many times to be completely accurate. But taken as a group, perhaps there was some truth in what he said."

Shit.

I got a cold shiver. The interview wasn't going the way I thought it would. "It's never been my intention to have anything to do with your group. I just seem to keep being drawn into it, like today."

"You have a relationship with Tony DiCenzo and his top lieutenant Maximillian?"

"I know them socially."

"From what we know about you, it is somewhat more than a casual social relationship. We know you meet with them on a regular basis and you've even had a brief romantic relationship with Maximillian."

"What does that have to do with anything?"

"Sergio has accused Danielle with crossing over to Tony DiCenzo's group and betraying the Black Death. Now, I find Danielle is indeed living with a close associate of Tony DiCenzo. It gives Sergio's accusation some weight."

"Your niece is living with me because Sergio's trying to kill her. I was the only friend she had who already knew her secret. I won't deny I know Tony and Max, but I'm not in their organization, any more than I'm in yours because I know Danielle."

Tio Francisco paused and looked at me. His gaze was more than a little creepy and I could sense the presence of Largo standing in the corner of the room. When he finally spoke, it was a question I wasn't expecting. "Would you consider my niece to be your friend?"

I looked at him for a moment. I wasn't sure how to answer that. He'd posed it as a casual question, but I got the feeling Francisco Salazar never asked casual questions during an interview.

"It's complicated," I said. "When I first met her, I didn't know who she was and we became friends. Later, I learned her secret and she almost had me killed as a result. That's something I find very hard to forget or forgive. When she came to me, looking for a place to hide from Sergio, it was a close thing, but our former friendship won out. Like I said, my feelings for her are complicated, but yes, I consider her to be a friend."

"Alright, I understand," Tio Francisco said. "Danielle told me much the same thing. I appreciate your honesty and I also appreciate the way you took in my niece. We are a very efficient organization. If you hadn't sheltered her, she likely would have been assassinated."

"I couldn't have lived with myself if I'd turned her away and something had happened to her."

"I believe I understand your position in this. But now, since you're already involved, I may call upon you to provide additional assistance to help me clear up this matter. Would you be willing to do so?"

"Um, sure. I guess it depends on what it is."

"Sensible answer. Now then, since you're a friend of my niece, I'll tell you a small secret of our group. Even after all that has happened, my brother does not wish to have Sergio punished. He blames himself for putting Sergio in such a position. Sergio wishes to lead, but he must take instructions from Danielle. Part of the problem is that we never had a formal handover of power to Danielle when Escobar sent her up here to lead the group. Everything was done quietly. Carlos took it well, as we knew he would. But after Carlos was killed, we notified Sergio of the situation hurriedly, over the phone. You may not know this, but ritual plays a large part of what we do. It's the ceremonies and rituals that bind everything together."

"So, you're going to have a formal ritual that says Danielle is head of the group and Sergio will remain the figurehead?"

"Not exactly. For what he has done, Sergio will need to return to our corporate offices for a while to atone. I said Escobar doesn't want Sergio to be punished, but that doesn't mean he can stay here to work with his daughter."

"So, what will the ceremony be for?"

"Danielle must take her place as the formal head of the Black Death here in Arizona. It must be done quickly and it must be done in view of our entire leadership team. Sergio will be seen freely giving his leadership and his endorsement over to her. There must be no mistake about who is in charge."

"Is that what she wants? I didn't think direct leadership was what she was looking for."

"It's true Danielle came to Scottsdale only to report and observe for her father, but now she must be strong enough on her own to openly lead the group. If not, she must back away completely. We've learned the lessons of half-truths and deceptions when leadership is involved."

"From what I know, everyone in your group is very competitive. Will Danielle be able to hold on to her power?"

"I did not say she'd be alone. Largo will stay here to protect her position. There is no one in the entire Black Death who is foolish enough to challenge Señor Largo. Plus, she has friends like you who are willing to place themselves in danger to protect her. That makes her very formidable."

"Yes, but like I said, I'm not doing any of this for the Black Death, I'm only doing this because a friend of mine needed help."

Tio Francisco looked at me for a moment and smiled. It wasn't exactly a friendly smile. It was more cunning and devious.

"You are in an interesting position, Laura Black. You know secrets of both the Black Death and Tough Tony's organization, even if they are only the unimportant ones. Danielle says you are very good at keeping these secrets and so I will believe her. However, there may be some, from both groups, who will perceive your knowledge as both a threat and an opportunity. They may wish to take you to extract all you know. I would be careful with how closely you associate with people from either group. I would also not rule out something similar happening from the police or even your federal agents. They may see you as a great prize and not be as concerned for your liberty or well-being."

~~~~

Danielle was very quiet as we walked back to my car. We drove to the black gate and waited while it swung open. I drove down the dirt road to Dynamite Boulevard and turned west. I heard a soft noise and looked to see Danielle crying.

"Hey," I asked. "Are you alright?"

"I'll need a minute. I received some unwelcome news from Tio Francisco. It's going to take me a while to figure out what I'm going to do."

When we got to Pinnacle Peak Road, I pulled into a strip mall and found a space in front of Boss Coffee. When Danielle didn't object, we went in and I ordered us two sweet cream Nitro Cold Brews. Danielle picked out a table away from everyone else while I got the coffees.

When I came back to the table, Danielle had stopped crying, but her face was still a study in misery. As she absentmindedly sipped her coffee, I went over what had just happened. It didn't take long to figure out what the problem was.

"You don't want to be head of the group, do you?" I asked. "You weren't all that comfortable giving orders from the background. Now, they aren't giving you a choice. You've got to go through with this ceremony and become head of the group in Arizona."

"I'm not sure how it's come to this. When I was a little girl, my mama said my father had died in the drug wars and I was okay with that. Lots of kids had fathers who died that way. But when I was a teenager, my mama told me the truth. That Escobar Salazar, the
~~~~

biggest of the bosses in our part of the country was my father. The reason we had to move every year or so was to prevent anyone from finding me. We always had to live out in the country so no one would recognize who I was. When I became an adult, I went to meet him. My mama didn't know I was going to do it, but she would have only forbidden it. When I met him, he knew who I was. He had apparently been getting regular updates on my progress and we had been living under his security protection since I was a small child."

"How was that? Meeting your father for the first time."

"It was nice. I didn't see him as the leader of a powerful cartel, I only saw him as my father. He seemed glad to see me too. I said I wanted to work for him. He put me in the main office in Guadalajara where I learned about the company and eventually became the office manager. It was wonderful. Even though we still had to keep our relationship a secret, I got to see him when he was in town. He even took me to dinner a couple of times, on the pretext we were talking business."

"How'd you end up in Arizona?"

"It was like I've told you before. About ten months ago, Carlos had lost an entire shipment to the police and several of our men had been arrested. My father asked me to come up to Arizona, take charge as the office manager at the Scottsdale branch of Southwest Desert Transport, and to report back to him with whatever I saw. After a couple of months of reporting, my father told Carlos that he would be putting me in charge and I would be the only person to have direct contact with the corporate offices in Mexico."

"Was Carlos alright with that?"

"He didn't mind. He used to call on our family when I was a child. He was always Tio Carlos to me. I remember whenever he came, I would get a new toy. I think it was part of my father making sure we were doing alright. Carlos knew I had no desire to be in charge and I think he looked at it as a way to shed some of his responsibilities."

"But after he died?"

Danielle got quiet for a moment. "Yes, well after he died, Sergio was told who I was and what my real position in the group was. Unlike Carlos, he was never going to be satisfied with the arrangement. He looked at Carlos' death as a way to become head of the group, not the new number two. I knew from the beginning I'd have trouble with him."

"Now they want to openly put you in charge. When is the handover ceremony? It sounds like a big deal."

"Wednesday night. Yes, we're supposed to have the ritual whenever there's a change of leadership. It's a way to acknowledge everyone from Escobar on down approves of the change. It keeps upstarts from trying to take over through assassination. On Thursday, both Tio Francisco and Sergio will go back to Mexico and I'll have the group, well, along with Largo anyway."

"This isn't what you wanted?"

Danielle laughed and shook her head. "I never wanted this. I joined the group to be close to my father. When he asked me to come up to Arizona, I gladly did it because I knew it would help him and I'd do anything for him. But, being head of a drug cartel? No, I have no desire to do that."

"What can you do? We have until Wednesday night to figure something out."

"I don't think there is anything we can do. My father wants me to be head of the group, so I'll do the best I can. I'll try to make him proud of me."

"If you're about to be in charge, do you still need to hide? I mean, it wouldn't make a lot of sense for the order to still be in effect now."

"Word will go out to back off the kill order, but it might take a day or two for the news to get out to the troops on the street. I should be okay with Sophie for a couple of nights. Tio Francisco wants me back out at the house on Tuesday night. They'll have the ceremony sometime on Wednesday."

~~~~

After we finished the coffees. Danielle's mood had greatly improved. We made it to Sophie's place at about nine. When we walked in, I was a little shocked at how clean and organized it looked. It even smelled nice. Every other time I'd been here, the apartment had been a disaster. Even though Sophie was my best friend, and had many wonderful qualities, being a good housekeeper wasn't one of them.

Danielle looked around the apartment with approval. When she saw Sophie had placed a heavy blanket on top of the cushions on the couch, she smiled and gave her a thumbs-up.

Sophie came back from the kitchen holding three Coronas with a wedge of lime in each one. Danielle eyed Sophie as she squeezed the lime in. She shrugged her shoulders. "When in Rome," she said, then squeezed the lime into her beer as well.

Danielle and I each took turns describing what had happened with Tio Francisco. Sophie's eyes got big a couple of times when we discussed Señor Largo and the handover ceremony. But then, after another round or two of beers, our joking soon had a gallows humor feel to it.

Sophie had made some loaded nacho's and we sat around drinking, eating, and laughing until almost midnight. Being surrounded by friends made me feel great. It made me glad I'd taken the chance to help Danielle.

After Sophie got done telling us the latest with Milo and Snake, she asked Danielle if she was dating anyone.

"Well, no not yet. But there's this man I've had my eye on. He's only a lower level soldier in the group, but I think he's got a great smile."
~~~~

"Well," I asked. "Does he like you too?"

"I think so. His name's Roberto. He came up from Mexico when they first started the office in Scottsdale. We've had several long conversations in the office and I've been waiting for him to ask me out."

"Men are stupid," Sophie said. "All of them are dumb as rocks when it comes to dating. If you want him, ask him out the next time you see him. If he has an interest, he'll say yes. If not, you'll know he's a loser right away and you can move on to the next one."

"Maybe I will," Danielle said. "I've been a little worried about what would happen if he found out who I really was. But I hate being alone and I suppose I'll need to trust someone."

"If I had a superpower," Sophie said, as she got up to go to the bathroom for about the fifth time. "It would be the ability to drink beer all night and not have to pee. I swear, it's like I have to go to the bathroom twice for every beer I have."

~~~~

I made it back to my place around twelve thirty. I'd stopped drinking an hour before I left, but still fell asleep the moment my head hit the pillow.

~~~~

I was awakened by the sound of Rihanna's *S&M* playing throughout the room. It took me a while to find my phone, still in the back pocket of my capri's from the night before.

"Hey Sophie," I said when I finally got to the phone. "What time is it?"

"It's almost nine thirty. Why didn't you tell me Danielle could cook? She gave me a list of things to get from the store this morning, then she made me a breakfast like my grandmother cooks back in Mexico."

"Sorry, until yesterday, you weren't supposed to know anything about her at all."

"Well, I'm starting to know all about her. She's a light sleeper for one. I heard noises in the living room at six fifteen. When I came out, she was drinking coffee and watching the TV news."

"She's worried Sergio might start a war with Tony. I think she watches the local news to look for carnage."

"Yeah, that's what she said. I'm going into the office about eleven thirty. I should have some results on your billionaire by then. Swing by around noon and we can go over the information."

I got up and crawled into the shower. It was great feeling the hot water splashing against me. When I got out, I was vaguely disappointed when I didn't smell coffee brewing. I went out to the living room and it seemed very quiet and empty after the commotion of the last week. Even after I put on the coffee, the room didn't seem right. Marlowe followed me into the kitchen and looked up as if to ask, "Well, where is she?"

~~~~

I drove down to the office to find Sophie hunched behind her desk, sipping a big gas station coffee. She looked half asleep.

"Hey, Sophie. How are you doing?"

"I'm so tired. We stayed up for another hour after you left and she had me up a little after six. I was at the grocery store buying stuff for breakfast at seven. I just threw on some sweats and walked out the door. I'm glad no one saw me."

"I'm sure it's a relief for her being somewhere safe. I thought my apartment was secure, but you know how that worked out. Thanks for coming in on a Sunday."

"No problem. I'd still rather come in than have the software installed on my home computer."
~~~~

"How was it yesterday, typing instructions into the secret database? Did you feel like something was holding you back?"

"No, maybe you're right. Or, *maybe* they did plant a device and they're only monitoring my activities rather than actively controlling me."

"Couldn't they monitor what you're doing by looking at their database?"

"Maybe it's not only the secret software they're interested in. Maybe they want to control some other parts of my life. Do me a favor, let me know if you see me acting weird."

At that, I simply looked at her.

"Hey, you know what I mean. If I start to act *Night of the Living Dead* zombie weird."

"Okay, I can do that. What'd you find out on everyone?"

"Caroline Holiday was easy. She has her Facebook profile set to public and she's posted a lot of pictures of what she does with the Charles and Susan Barton Foundation. I'd say she's legitimate."

"And Charles Barton? Did you learn anything the world doesn't already know?"

"Not really, but I only did a Google search for him. He made his first fortune in video games then started buying and selling computer and internet related companies. He bounces between number five and number eight on the Forbes list of the richest people in the world."

"What about Derrick Root. I've heard his name before, but I don't know a lot about him."

"He's a lot more interesting. He started out by writing computer games and co-founded Mammoth Gaming Systems, along with Charles Barton. Where Charles was the business genius, Derrick was the guy who wrote the first half dozen games. Unfortunately, after he became rich, Derrick turned to partying and his games suffered. That's when Charles stepped in and took control of all programming at the company. Derrick got pissed, sold his half of the company to Charles, and started his own company. Unfortunately, his new blockbuster game was delayed several times and by the time it was issued, gaming consoles were switching over to a newer technology. After that, Derrick lost interest in designing video games and simply lived off his billions. He's bought and sold a few companies over the years, but he's mostly dropped off the map."

"From what Caroline says, he finds it fun to piss off Mr. Barton."

"Most of this is only surface information on Caroline and Charles Barton. I could use the secret software to go deeper, if you need me to."

"That should be enough for now. I don't want you to annoy your government handlers on a Sunday."

"You know, you think you're being funny right now, but you're not."

~~~~

I went home and it seemed very empty. Marlowe was next door and the TV was off. I sat at the kitchen table and again tried to organize my notes. When that didn't work, I called Max. Unfortunately, his phone only rolled over into voicemail. I remembered him saying he was having meetings all day, but it was still great hearing his voice.
~~~~

Chapter Ten

I made it into the office the next morning a few minutes after nine. Lenny and Sophie had beaten me in, while Gina was off doing other things. I walked up to the front and was momentarily startled to see Danielle sitting in one of the red leather chairs in reception. Both she and Sophie were holding big gas station coffees. I'd forgotten about Sophie's offer to have her come in to file some of the folders for pocket money.

"Hey, Laura," Sophie said. "Meet our new temporary admin, Jessica."

"Jessica?"

"Sophie didn't think I should go by my real name," Danielle said. "Just in case."

"But why Jessica?"

"I have a fake social security number and identity for Jessica Mongolivitch," Sophie said.

"How'd you get that?"

"Um, let's just say you should monitor me extra closely for the next day or two, okay?"

"You know, I'm starting to think you might be right about using the software too much. Have you told Lenny about Jessica yet?"

"No, when we got here, his door was closed and he hasn't come out yet. But the paperwork will go through as legitimate and I know he wants the place to be organized."

"What are we going to tell Gina?"

"The truth, of course. Danielle has temporarily lost her job at the truck company and needs some cash until she gets it back. The Jessica ID is legitimate, it just doesn't belong to any one person in particular."

"Gina knows not to dig too deeply into one of your stories. We should be good."

"I was thinking about going back to Guerilla Bootcamp class today," Sophie said. "Danielle says she can't risk the exposure, but do you want to come along?"

"It's not just the exposure," Danielle said. "I'm not all that into standing in a room with a bunch of sweaty women and purposefully hurting myself for an hour."

"You want to go back to Crystal's class?" I asked. "She knows you were with me the first day. Don't you think that'll cause a scene?"

"Hey, I'm paid up for a month. That's another three weeks of classes. I bet I could get my ass down two sizes if I go three times a week. Besides, I don't see what the big deal is. You filmed Crystal having sex with some married guy, but it's not like we're going to put it on the internet or anything. I'm sure she'll be fine with me taking her class. So, what do you say? Want to come with me?"

"Thanks, but no. I'm really not up to it today. Remember how you thought I might be pregnant last week? Well, um, it turns out that I'm not. And after last week, I'm hoping to avoid anything that even looks like exercising for the next few days."

"Oh, that's a bummer, about not exercising, I mean. I'm glad you aren't pregnant and all, but after going the two times, I'd think you'd be getting the hang of the class."

~~~~
~~~~

About an hour later, I was in the conference room looking for some information in one of the piles of folders, when Lenny came out of his office. Danielle was talking to Sophie at her desk and he walked up to them. "Laura," he said, looking at Danielle. "Come in when you get a chance. I need to know where we are on the gold mine thing."

Lenny stopped and gave Danielle a weird look.

"What'd you do to your hair?"

"I'm here," I said, as I stepped out of the conference room. Lenny's eyes grew big as he looked at me, then back at Danielle, then back to me.

"Um, Lenny," Sophie said. "This is Jessica, I've brought her in for a few days as casual labor to help me clean the place up."

Lenny looked at Danielle, still with the strange expression on his face. "Alright, um, good. It will be nice not having these piles of folders everywhere. Um, Laura, come in and talk to me about the gold mine."

I followed Lenny into his office and sat on one of the short wooden chairs in front of his desk.

"Well?" he asked. "Where are we? You said you recovered the statue."

I took out my phone and forwarded him several of the pictures I'd taken of the Lost Sister in the basement of the engineering center. When his phone dinged, he spent two or three minutes examining the photos. Lenny seemed to be impressed at what Mindy had found.

"And it's made of solid gold?" he asked.

"I don't know if it's completely solid or not, but it's pretty heavy. I've also got a pretty good idea of who else is after it."

"Well?"

"Charles Barton and Derrick Root."

"What? The billionaires? You're serious? Are they in a bidding war or what?"

"Not really. Charles Barton sent the head of his charity foundation to offer ASU a million dollars to be able to direct which museum it ends up at. Derrick Root sent some thugs to steal it."

"Why would a billionaire need to steal anything? He could offer Mindy a couple of million dollars and walk away with it."

"From what we've been told, Derrick Root is cheap and would rather pay someone to steal it rather than buy it outright. Besides, I don't think Mindy would sell it to him. She's more interested in making sure the Lost Sister gets into a proper museum than in money."

"Everyone's interested in money. Wave a couple of million under the professor's nose and I'd be surprised if the statue didn't accidently disappear. Where is it now?"

"We're keeping it in an old bank safe on campus. I don't think anyone will be able to get to it."

"Good. Charles Barton and Derrick Root, huh? And they both want it?"

Lenny's words trailed off as he stared into space. I knew he was busily trying to figure out how he could make some money off an exchange of the statue with one of the billionaires. "Alright," he finally said. "Let me know if anything happens on it. We're still working on the paperwork to make everything legitimate."

I got up to leave and was about halfway to the door. "Oh," Lenny said. "Good job on the aerobics instructor thing. It was a good quality video and having the husband threaten you was a stroke of genius. I'm setting up a meeting with opposing counsel and we'll be able to wrap it up in a couple of weeks."

"Um, thanks."

I walked back out to reception where Danielle was sorting through a stack of file folders with her back to me. My phone started to ring with the theme to *The Love Boat.* Sophie looked at me with a knowing smile, then glanced toward Danielle. I shook my head to let Sophie know not to say anything. I then hit the accept button and headed back to my cubicle.

"Hello, beautiful," Max said. "I'm sorry I didn't return your call last night. By the time we were done, I assumed you'd be asleep."

"No problem, I went to bed early last night."

"Can I make it up to you?" he asked. "I'm free for lunch today."

"Yes," I said. "That will work. I should be good today."

"Perfect. Come to the lobby about twelve thirty. I'll send someone down to bring you up."

~~~~

I drove up Scottsdale Road to the Tropical Paradise and parked in the main guest lot. Now that my legs were feeling better, walking up the hill to the reception building didn't seem so bad. All the exercising over the past week seemed to make the climb easier. Maybe there was something to what Sophie had said and perhaps I should try to keep it up.

Naaah. That's not me.

I searched the lobby for a friendly face. Milo came down the staircase from the second floor and walked over to me.

"I'm here to escort you to the Headhunter Lounge," he said. As always, his gold tooth shone out when he talked.

"I already know the way, but lead on."

Milo led me across the main lobby and down the short hallway to the Headhunter. When we got there, it was closed, but two beefy guards in black hotel security polos opened the door to let us in. Milo and I went to a table and chatted for a few minutes when Johnny Scarpazzi appeared in the doorway, pushing Tony in his wheelchair.
~~~~

Milo said he had some things to take care of and he left. At a wave from Tony, Johnny stopped the wheelchair twenty feet from my table and handed Tony a purple aluminum cane. Johnny then bent down and gently assisted Tony up.

I stood up and started to take a step towards him, but Tony lifted a hand to stop me. Leaning heavily on the cane, he slowly walked over to where I was standing.

"Wow," I said, as I gave him a hug. "You're doing great."

"Laura Black," Tony said. "It's good to see you again. I hear you've had a few adventures since we last met. And yes, I wanted you to see it takes more than a bullet to keep me down."

He glanced over at the woman patiently standing behind the bar. He held up two fingers and the woman set up a couple of glasses and poured out drinks. She brought them to our table and went back to the bar.

"I think you're going to like this," he said. "It's a Macallan 25-year-old sherry oak scotch. I first tried it last week. It has tons of fruit, it's like you're smelling and tasting your way through a summertime farmer's market. Oh, and the honey, there's plenty of that."

I picked up the glass, swirled the single ice cube around for a moment, and then smelled the scotch. It was everything he said it would be. I took a sip, felt it dissolve in my mouth, and travel warm all the way down. I gave an involuntary shudder of pleasure.

Tony must have seen the look on my face. "I'm glad you like it. I know I've told you before, but I do appreciate you getting me into these scotches. I don't drink a lot anymore, so when I do I prefer to have something memorable."

"Well, this is more than memorable, it's wonderful."

We spent a few moments sipping the amazing scotch. Before Tony told me whatever he was here for, I thought I should first apologize in person for the car.

"Um, I know Max already told you, but your beautiful car is gone. I'm sorry I wasn't able to take better care of it."

Tony gave a small wave of his hand as if the subject wasn't important. "When I gave you the car, I knew very well the kind of work you do. I understand it was lost as part of one of those cases. It's fortunate you weren't injured when it blew up."

"Luckily, the car was sitting in the middle of an empty parking lot. It was so badly burnt, the only thing I was able to salvage was the license plate."

Tony chuckled and shook his head. "You have the lifestyle I myself used to lead. Hearing about your exploits makes me think of times gone by. Enjoy these carefree days. I know as you live them, they may seem like a pain in the ass, but I don't doubt someday you'll look back at this time of your life with great fondness."

"Thanks, Tony. That's good to know, especially since you're already right about one part. Working investigations for Lenny definitely seems like a pain in the ass."

"Alright, to why I'm here. Originally, I was going to ask you to have another negotiation meeting with your contact at the Black Death. But over the last few days, I've felt something amiss in the city. As usual, I can't put my finger on it, but something seems to have changed."

"Um, what have you heard?"

"Nothing on the surface that would mean anything specific. However, Sergio has refused to take our calls over the past week. The negotiations have been going rather smoothly and I had hopes we could settle things between our groups. Now, I'm not certain. Not that I was naive enough to think something like this would happen without problems, but I've sensed a sudden pull-back from their side. My guys on the street tell me the Black Death seems to have disappeared over the last few days. In addition, I have reports of some arms shipments coming up from Mexico. That in itself is very unusual and would cause me pause. As you know, the money is to be made by shipping weapons south of the border, not bringing them north."

"What can I do to help?"

"All I ask is you keep your eyes open. You know the city in a way Max and I don't. You have contacts who are out of reach to us. You've been the go-between for our two groups and you know our situation. My fear is the Black Death has given up on settling things through negotiations and have instead decided to carve out their piece through force. It's what they know, and I can see them reverting to their tried-and-true ways."

"You're talking about the two groups going to war. You don't really think it will come to that, do you?"

"I'm hopeful we can avoid it, but things like this occasionally happen. It's part of the cost of doing business. Neither side ultimately wins, but it's how disputes sometimes need to be settled."

Tony picked up his glass and downed the last of his drink. "Alright," he said, "to happier things. I'm glad you and Max have decided to date. He thinks highly of you, as do I."

"Thank you, Tony. I'm also glad we're together. The only frustration is we can never juggle our schedules to have more than the occasional dinner."

"I know Max is concerned he can't spend more time with you. I've encouraged him to take some time away from the position, but as we both know, that's not his style. Truth be told, he's assumed the leadership role so smoothly, the company hasn't missed a beat."

"Honestly, Tony, I'm not worried about it. When Max first told me he'd be the temporary head, I knew it'd be like this, at least for a while. Max puts so much of himself into the job. I'm not going to make a fuss when we can't always be together."

"Max is more than capable in his role as the leader of our

organization. Honestly, I've been thinking maybe it's time I relinquish total control to him. This is especially true now that it appears we'll be having trouble with the Black Death. In such a conflict, there can't be any question of who's in charge. Please don't repeat this. I haven't totally made up my mind and I haven't yet fully confided this to anyone, not even to Max."

Oh shit.

"Um, sure, Tony, I won't breathe a word. But why are you telling me?"

"Now that you and Max are growing closer, I wanted you to understand the position he'd be in if he fully assumes control. I know both Max and the pressures of the position. I'm not sure how he would feel about being both the leader of our group and your open boyfriend. Honestly, it's one of the factors that's kept me from turning the company over to him already."

"You're saying if you step down and Max becomes permanent, he won't want to be with me anymore?"

"Not at all. Of course he'll still want to be with you. What I'm saying is being head of a group such as ours carries certain responsibilities and commitments. That alone will make it hard for him to have an active social life. But it's more than that. If you become a known associate of someone in that position, it carries a certain level of risk, both from the authorities and from outside groups that mean us harm. It's one of the reasons I haven't had more than an occasional relationship with any woman over the last twenty years. If it became widely known a woman was dear to me, she'd become a target."

Shit.

"Okay, thanks for telling me. But nothing's for certain yet?"

"In our business, nothing's ever for certain. However, I wanted to personally alert you to the possibility."

"Thanks, Tony. I appreciate that. And I'll keep my eyes open about things in the city."

Max walked into the lounge, followed by Gabriella. She took up a position in the corner while Max walked to our table. I stood and gave him a hug. As always, it felt great to have his arms around me, even if it was just for a few seconds.

Tony stood and Johnny helped him back into his wheelchair. "It was good to see you again, Laura Black. I look forward to you returning here."

"I'm sure I'll be back," I said. "Hopefully soon."

Tony and Johnny left and Max sat. "I only have time for a quick lunch, but I wanted to see you today."

"I appreciate it," I said. "I always hate the days we can't get together. Are you still going to have time to get together this weekend?"

"So far, so good. When I told Tony about it, he thought it was a good idea. I think he's actively rearranging things to make sure I'll have the time off."

"That's nice of him. I'm hoping nothing comes up on my side. I'm finished with my cheating spouse and the gold mine thing seems to be coming along."

"Well don't jinx it," Max said. "I know how your work assignments have a way of blowing up on you."

"Don't say blowing up. I had to apologize to Tony about what I did to his car."

"Okay, you're right. What should we have for lunch?"

~~~~

I got back to the office about three o'clock. When I walked up to reception, it looked great. The stacks of file folders were gone.
~~~~

"Wow," I said. "It looks great up here. Where's, um, Jessica?"

"I paid her and took her back to the apartment. I was planning on having her stay all day, but she's too efficient. She filed everything out here in a couple of hours and was about to start on the conference room. If it's too clean in here, Lenny'll never hire anyone."

"You're probably right. How was the fitness class?"

Sophie got an annoyed look on her face. "Well, everything was going okay. Timothy wasn't there, and I was in the back of the class in the corner. Crystal didn't recognize me until our third pulse-check. But then, you could tell she knew who I was. At first, all she did was make some weird expressions with her face. But then, there was some yelling, and then some crying, and then the class sorta stopped. Crystal ran out of the room and after a while everyone else in the class left too. I got lunch for Danielle and me, then came back here."

"I guess you won't be going back."

"Not until they get a different instructor. I guess Crystal's still a bit emotional after you filmed her having sex with a married guy while she was bent over a stack of towels. Maybe she was worried you caught her at a bad angle or something."

My phone rang with the theme from *Raiders of the Lost Ark*. When I answered, Mindy sounded upset.

"Laura, I think someone followed me home."

"Tell me what happened."

"I left my office and walked to my Jeep in the faculty parking garage. I didn't think anyone was following me, but when I got to the street, I saw a red Chrysler pull into traffic as soon as I drove by. They weren't even very subtle about it. They stayed close behind me the entire time, until I was a few blocks from my house, then they veered off. I imagine they're probably still out there."

"Could you see who it was? Was it Caroline?"

"No, there were two men in the car. I couldn't see their faces very well, but the guy in the passenger seat sort of looked like the creep with the gun who fell down the stairs the other day."

"You mean Tad Murphy? Where are you?"

"I'm at home, in my bedroom. I've locked every door I have."

"Okay, stay there. Where do you live?"

"I have a rental house in Tempe, a little west of campus. It's the same place I've lived for over ten years."

"Do you have a gun or anything to defend yourself with?"

"No, I've never believed in guns. But honestly, I'm currently questioning that opinion."

"You'll be fine, but maybe it would be best if you stayed in a hotel for a couple of days. I know a place where you'll be safe. Start putting together an overnight bag. Give me your address and I'll be right there."

I hung up with Mindy and called Max. "Hey," I said when he answered. "I have a friend who needs to stay someplace safe for a few days. She's the client with the gold mine and she's being followed by a couple of creeps. Do you think you could get me a rate someplace?"

"Sure," he said. "Bring her to the Tropical Paradise. Check her in at the front desk and we'll take care of her."

~~~~

Mindy lived in a house off South Hardy Drive and West 12th Street. The neighborhood featured small, but well-maintained houses, mostly with desert landscaping. I drove up and down the nearby streets but didn't see a red Chrysler or any big men lurking about.

I pulled out my phone and called the professor. "Mindy, I'm about to pull into your driveway. I drove around the neighborhood but didn't see anyone matching the description you gave."
~~~~

"Okay, I'm almost done packing. I'll let you in and we'll both be out of here in five minutes."

I walked to the front door and it opened. As I went in, Mindy locked the deadbolt behind me. Without saying a word, she walked into her bedroom and I followed. She then busily continued packing makeup and clothes into a small bag.

"This is a nice place," I said, mainly to break the silence.

"Thanks," she said as she continued to stuff items into her bag. "I used to have roommates, back when I was a grad student, but they all eventually moved out. I'm able to make enough as an assistant professor to pay the rent, but that's about it. I'm trying to save up for a down payment on a place of my own."

Mindy shoved in the last shirt and zipped up the bag. "Okay," she said. "Let's go."

There was the loud sound of breaking glass as something came crashing through the bedroom window. A tear-gas canister hit the far wall, then dropped to the floor, spewing out a cloud of thick white gas.

Tear gas? What the hell?

I'd sometimes seen these canisters on the news, when the police would lob them into crowds of protesters. I knew we'd need to get out of the bedroom before we started coughing and our eyes began to water.

I reached into my bag to get my Baby Glock. The bad guys were nearby, and they'd be on us quickly. As the vapors spread out, I got my first sniff and realized it wasn't tear gas. Instead, it had a strong medicinal smell. Mindy was standing transfixed, looking down at the canister as the thick smoke bellowed out.

"Get out," I croaked. "It's something bad."

I turned to run, but I was already becoming dizzy. I took two wobbly steps into the living room, then went down to a knee. I managed to stand and take another step towards the front door before the darkness descended.

~~~~

As I slowly came to consciousness, it took me several seconds to remember what had happened. My head was swimming, but I didn't have the headache I've come to expect when getting knocked out with drugs.

As my eyes came into focus, I was sitting on a wooden chair in what appeared to be a crappy hotel room. I tried to move my hands and realized I was handcuffed into place.

"Laura, I'm glad you're up," Mindy said. She was also handcuffed to a chair, about five feet from me. "I was hoping you were okay."

"Yeah," I mumbled, still feeling fuzzy. "I'm doing great. What time is it?"

"The sun came up about two hours ago. So, maybe eight thirty."

"We've been here all night? Shit."

Max isn't going to be happy with me.

"What are we doing here?" she asked. "We were in my bedroom, then we were gassed."

"I assume someone who wants the statue has decided to take direct action."

"I was thinking the same thing. But why bring us to a place like this?"

"I don't know," I said. "Maybe they were spotted when they broke your window and needed to get us out of the neighborhood."

"I was thinking. If we both start screaming, perhaps somebody will call the police."

"Wherever we are, I get the feeling they're used to women screaming. The bad guys are likely nearby, and I'd hate to be gagged.
~~~~

Let's see what they want first. Then, we'll scream our lungs out."

~~~~

Five minutes later, I was still a little groggy, but at least the room had stopped spinning. The door opened and a big man walked in. He was in his forties, had long stringy hair he kept pulled back with a rubber band, and he looked mean.

"About time you're up," he said, looking down at me as if I were trash. "You both know what I want." He pointed a dirty finger at Mindy. "I know it's not at your house and it's not in your office. So, where is it?"

"Who are you?" I asked. "You kidnap us, then start making demands?"

"My name's Seth, Tad will be back soon, and I'm going to start making a lot more demands if I don't get what I want. So far, Tad and I have been very polite towards the two of you. But if you knew the things Tad was talking about doing to you while you were both unconscious, you'd likely be a little shocked."

"Sure," I said. "I can imagine."

Seth had a long military knife in a metal scabbard on his belt. He reached down and pulled it out. He looked down at the blade, then slowly walked towards Mindy. Her eyes got big as he stopped directly in front of her. He reached out and lightly touched her face with the flat part of the blade. He then slowly rubbed the knife against her face, like a lover gently caressing her cheek with his fingers.

"You know what I want," he softly said. "Now then, am I going to get it, or do I need to start slicing off body parts?"

"Okay, okay," Mindy said, a trace of panic in her voice. "We'll get it and bring it here."

"That's a good girl," Seth said, then he looked at me. "You get it and bring it to me. Otherwise, I'll cut off her ear. If I enjoy the way she screams, I'll start cutting off other things."
~~~~

"No, Mindy," I said. "There's got to be another way."

"Honestly," Mindy said, speaking in a low shaky voice. "For the last two hours I've been thinking about this. I've already fully documented the Sister, and everything's been uploaded into the campus computer systems. I'll be able to publish based on what I have. The only question is which museum the statue will end up at. I thought I'd be able to keep it at the anthropology museum at ASU, but I doubt that'll happen in either case. I think you'll have to get the Sister and bring it to them."

"I'll give you two hours," Seth said as he looked back at me. "You work for the professor here, don't you?"

"She's a client of the law firm," I said.

"Good, I'd hate to think you'd run and not return."

"I'll come back, and I'll have your statue."

"I don't think I need to tell you what'll happen if you bring the police," Seth said. "So far, everything's been nice and friendly. But keep in mind, I chose this place because it has some handy escape routes in the back. If I even get a hint you've brought the cops, I'll kill your client, then be gone before the cops even knock on the door."

"I won't bring the cops," I said, trying to add as much sincerity as I could under the circumstances.

"You'll need to get my keys so you can get into the storage room in the Matthews Center," Mindy said. "I think my purse is still on the bed at my house, assuming they didn't also ransack it while they were there."

"What's the combination to the safe? Did you write it down somewhere?"

Mindy's face twisted with concentration as she tried to recall the three numbers that would help save her life. "I can't remember it," she said. "But it's in one of the lab notebooks in my office. I think it's still sitting on my desk, or maybe I already put it back on the bookshelf. Use the big key on the key-ring to get into my office. The smaller key next to it will get you into the storage room in the basement."

I took a deep breath. In my mind, I was organizing everything I needed to do to get the statue into the hands of the creep standing before me. I felt in my back pocket for my phone, but it wasn't there. I then remembered putting it in my bag after talking with Mindy, right before I went into her house the night before.

"Well?" Seth asked. "Are you going to stand there all day? Do I need to call you a cab?"

"No," I said. "I've got this."

I walked over to the phone, which was on a battered desk, and picked up the receiver. As I held it to my ear, I tried not to think of the hundreds of grimy hands that had previously picked it up.

I tried to remember Sophie's cell phone number, but I hadn't punched it in since I'd first put it into my phone. Fortunately, I remembered the office number. It was great when I heard her familiar singsong voice answer with, "Halftown, Oeding, Shapiro, and Hopkins. How may I direct your call?"

"Sophie, it's me. I'm glad you're in. I'm in the middle of a shitty day. Can you come pick me up?"

"Isn't it a little early for a shitty day? It's not even nine o'clock yet. But sure, I've already had my coffee and it'll be nice to get out of the office for a while. Where are you?"

"I'm at the Desert Breeze Motor Lodge. It's a crappy motel off Curry Road, about two blocks east of Mary Street. Mindy and I were kidnapped, but they're letting me go so I can get the statue."

"Why are you always the go-between whenever someone gets kidnapped?"

"Are you coming to get me, or do I need to call Uber?"

"Keep your shirt on. I'll be there as quickly as I can."

~~~~

It took Sophie about fifteen minutes to pick me up. As we drove over to the professor's house in Tempe, I filled her in on everything that had happened the night before.

"I guess that would explain it," she said.

"Explain what?"

"Milo's phone call. He called a little after midnight, wanting to know if I knew where you were. I told him, as far as I knew, you were at home."

"Great, I'll have to explain to Grandma why men were pounding on my door at midnight. Hopefully she didn't call the police on them."

We drove down Hardy Drive and when we pulled onto West 12th Street, I knew I was in trouble. My car was where I had left it in the driveway. But sitting in front of Mindy's house was a black MKT Town Car, one that looked familiar.

Sophie pulled in front of the Lincoln and glided to a stop.

"What's he doing here?" she asked, more curious than annoyed.

She opened her door and bounced over to the black car. Milo stepped out and gave her a long hug and a rather too obvious display of public affection. I got out and walked over to him.

"Hi Milo," I said. "I assume you're here looking for me."

"Hey Laura. Yeah, you really stirred it up last night when you said you'd show up at the Tropical Paradise, then you didn't. We've been looking for you since about midnight."

"I know. As soon as I get my phone, I'll call Max and let him know what happened."

"Would you mind if I called him first? That way he'll know I
~~~~

wasn't asleep when you showed up."

"Go ahead. How does the inside of the house look?"

"It's not too bad. The front door's busted and someone tossed the place. There's a broken window in the bedroom and there was some sort of shoulder-fired gas canister on the floor. It didn't smell like tear gas though."

"My client, Professor Parker, and I were in there when the canister came in. It was filled with some sort of knockout gas. It was fast acting but didn't seem to have caused any permanent damage. After we were unconscious, two guys kidnapped us. I'm only here to collect our purses and grab some keys."

"So, is everything alright?" Milo asked carefully. As if he wasn't sure what answer I'd give.

"Everything's okay, at least for the moment. When you talk to Max, let him know I'm getting my phone. I'll call him in a few minutes."

"Will do. Your purse is still in the bedroom, where we found it last night. We looked through it to see if your phone was there, but that's it."

We walked into Mindy's house. As Milo had said, it was trashed, but it wasn't as bad as I'd feared. All the drawers and cabinets had been opened and gone through, but since the box with the statue was so big, there was only a limited number of places where it could have been hidden.

When we walked into the bedroom, I found my bag. It was still on the bed next to Mindy's. My Baby Glock was still where I normally keep it. Apparently, I never even had time to pull it out. I searched Mindy's purse and pulled out a wad of keys on a key-ring that had a green plastic dinosaur on it.

With a sense of dread, I looked at my phone. As I expected, there were a half a dozen calls from Max, along with four new messages.

~~~~

We walked out of the house to where Milo was standing with his back against the black car, talking on his phone. He hung up and looked at us as we walked down to the street.

"Max is glad you're alright," Milo said, "but I don't think he's in a very good mood. I told him you'd call right away, so please do it or it'll look like I don't know what I'm talking about."

"I'll do it on the way over to campus," I said. "Thanks for looking out for me. I appreciate it."

"Let the boss know if you need us to do anything for whatever you're involved with. Now that Max knows you're safe, he's going to send over a crew to straighten the place here back up. He wanted to know if you'll be contacting the police or not, before he tampers with the scene."

"Thanks, Milo. Tell him to go ahead. I know my client would appreciate it. Hopefully, I'll be able to do this without the police."

Sophie spent another two minutes hugging and kissing Milo goodbye, then we took off.

As we drove over to campus, something started to bother me. "How did Max know to have someone stationed at Mindy's house?" I asked. "I never told Max the professor's name. Even if he could have figured it out, it was a longshot I'd have been over there."

"I bet he still has a tracker on your car, maybe one in your bag too."

"He'd better not. I don't need a babysitter. I've told him that before."

"Um, well, maybe you do, sometimes, I mean."

I pulled out my phone, took a deep breath, and called Max.

"Hey," I said when he answered. I did my best to sound lighthearted. "Sorry for disappearing on you. I guess you've already found
~~~~

out I had a little trouble over at Professor Parker's house last night. I didn't have a phone with me, so I couldn't call you to cancel the hotel thing."

The phone was silent. It was the kind of silent where I could hear him breathing, but he wasn't saying anything. It reminded me of talking to Reno.

I was about to say something else when he started talking. "Do you have any idea how worried I've been? You say men are following you, then you disappear. We go to your last known location and find your car and your purse, but not you. There's a forced door, a broken window, and a canister of knock-out gas. The place is trashed and it's obvious you've been taken somewhere against your will."

"Wait a minute. What do you mean, my last known location? Do you still have a tracker on my car?"

"We never took it off after we put it on. That was almost a year ago. We don't actively monitor where you are, if that's what you're asking. But yes, in an emergency we can find the location of your car. I used it last night, for your protection."

"I want it off and I want it to stay off. I don't want to think you're sitting in some dark room somewhere, watching to see where I am."

"Laura, I think I had valid reasons to fear for your safety. You'd disappeared from the face of the earth."

"Yeah, I do that sometimes. If we're dating, you're going to have to get used to it."

Chapter Eleven

Five minutes later, Sophie pulled into campus. We were having a hard time finding a space, so she parked in a no-parking zone.

We walked to the Matthews Center and quickly climbed the stairs to the second floor. As we walked down the hallway, I looked around to make sure we hadn't been followed.

We stopped in front of Mindy's office, but when I was about to insert the key, I noticed the door was already ajar.

With a sense of dread, I reached into my bag and pulled out my Baby Glock. With a light shove, I pushed the door open.

Mindy's office was trashed, just as her house had been. Fortunately, the office was small and there were no hiding places. Every desk drawer was open and the files in the cabinet had been pulled out and dumped into a pile on the floor. But that was the extent of the damage. After a quick peek under the desk, Sophie closed the door and I put the Glock back in my bag.

I looked on Mindy's desk, hoping to see a notebook, but everything had been shoved onto the floor. We looked all around and under the desk but didn't see the notebook.

We walked over to the bookshelf where Mindy had originally pulled the notebook from. On the floor were about fifty textbooks and a pile of fifteen or twenty identical lab notebooks.

"It's going to take a while to find the combination if we have to sort through all of these," Sophie said. "How long did the kidnappers give you?"

"He said if I'm not back in two hours, he'll start cutting Mindy. I'm hoping it was only bluster, but we've got to hurry in case he somehow wants to prove a point."

"Is it only the combination by itself on the page, or is there anything else on it?"

"Um," I said, thinking back. "The combination was underneath a sketch she had done of the safe. I remember after seeing the real thing, I thought her sketch was pretty accurate."

Sophie and I each picked up a notebook and started flipping through it, looking for a sketch of the safe and the combination. Five minutes later, we had gone through every page in both notebooks, without finding what we were looking for.

"This will take all day," Sophie said. "You were there when she looked up the combination. Was there anything unusual about the notebook?"

I again thought back to the week before and tried to remember Mindy going through the notebook. "Yeah," I said, having a memory come back to me. "There *was* something. The front of the notebook had a stain on it. It was a ring, like someone had set down a wet cup of coffee on it."

Sophie sat on the floor and started going through the notebooks. After she looked at one, she'd toss it in a separate pile. She was about four notebooks from the bottom, when she showed me a cover. "Is this the one?"

The stain was browner than I remembered, like hot chocolate had caused it rather than coffee, but it was definitely the right notebook.

"That's the one."

Sophie handed it to me and I set it on the desk. We both stood over the notebook as I rapidly flipped through page after page. There were pages of mineral descriptions, sketches of old watches, chemical equations, and even a sketch of a statue like our Seventh Sister. Towards the back, I found the page with the sketch of the safe. At the bottom of the page, three numbers were written with a dash between each of them. "Okay," I said, as Sophie started typing into her phone. "I think this is it: forty-two, twenty-five, ninety-six."

~~~~

We walked out of Mindy's office and looked to see if anyone was in the hallway, but it was still completely empty. I tried to lock the door, but the latch was broken. I ended up pulling it shut the best I could, then we left.

We raced down the stairs and to the storage room. I used Mindy's key to let us in. I then locked the door behind us.

The safe was sitting where it always had been. Only this time, it looked rather formidable. Even with the combination, I wasn't sure if I could figure out how to open it.

I started spinning the brass dial, but as always, I couldn't remember if it was left-right-left, or the other way around. While Sophie looked up safes on her phone, I spent ten frustrating minutes trying every combination of left and right I could come up with.

I was getting frustrated to the point of giving up and having Sophie try her luck. I was starting to doubt whether we even had the correct combination.

"Do you know if the safe has a group one or a group two lock?" she asked, looking up from her phone.

"What? How am I supposed to know that?"

"I thought maybe Professor Mindy might have mentioned it. It makes a difference on how you open it. According to the internet, if you have three numbers, you can usually assume it's a group two lock."

"Great, it's a group two lock. So how do I open it?"
~~~~

"Rotate the dial to the left, four times past zero," she said as she read off her phone. "That clears it."

I spun the dial and after the fourth time past zero, I stopped. "Okay, what now."

"Keep going left until the forty-two is directly under the top center notch."

I carefully turned the dial and made sure to stop at exactly the right place. "Got it. Next?"

"Turn the dial to the right, past the twenty-five twice, then stop on twenty-five the third time around."

"The third time?" I asked. "Are you sure this is how it works? I don't remember Mindy doing all of this."

"Do you want my help or not?"

I spun the dial and the third time I stopped on twenty-five. "Fine. What next?"

"Go back to the left, past the ninety-six once, then stop at ninety-six the next time around."

I carefully spun the dial, stopping at ninety-six. "Do we open it now?"

"Not yet, slowly turn the dial to the right."

"How far?"

"Just keep going."

I turned the dial, but after about half a turn, it stopped. "Nope," I said, "it's stuck."

"That means it's open," Sophie said. "Give it a try."

I reached out and twisted the steel handle. There was the sound of internal metal parts sliding against each other and the knob turned smoothly. I pulled hard on the handle and the heavy door slowly swung open.

I gave out a big sigh of relief. I hadn't realized I'd been holding my breath. "Sophie, you're a genius."

"I know. You'd be lost without my help."

We looked in the safe. Both the box and the bucket were still there. Knowing my luck, I half assumed I'd open the door, only to find the safe empty.

Sitting on top of the safe was the Bashas grocery bag Mindy and I had used before. Sophie helped me slide the box into it and we stood up to go.

"When you close the safe, make sure to spin the dial four times to the left," she said. "Otherwise, the internet says it's not really locked and anyone can come and open it up again."

I swung the door closed, turned the handle, and spun the dial half a dozen turns to the left.

"That should do it," she said.

~~~~

We walked out of the Matthews Center and wove through campus towards the parking lot. I was tightly holding the Bashas bag containing the wooden box and the Lost Sister. We both nervously looked around for signs we were being followed.

When we got to Sophie's Volkswagen, there was a ticket on her windshield, tucked underneath the wiper blade. Giving out a loud sigh of frustration, she pulled it out and shook it at me.

"In case Lenny asks you why he had to pay for my parking ticket, remind him it was work related. This is the first ticket I've gotten in like five years. If this makes my insurance go up, I'll need to charge him for that too."

With Sophie still grumbling, we got into her car. She pulled out of her parking space and we took off.
~~~~

"Back to the professor's house?" she asked. "I'll drop you off so you can get your car, then I'll need to head back to the office."

"Um, would you mind coming with me to get Mindy back?"

"Hey, I thought I was only picking you up so we could get the box. Now that you have it, I figured you'd be good."

"I know, but I don't know what kind of problems I'll have exchanging the statue for Mindy. Things always seem to go better when you're there to help."

"Things go better? You mean you always feel better when there's another target for them to shoot at."

"That's not it at all. You're a calming influence."

"You want me to go up and be in the room while you negotiate with a bunch of thugs and criminals?"

"Well, yeah."

"That never goes so well. Remember the time you had me go up with you to exchange the diamonds with those Consortium brothers and the Russian mafia? What happened then?"

"Well…"

"There was a big shoot out and the building exploded, in case you forgot. And what about the time you and Amber went up to the Black Death headquarters when Tough Tony was having his negotiations with Carlos. How did that end up?"

"Well…"

"When Gina and I came to rescue you, you were dangling from a chain in a torture chamber. You said Raul had wanted to slice you up like a Christmas ham."

"I know, but Sophie, I need you."

She thought about it for a moment, then let out a frustrated sigh. "Okay, fine. But if I get killed, you'll have to promise you'll take care of all my plants. Not just water them occasionally, I mean actually fertilize them and keep them pruned and stuff."

"Fine, I promise."

"Back to where I picked you up? That crap-hole motel?"

"Yeah, and, um, we're sorta in a hurry."

~~~~

"Uh oh." Sophie said as she turned north onto Scottsdale Road.

"Uh oh, what?"

"Uh oh, we're being followed. A woman in a white rental. She started following us when we pulled out of the parking lot. She's been on my back bumper ever since. I thought maybe it was a coincidence, but she just turned with us again."

I didn't need to turn and look, I knew who it was. "Is she a woman in her forties? Short blonde hair?"

"How'd you know? Is that the woman you had me look up? Caroline Holiday? She's too far back for me to make out her details, but from her pictures on Facebook, it could be her."

"She must have been hanging out at ASU, probably watching Mindy's office."

"Should I try and lose her? It shouldn't be too hard. It doesn't look like she's ever tailed anyone before."

"No. In fact, if I tell her where were going, she might want to come with us."

"Another calming influence?"

"Maybe."

"You don't think she'll pull out a gun and take the box?"

"I don't think so. She's hoping to buy it, legitimately."
~~~~

I pulled out my phone and called Caroline from the number on her card. When she answered, I told her where we were going and what we were doing. As I suspected, she wanted to come with us, even after I explained the danger it would put her in. I then asked if it wouldn't be better to all go in one car.

"Let's take her rental," Sophie said. "I don't want my baby getting shot at."

"Okay," I said. "Pull over when you find a decent parking lot."

There was a strip mall coming up on the right and Sophie pulled into it. I grabbed the Bashas bag and we got out. Caroline was out of her car and I quickly made introductions. I climbed into the front seat while Sophie took the back.

"Are you sure you want to come with us?" Sophie asked. "There's guys with guns and knives up there."

"Mr. Barton won't be happy if the statue disappears or if the professor is harmed. Maybe I can outbid whoever the criminals are working for."

We told Caroline how to get there and she dropped the car into gear.

~~~~

Five minutes later, we pulled into the motel parking lot. In addition to the typical cars you'd expect to see at a place like this, there was also a black limousine.

"Interesting," Caroline said. "There's only one reason there'd be a car like that here. But I didn't think he'd directly involve himself in this."

"Who?" I asked.

"Derrick Root."

We got out of Caroline's car and walked to the room. I knocked and Seth opened the door.
~~~~

We went in to find they had released Mindy from the chair. She was sitting on the edge of the bed with Seth standing next to her. Sitting on one of the wooden chairs was a skinny, pale, middle aged guy. He had curly brown hair and big round glasses. He was dressed in a black T-shirt, blue jeans, and brown loafers. From the pictures Sophie had looked up, I knew this was the billionaire, Derrick Root.

Before anyone could start speaking, there was a clanking noise and the door to the bathroom opened. With more clanking and scraping, Thaddaeus Murphy shuffled out.

He looked even worse than the last time I'd seen him. The doctors had reattached the casts on his leg and his arm, but now he also had a neck brace and a cast on his hand, the one that had previously been undamaged. When he saw me and what I was carrying, his eyes grew large in terror and he gasped. He clanked and scraped backwards until he was against the far wall.

Seth started laughing as he watched Tad cower in fear.

"Tad, quit being so dramatic," Derrick said in a high-pitched voice that sounded a little like Pee Wee Herman. "It's only a little gold statue. It won't bite you."

"You don't know what that thing can do," Tad whined. "I don't want to touch it. I don't want to be anywhere near it."

Derrick looked at me. "Don't tell anyone, but he's married to my cousin. They say to hire family and they'll be loyal. But I don't think it works so well in my family."

He then looked at Caroline. "I'm really not surprised to see you here. Charles always had his eye on the Mexican statues. He already controls five of them. Or is it six by now?"

"As I'm sure you're aware," Caroline said. "The Charles and Susan Barton Foundation is on the boards of the museums that hold six of the statues."

"Oh, that's right," he said. "It must have slipped my mind. So, he's sent you out to fetch it for him? Well, it won't be that easy. Did you forget, I know how Charles thinks. I've anticipated his every move. It's why I'll always come out on top."

He turned to me. "Well? Did you bring me the seventh statue? The one Charles has spent fifteen years looking for? Or do I need to have Seth begin torturing each of you to get what I want? Personally, I don't believe in pain and violence. But Seth enjoys hurting women and I like to keep my staff happy."

I looked at Mindy. Her face was anger mixed with sadness. She paused for a moment, then nodded her head.

"Yes," I said, holding out the grocery bag. "Here it is. It's still in the original Spanish chest."

Derrick looked at me with suspicion. "How do I know it's in the box?"

"Hold on," I said. "I have the pictures we took when we opened it."

I pulled out my phone and flipped to the pictures of Mindy and I with the statue in the basement of the engineering center. Derrick looked at them but didn't seem all that interested.

"These are just pictures. How do I know the statue's actually in this box right now?"

"What else would be in it?" I asked.

"Could be anything," he said. "Maybe you put a bomb in it to try to kill me when I opened it."

"That's nuts," I said.

"I don't think so. Do you know what? I'm going to make you open the box while we stand outside of the room. You'll show me the gold statue, then you can go."

I pulled out Mindy's keyring, but the key to the antique lock wasn't on it. In my rush to get the box, I didn't even think about the padlock key. "Um, Mindy?" I asked. "Where's the key to the padlock?"

"Oh damn," Mindy said. "The key. I didn't think we'd need to open the box. It's probably still in the top right-hand desk drawer in my office."

"It's no problem," I quickly said. "I'll be back with the key in twenty minutes. Thirty minutes tops."

"I don't think so," Derrick said. "You aren't going anywhere. Seth, find a hammer. We'll let this girl open the box with that. There'll either be a statue in it, or she'll be killed in the explosion."

Mindy's eyes got wide as she jumped up from the bed. "No! Please don't do that. The wooden chest is almost four hundred years old. It's a priceless artifact. Using a hammer would not only destroy the box, but you could damage the statue. Its carved from a block of solid gold and it's very, very, delicate."

Derrick looked at Mindy and laughed. "Ha, I knew the statue was in the box all along. I only wanted to see your reaction when I said I'd take a hammer to it. Handling you is so simple. It's like talking to a child. You're pathetic."

"Promise me you'll place the statue in a reputable museum," Mindy quietly said. "One that will have the facilities to maintain it properly."

"Museum? No, no, no. I'm thinking it would look better on my desk. And the best part about all of this is you can't do anything about it. You can't even complain to the police. After all, it's not like it can be considered stolen property when I take it from you. All you did was dig it up, in a Federal wilderness area without the proper permitting, I might add. That makes you a common felon. Maybe I'll turn you over to the police myself. I have a big charity organization, just like Charles, only mine's much better than his. My lawyers will take care of the paperwork, then this is going on my desk. Every time I look at it, it'll remind me how I took something valuable from my old friend, the one who always had so much fun screwing me over."

There was a pause while Derrick waited for another outburst from Mindy. Instead, Sophie started to giggle. Everyone turned to her.

"No, you're right," she said. "Take it."

"What the hell is so funny?" Derrick asked.

"Nothing," she said, still giggling. "You beat us, fair and square. You got us to bring the statue to you. You have it and we can't stop you. You won. Take it and go. We promise not to say a word about it. Not the kidnapping, not the guns, not your shitty attitudes. In fact, you're right about everything. I even bet it *would* look good on your desk. Just take it and go."

Mindy and Caroline looked at Sophie like she was nuts.

Derrick seemed to think about it for a moment, then he made up his mind. "You're right," he said. "This talking is pointless. I have won. The statue is mine and there's nothing you can do about it. Take it Tad. We're leaving."

"I don't want to touch it," Tad whined. "That thing almost killed me, twice."

"You're such a little wimp," Seth said as he stepped forward and took the grocery bag containing the box. "I don't even know why Derrick brought you here. All you ever do is hurt yourself and whine."

"We're going now," Derrick said to the three of us. "Don't get any cute ideas about reporting any of this to the police. It would be my word against yours and believe me, my word is much better than yours. Plus, I have a dozen honest witnesses who'll say that myself, Seth, and even Tad were in California the entire week. No one will believe your story and my lawyers would take extreme pleasure in suing you every possible way there is. I'd make sure the rest of your lives would be spent bouncing between civil and bankruptcy courts."

They filed through the door and we watched from the window as they got into the limousine. Seth was the driver, while Derrick and

Tad climbed into the back. It took Tad a couple of tries to figure out how he could fit through the door, but he eventually made it. The black car then smoothly pulled out of the parking lot.

Mindy sat on the edge of the bed and started shaking. Sophie sat and put an arm around her. Caroline turned toward me, anger in her voice.

"How could you let them walk out with the Seventh Sister? I doubt they would've done anything they threatened to do. With the statue gone, it will be years before it comes onto the open market again."

"How well do you know that little statue you've been chasing after?" Sophie asked. "She's more than just a hunk of gold in a box. I've only known about her for a week, but I've found out she can take care of herself."

"What do you mean by that?" Caroline asked.

"Let's follow them," I said. "They're likely headed back up to the Scottsdale Airpark."

We piled into Caroline's rental car and headed in the direction of the Airpark. We'd gone about two miles when we were met with a line of brake lights. After waiting in traffic for about a minute, a fire truck and a police car wove through traffic and went past us, lights flashing and sirens blaring. Through the traffic, we could see they came to a stop about a quarter mile ahead of us.

"You know what I'm thinking?" Sophie asked.

"I'm thinking the same thing," Mindy said.

"Find somewhere to pull over," I said.

Caroline was able to move her car out of traffic and head into a gas station parking lot. We all got out and started to walk down the street, in the direction of the flashing lights. After we'd walked a hundred yards, we could see the black limousine. It had rolled and was flipped over on it's top.

"It will only take us a few minutes to get to the car," I said. "Be careful. They may be injured, but they'll still have guns."

We hurried down the road and in five minutes we'd made it to the scene of the accident. From the skid marks and the items spread over the road, it was obvious the limousine had not only flipped over, but had rolled a couple of times as well. It looked like the trunk lid and at least two of the doors had opened while the limo rolled. The area around the car looked like a yard sale.

As we got closer, I could see the police officers at the scene were my friends Chugger McIntyre and Arny Montoya. Arny had his orange vest on and was starting to direct traffic around the scene. Chugger was busy setting up road flares.

"Don't get too close," I said. "They may be stunned, but I imagine they're going to be pretty mad and I don't want them shooting at us."

"I don't think they'll do that," Caroline said. I looked at where she was pointing, a spot on the pavement about twenty yards behind the limo, where a pistol was laying in the street next to a tire iron. Several feet from it was a piece of a cast. It looked like the one that had been on Tad's leg.

"There's another gun over there," Sophie said, pointing to a spot about ten yards further back.

When we got to the limo, everyone was a mess. They'd obviously been bounced around badly when the car rolled, but fortunately they were all still moving. They were efficiently being attended to by two paramedics. An ambulance had come to a stop beside the limo and two EMT's were pulling equipment out of the back.

"Go figure," Sophie said. "It doesn't look like either billionaires or street thugs like to wear seatbelts."

"I don't see the box anywhere," Caroline said.

"We might need to wait until they take everyone to the hospital, then somehow search the limo before it's towed," I said. "But just in case, let's look around."

A small crowd had started to gather around the scene of the accident. We fanned out and started searching through the debris on the road.

Mindy was the first to spot the box. She waved us over and pointed. It was sitting on the pavement at the very edge of the road, perhaps twenty feet from the car. As usual, it seemed to have survived without getting a scratch.

I looked at Mindy, Caroline, and Sophie. "I'll go talk to Chugger and keep him distracted. You three figure out a way to get the box without causing a scene. I'll meet you back at the car."

"Hey Chugger," I said as I walked up to the large officer with the short red hair, sun freckles, and the permanently sunburned face. He was digging through the trunk of his cruiser to get another handful of road flares.

"Hey Laura, what are you doing here?" He pointed to the people being treated in the wrecked car. "Are those some of yours?"

"Sort of. I know who they are. They're mostly harmless, but I'd keep an eye on them. Most of their guns are scattered along the road back there, but they may have more. Make sure the skinny guy in the back with the glasses and the black T-shirt gets looked after well. He's worth a lot of money and he'll raise a ruckus if he thinks he was mistreated. Is everyone alright?"

"I think so. It could have been a lot worse. Probably some broken bones and stitches for all of them, but the EMT's aren't running around like anything's life threatening.

"What happened?"

"I've already talked to one witness. It was a single vehicle accident. The car was heading down the road at a high rate of speed, then suddenly turned hard to the left, causing it to flip over and roll. Drivers typically don't perform a panic turn maneuver when the road is dry and clear, so I'm guessing a mechanical failure. Maybe a tie rod broke."

Or maybe they had some help from a little gold statue?

~~~~

I talked with Chugger while he set up the rest of the flares, then went over to say hello to Arny.

"This accident is the craziest thing," Arny said. "But it's a good thing no one died. I have you down for finding the next dead body in three weeks. Chugger says it'll take you six weeks." He started laughing. "He has no faith in your abilities."

The girls had disappeared, so I assumed they had gathered up the box. Nobody had raised a ruckus, so it seemed we were good. I said my goodbyes to Arny and Chugger, then power walked back to the gas station.

When I got there, everyone was standing next to the car. Caroline and Sophie were smiling and laughing, while Mindy had both arms wrapped around the wooden box.

"Where to?" Caroline asked. "We need to get this sorted out before someone else tries to make a go at it."

"We could go to my house," Mindy said. "It's not too far."

"The bad guys know where you live," I said. "We might have taken some of them out, but there may be more. Let's head up to the Scottsdale Tropical Paradise. It will be a quiet place to sit and talk."

"A golf resort seems rather open," Caroline said. "Are you sure we'd be safe there?"

"Oh yeah," Sophie said. "It doesn't look like it, but that place is guarded like Fort Knox."

"Sounds good to me," Mindy said.

The four of us climbed into the rental car and I gave some
~~~~

directions on how to get to the resort. Caroline dropped it into gear and we took off.

~~~~

Twenty minutes later, we were parked in front of valet at the Tropical Paradise. Before they drove away with the car, Caroline had gone into the trunk and pulled out a black leather bag and a slim briefcase. She handed Mindy the bag.

"This is for the box," she said. "We had it made up based on the measurements in the pictures you showed me on Saturday. The interior is padded, chemically neutral, and non-abrasive. It will be better than trying to carry around the chest in the open."

Caroline unzipped the bag and Mindy slipped in the box. It fit perfectly.

"Wow, this is nice," Mindy said, as she felt the weight of the bag. "Thanks."

"What will it be?" I asked. "Talking or talking and lunch?"

"I'm starving," Caroline said. "We'll let Mr. Barton buy."

"In that case, I know just the place."

We walked through the beautiful lobby and over to the Dreamland Cove Bistro. We asked for a table outside on the patio. It was a beautiful sunny day, with temperatures in the low eighties, a few fluffy clouds, and only a light breeze. We got a table that was close to the waterfall, but also had a nice view of the upper pool.

When the waitress came to the table, Sophie said she'd had a crappy day and needed a margarita. As soon as she said it, I realized I needed one too. To keep it simple, we got a pitcher to share.

"From what you said at the meeting the other day," I said to Caroline, "you run the Charles and Susan Barton Foundation."

"That's right. Although, I don't really manage it. There's a staff of several people who run the place on a day to day basis. I'm Mr.
~~~~

Barton's voice to the board. I make sure his wishes are put into action."

"And since Charles Barton's been looking for the Lost Sister for some time, it's been your job to help him find it?" Mindy asked.

"Yes, he's been searching for the Lost Sister for over fifteen years and we've been financing Professor Babcock for the last ten. From the professor's previous work, we thought he'd have the best chance at finding the statue."

Caroline looked at Mindy and there was some shame in her voice. "Although, in retrospect, it seems we should have been financing you as well. But from what Professor Babcock told us, you weren't really looking for the statue, but were merely a talented post-doc looking for lost gold mines."

"Typical," Mindy said.

The waitress came out with the margaritas and Sophie poured everyone a stiff drink.

Caroline held up her glass in a toast. "To the archaeological find of the century." We all clinked our glasses together and Mindy's face turned bright red.

After everyone had taken a sip, Sophie held her glass up again. "To our little Lost Sister. She knows how to take care of herself and kick the bad guys' asses."

Everyone laughed as we clinked our glasses together again.

"Well," Caroline said to Mindy. "Have you decided what you're going to do with the Seventh Sister?"

"I've been thinking about it," Mindy said. "As an archaeologist, my first job is to make sure the artifact is handled properly and sent to a reputable museum. One where it can be both viewed by the public and properly preserved. If that happens, I suppose it really doesn't matter which museum she goes to."

"We were hoping you'd feel that way," Caroline said. She reached into her briefcase, pulled out a multi-page contract, and handed it to Mindy.

"This is a transfer of the Lost Sister from yourself to the Charles and Susan Barton Foundation. The contract acknowledges the statue was found in a federally-controlled wilderness area and we will merely keep it safe until a decision is made by the government on where best to display and preserve the statue. The contract further acknowledges you as the sole finder of the object and fully authorizes you to publish news of the finding in scientific journals or any other means, as you see fit."

"Wow," Mindy said. "This is a little overwhelming."

"The contract also grants the sum of one million dollars to be given in your name to the archeological museum at Arizona State University, in the form of a perpetual endowment, to be used for scholarships to the further study of archeology, or an any other way the museum trustees wish."

Mindy flipped through the contract then looked over at me. "I don't know, this all seems rather sudden."

"You have the services of an attorney, I believe," Caroline said. "Have him look it over and convince yourself of our sincerity. I'll inform Mr. Barton that we'll meet here tonight and have a formal handover. If we can have someone representing the university meet us here, we can even present the endowment check tonight."

"Charles Barton would come here?" Mindy asked, a little awestruck. "I'd give the Seventh Sister to him? In person?"

"That's right," Caroline said. "It will be done in the open and we'll even invite the press. It would be Mr. Barton's way to introduce both you and the Seventh Sister to the world.

Mindy was thinking about it, but she seemed unsure. "What's the alternative?" she asked.

"I assume the alternative is you'd keep the Lost Sister at the museum on campus," Caroline said. "However, given the nature of the people who want it, I imagine it will be stolen within a few weeks of the time you put it on display. Since it couldn't be sold in the open, it would likely go underground for several years before it showed up again on one of the dark auction sites. We'd attempt to purchase it through one of those sources, then spend a lot of time and resources straightening out the paperwork on ownership and who had rights to it."

Mindy seemed to think about it for a moment. "Alright, I'll have Leonard look over the contract. So far, I think this is the best alternative. Plus, if anyone could introduce the Lost Sister to the world, it would be Charles Barton."

"I'm glad," Caroline said. "I'll start making the arrangements. Let's tentatively plan on eight o'clock tonight. Mr. Barton left me strict instructions. He wants the statue in his hands the same day you agree to transfer it. He's been keeping his schedule flexible for the past few days, in case we were able to recover the Sister."

Sophie pulled out her cell phone to talk with Lenny and I called Max.

"Hey," I said when he answered. "I wanted to let you know that Charles Barton, the billionaire, will be at the Tropical Paradise in a few hours. He'll be wanting a space where he can have a reception. I think they're inviting the press."

"Really? How do you know that?"

"It's part of the gold mine thing I've been working on. We're going to be handing over a treasure to him tonight, here in the hotel, if you have anywhere we can do something like that. It would be your chance to meet him."

"Thanks for the head's up, but Tony's always had a policy of keeping a low profile and I think it's best I do the same. I'll let the staff know we've got a VIP heading in and I'll have my hotel manager handle the customer service on this one. Men like Charles Barton don't want to be seen in public with men in my profession. Things like that can end up in the papers."

"Um, there's one last thing. You know how I told you I don't need a babysitter?"

"Yes, you've mentioned it before."

"Well, I need a babysitter. For the afternoon anyway and maybe a car."

"Are you expecting trouble?"

"Expecting? No, but you know how things sometimes come up. Mindy and I both need to clean up and change before Charles Barton gets here. We'll be carrying around a gold statue worth several million dollars and I don't want to be looking over my shoulder the entire time."

"I have a safe here at the hotel you can use and I'll even give you a receipt. But if you're expecting an emergency, I know just the person. Where are you now?"

I hung up with Max. Sophie poured everyone another margarita and the four of us quickly made plans for how we were going to get everything done by eight o'clock.

Chapter Twelve

Ten minutes later, Gabriella appeared next to our table. I didn't see her walk in and it was a bit of a shock to see her suddenly standing there. I realized she must be the babysitter I requested. As always, her black Farucci spy bag was hanging from her shoulder. There were no obvious bulges in it, but I knew it contained her Uzi, along with enough ammunition to start a small war.

Winding his way through the restaurant was a man who I recognized as Mr. Nevil, the hotel manager. Trailing behind him was his admin, Tonya. When they got to our table, I made introductions to everyone. Mr. Nevil seemed a little nervous at the thought of hosting an event for Charles Barton on such short notice, but he assured us that it could be done and we'd be delighted with the results.

Caroline said she was going to stay to work with Tonya on the preparations for the handover. She then got on her phone and started making arrangements with Charles Barton's secretary.

With Gabriella trailing us like a mother lion watching over her cubs, Mr. Nevil led us to a small room behind the front desk. We then watched as he placed the bag containing the Lost Sister in a safety-deposit box in the hotel safe. As Max had promised, he even gave us a receipt.

~~~~

The four of us went out a back door, then down to a side street
~~~~

where Milo was standing next to a black Cadillac SUV. He was a flawless professional as he opened the door and let Mindy slide in first. When he thought no one was looking, he covertly blew a kiss to Sophie. She responded by giving him a quick kiss on his cheek before she slid into the back seat with Mindy and me. After everyone settled in, Gabriella climbed in the front next to Milo.

~~~~

Milo first drove us to the strip mall to pick up Sophie's Volkswagen. The plan was for her to deliver the contract to Lenny. He'd review the paperwork and, assuming there was nothing to negotiate, he'd come to the Tropical Paradise for the handover. Sophie got into her car and took off towards the law office.

Our second stop was the university. Milo drove to the Matthews Center and waited in the car while Mindy, Gabriella, and I got out. We went up to Mindy's office and grabbed the key to the antique padlock, which was still in Mindy's desk drawer.

Milo then drove us towards Mindy's house. As we approached the professor's neighborhood, Gabriella smoothly unzipped her bag and intently began to scan the area. I silently hoped no one would be there to start trouble. I wasn't so much worried for our safety, it was more for the poor bastards who wouldn't know what had hit them if they tried anything.

Milo parked in front of the house and we all got out. There was another car there and one of Tony's guys was sitting in it. He also got out and chatted with Milo for a moment before handing over a key.

Someone had fixed the lock on the front door and Gabriella used the key to open it. She then went in to do a quick search of the house. Once she declared it to be clear, Mindy and I went in.

Mindy stood in the doorway and surveyed the damage. I'd warned her ahead of time, so the shock wasn't as bad as it could have been. Max's team had come in and had done a good job of putting everything back in order, but even at that, it was obvious what had
~~~~

happened.

While Mindy went to her bedroom to take a shower, I tried to make small talk with Gabriella. I quickly learned she didn't talk a lot while performing active guard duty. She spent most of her time looking out of the windows and checking the back yard. I eventually sat on the couch and flipped channels on the TV.

~~~~

Half an hour later, Mindy called me into the bedroom. The glass had been cleaned up, the gas canister was gone, and a piece of plywood covered the broken window. Mindy was in a robe and slippers, looking into her closet.

"I don't know what to wear. I have a couple of dresses for when there's a reception at the university, but nothing for something like this."

I sorted through her closet and found a gorgeous blue silky A-line gown. I pulled it out and held it up to her. "What about this one?"

"I don't know," she said. "It was from when I was a bridesmaid a couple of years ago. It seems a little over the top."

"No, it's perfect," I said. "You'll look great."

~~~~

Thirty minutes later, I'd helped Mindy with both her hair and makeup. I then stepped back to get a look at her. "Not bad," I said.

Mindy looked at herself in the mirror. "It doesn't even look like me, so I'll take your word on it. I'm not much into dress-up. I'd rather be outside, digging through a pile of rocks and dirt."

~~~~

Milo drove us to my apartment and Gabriella again went in first to make sure there were no bad guys around. I was grateful Danielle had moved out. Even though her real identity was still a secret, I didn't think it would be a good idea to have Danielle and Gabriella together
~~~~

in the same room. Too many things could go wrong.

I'd been so worried about Mindy, I hadn't thought about what I'd wear. To avoid making a decision, I pulled out my black skirt with the silver sparkles and my red top. Perhaps I should have worn a gown or something more formal, but I felt comfortable in this outfit. I thought about it for a second, then pulled down my jewelry box and put everything on. I figured I'd be safe at the Tropical Paradise, especially with Milo and Gabriella as our escorts. I'd just need to keep a lookout for exploding wedding cakes.

Ten minutes to fix my makeup and we were ready to leave.

~~~~

When we got to the Tropical Paradise, we again went around to the back entrance. This time, there were three local news vans parked outside and technicians were laying cables and positioning their satellite dish antennas.

The inside of the hotel was a buzz of excitement. Fortunately, the Tahiti Ballroom had been free for the night and it was a perfect venue for the event.

Mindy and I went into the room and watched as a dozen hotel employees scurried around, transforming the venue into a large but elegant reception space. Two full bars had been set up and an area off to the side was being prepared for a band. In the front, workers were setting up a low stage with a podium, a microphone, and a blue background with the Charles and Susan Barton Foundation logo plastered all over it.

We went back into the main hallway, where a long table was being prepared where people could sign-in. Tonya was busily printing up name badges from a list of about two hundred people. Next to her, three women were making phone calls and typing on laptop computers.

Tonya let me look at the list to see who was invited. In addition to every television and radio station in The Valley, it looked like Charles
~~~~

Barton had invited the president of ASU, along with most of his staff, the entire ASU anthropology department, two dozen people from the Arizona Museum of Natural History, and another dozen from several of the smaller museums in the area.

There was also a separate group of about a hundred and fifty people tacked on to the end of the list. I had no idea who they were until my eyes drifted down and I noticed Margaret Sternwood, along with several of the cougars. When I saw this, the list made more sense. These were the old money and glamorous people of the Scottsdale charity circuit. The kind of beautiful well-dressed people you'd want to have show up at an event like this. I wondered who kept the master list of these people and what you had to do to get on it.

Caroline walked up to us with a smile on her face. "Thanks for recommending this hotel. You're right about the security. Mr. Barton's advance team is already here and they say it's solid."

"I see you already had a list of people to invite," I said. "But it's such short notice, do you think anyone will show up?"

"We've been working on the list for over a week. Mr. Barton likes to be prepared. And yes, even with the short notice, people will show up for a Charles Barton reception. Having it happen so quickly will only add to the air of mystery and excitement over the event."

~~~~

Lenny showed up ten minutes later, looking every inch a Scottsdale attorney heading to court. He had on a black Armani suit, a red silk tie, and his black shoes were so shiny they almost glowed.

The three of us found a quiet corner to talk, out of the way of the main activity. Lenny said the contract looked solid and if Mindy wanted the Lost Sister to end up in a reputable museum, this would probably be the best way to do it.

Sophie and Gina arrived together about an hour before the press conference was scheduled to begin. They dressed for the event and
~~~~

they both were wearing Elizabeth's jewelry.

"I got a call from somebody from Charles Barton's office," Gina said. "They said Charles Barton was holding a press conference and reception tonight to announce the archeological find of the century and that my presence was requested. I called Sophie and she confirmed Professor Parker was transferring the Lost Sister to the Barton Foundation tonight."

"And I'm letting Gina be my designated driver tonight," Sophie said. "I figured the drinks here would be pretty good and I think I've earned a few from this assignment."

The guests were starting to arrive, and the four-piece band began playing upbeat jazz. We milled around, bouncing between the bar and the buffet table, while we watched the TV stations set up their cameras and lights. A long table had been set up in front of the TV cameras and several newspaper and internet journalists were setting up their laptops. At about ten minutes to eight, everything was ready and people started looking around for Charles Barton to make his appearance.

The first sign of activity was when eight or ten large men in black suits came in from a rear door and quietly took positions around the stage. It reminded me of the secret service coming out to protect the president.

The crowd fell into a subdued hush while we waited for the press conference to start. We knew Charles Barton had arrived by the cheers and applause from the crowd. He came in from the same rear door as his security detail and he quickly took the stage.

He started out with general introductions and comments. He then went into a ten-minute history of the Seven Sisters. He started with their early history, when they were revered as gods in the temple in central Mexico. He talked about them being stolen by the Conquistadors in the late fourteen hundreds. He then went into a brief history of how each of the previous six sisters had been recovered and which museum each now resided in. He talked about the world tour he had planned for the six known sisters and of the mystery of the lost Seventh Sister. "But now," he said, "I'm pleased to announce to the world, with funding from the Charles and Susan Barton Foundation, the long lost Seventh Sister has now been found by Professor Mindy Parker of Arizona State University."

The crowd broke out into cheers and applause. "And now," he continued, "Professor Mindy Parker will show her finding, the Lost Sister, to the world."

Charles Barton made a sweeping gesture and a spotlight fell upon a table with blue velvet drapes. It must have been brought onto the stage while he was talking, but none of us had noticed it. The black bag Caroline had given Mindy to hold the Lost Sister sat in the middle.

There was another round of clapping and a lot of cheering. Mindy awkwardly walked onto the stage. She was blushing so hard her face must have hurt. Caroline followed her up to the stage and together they unzipped the bag. They then each put on a pair of white gloves and took out the wooden box. Caroline extracted a key from her pocket and Mindy used it to open the old lock.

With the box open, Mindy carefully took out the cross and sat it on the table. She then took out the wrapped bundle and sat it next to the cross. She and Caroline unwrapped the layers of yellowed cloth and carefully laid them in a pile next to the bundle. The crowd was getting louder and more excited with each layer that came off.

When they got to the last layer, Caroline stepped back and let Mindy have the stage to herself. With a slow and deliberate movement, Mindy pulled off the last cloth layer. There was a sharp intake of breath from everyone in the crowd as lights danced and sparkled off the brilliant gold statue. It was so beautiful that no one did anything for a moment. Then there was a sudden outburst of cheers and clapping from everyone in the room. Charles Barton was clapping as he walked over to stand next to her.

Mindy took the Lost Sister and held it over her head for everyone in the room to see. Her face had gone back to its normal color and she had a huge smile on her face. I think this was the first time she realized the statue would be safe and she could finally relax. Dozens of flashes went off at once, as everyone wanted to get a picture of Charles Barton with the now famous Professor Mindy Parker and her Lost Sister.

Charles opened the floor to questions and the reporters asked how the professor had found the Lost Sister and if she really had found it in the famous Lost Dutchman's Mine. When Mindy said it appeared the cave was in fact the legendary mine, you could see the news people scrambling to get the story onto the wires as soon as possible.

After the press conference, the official reception began. A line had formed for everyone to walk up to the table to get a closer look at the Seventh Sister. People then broke up into smaller groups while the journalists worked to post their stories. All the TV stations were giving live reports and there were now lights and cameras set up everywhere.

Sophie and Gina scattered to freshen their drinks. I felt a tap at my shoulder and there was Max. He turned and walked out of the ballroom and I followed. He opened a side door and went down a service hallway. He opened another door, then turned and beckoned me to follow.

We found ourselves in a quiet room that was storage for the conferences and conventions. An area off to the side had several couches and oversized chairs. Max sat on a couch and patted the seat next to him. I sat on the couch then melted into his arms. His lips were all over my face and his hands were all over my body.

"I only wanted to see how everything was going in there," he said. "But I saw you and thought I should kiss you for a while."

"Good move on your part. How long do you have?"

"Oh, not even ten minutes. I shouldn't have even stopped by. Mr. Nevil is handling things tonight. But I was hoping to see you before you left. Not for anything specific, I just needed a kiss."

"But you have ten minutes?"

"Yes, ten minutes."

~~~~

Eleven minutes later, I was back in the ballroom and had regrouped with Sophie and Gina. The three of us ended up in a back corner, trying to keep out of the way, but still with a good view of the room. I had started on my third or fourth scotch of the evening when Sophie nudged me.

When I looked up, Caroline was directing Charles Barton, along with three or four of his staff, in our direction. I had a brief panic attack, not knowing what to do when meeting one of the wealthiest people in the world.

The group stopped in front of us and I took a deep breath.

"Mr. Barton," Caroline said. "This is Sophia Rodriguez, Gina Rondinelli, and Laura Black. They work for Leonard Shapiro, the attorney handling the paperwork for Professor Parker. They're the women I've been talking about. The ones who played such a large part, not only in recovering the Lost Sister, but also in keeping it out of the hands of Derrick."

Charles Barton didn't say a word. Instead, his eyes flickered over each of us; our faces, our bodies, even down to our shoes. It wasn't like he was sizing us up for sex, it felt more like we were being inspected. We awkwardly stood there, not knowing if we were supposed to talk or not.

"Interesting group," he said at last, as he reached out and shook Sophie's hand.

"The symmetry on your pendant is remarkable," he said. "The setting appears to have been made in the late nineteen sixties or early seventies. The emeralds are well-matched and the three-carat center diamond is nicely cut."
~~~~

"It used to belong to Raquel Welch," Sophie said. "She was a movie star from before my time, but I looked her up and she was really famous."

"Yes, I've met her," Charles said. "She's been active for some time in the philanthropic community. I'm sure she'd be glad to know the pendant was being cared for so well. Don't you agree that having a compelling backstory on a piece of jewelry only adds to its value?"

He then turned to Gina. "Three carat drop-down diamonds with baguette clusters in modern clip-post gold settings. I've always thought the drop-down was the most elegant of all the earring styles. The pair you have is nicely matched and you wear them well."

"Thank you, Mr. Barton," Gina said.

He then looked directly at me. "Laura Black," he said in a warm friendly voice as he held out his hand. "I can see you have some stories to tell."

I awkwardly shook his hand. "Me? Um, no, not really. I don't get out all that much."

"No? You have a splendid five carat diamond pendant hanging from a hundred-dollar gold chain. You have a thirty-two-stone diamond and ruby tennis bracelet. The rubies have been heat treated, but it's a nice piece regardless. But the thing that really intrigues me is your ring. Would you permit me to inspect it?"

I held out my hand and he lifted it to get a better look. From his pocket, he'd extracted a jeweler's magnifying glass that I knew was called a loop. He spent fifteen seconds turning my hand to the right, then to the left, while looking at the ring through the magnifying glass. He then released my hand and the jeweler's loop disappeared back into his pocket.

"You have an untreated eight-carat Burmese pigeon-blood ruby in a Georgian period bezel setting, making the ring approximately two centuries old. The diamonds and rubies surrounding the center stone appear to be high quality and the center ruby is magnificent.

Imitation rings of the period often have a paste center stone, surrounded by lesser quality diamonds, along with artificial tool marks and wear patterns, but this piece appears to be genuine. I would imagine this ring was originally commissioned in the early seventeen hundreds to be an engagement ring for one of the royal families of central Europe, perhaps the Hohenzollerns or the House of Wittelsbach."

"You're serious?"

"That ring belongs in a museum. If you'd ever like to know more about the piece, give it to Caroline and she'll have its history investigated. She could even give you a rough appraisal, in case you'd like to sell it to my foundation at some point."

He then stepped back and took us all in. "Yes, you're a group of women with some interesting stories to tell. Perhaps we'll all meet again someday, and you'll be able to fill in some of the missing pieces for me."

When we all agreed we'd like that very much, Charles said his good-byes, then both he and his entourage drifted to the next group to be greeted. I think we were all a little awestruck after talking to the billionaire in person. As usual, Gina was the first to bring herself around.

"Well, he was nicer than I thought he'd be."

"Yeah," Sophie said. "It seemed like he had a personality."

"He certainly liked your ring," Gina said. "I wonder if Elizabeth knew any of its history?"

"I don't think so," I said. "The jewelry in her grandfather's collection were mostly happy memories from her childhood, rather than valuable investments or antiquities."

"The bigger question is why she doesn't sell the ring, get rid of her piece-of-crap car, and use the money to get something new," Sophie said.

The only incident happened towards the very end of the event, when Charles Barton, Caroline, and Professor Mindy were circulating through the room, chatting with reporters and the guests. One of Charles Barton's huge security guards got a little too interested in Gabriella and the black bag she had slung over her shoulder. She'd explained she was with hotel security and even showed him some identification. But rather than check into it, the guard grabbed Gabriella and marched her to the hotel security office. I saw the incident happen from across the room and was amazed Gabriella allowed herself to be manhandled through the hotel. I guess she didn't want to escalate the situation and cause a public scene.

With a sense of increasing anxiety, I followed them to the security office. I got there in time to hear the security manager on duty explaining that Gabriella was in fact head of security for the entire resort. The guard who'd grabbed her stammered out an apology. Gabriella suggested they go into an empty conference room and discuss the incident in private.

The confused guard agreed, so I followed them both down a hall to a conference room. Gabriella opened the door, let the guard in, then took off her shoes and handed them to me.

"Hold these for me, please."

"You're going to talk barefoot?"

"I talk better barefoot. Wait in hall and see that no one disturb us." She then walked in and closed the door.

I stood in the hallway for about ten minutes, listening to the sounds of thuds, crashes, and moans from inside the conference room. Some of the moans were from the man and some were from Gabriella. From what I could tell, the man was moaning in pain, while Gabriella's moans were something completely different.

When all again became quiet, the door opened, and Gabriella stepped out. Her face had a bright pink glow and she had a huge smile.

"He apologized," she said, as she softly closed the door behind her.

~~~~

As I walked down the hallway to my apartment, I heard the TV on at Grandma's. I knocked and waited for her to open the door. I was going to tell her that I'd be gone all weekend and to see if she could take care of Marlowe. When she opened the door, Marlowe was asleep on his chair. He didn't even wake up long enough to meow at me.

"Hello, Laura. You look nice tonight."

As Grandma started talking, she had the strangest look on her face.

"Hi, Grandma," I said. "Thanks. I was at a big reception at the Tropical Paradise tonight. Is everything alright?"

Grandma didn't say anything. Instead she held up her left hand. There was a shiny diamond ring on her fourth finger.

"Wow. Pretty ring."

"It was his mother's and it's nice." Grandma said as she held it up to the light.

"Um, congratulations?"

"I suppose so," she said. "I'm still trying to decide if I'm doing the right thing or not. I've had a few days to sleep on it and I still don't know what to do."

"Have you set a date yet?"

"No, we've only gotten to the ring part. We've both been married before so neither of us is talking about a big church wedding. I know I should be happy about this, but I still don't know if I'm ready to live with a man full time again."

"Well, let me know if I can help or if you'd like to talk."

"Of course, I'm mostly fretting about what to do. We might need to talk this out over a couple of Jerks sometime."
~~~~

I then told her about my date and asked her about feeding Marlowe. She said she'd be home all weekend and that she usually feeds him, whether I'm home or not.

~~~~

When I walked into my apartment, it was very quiet and a little lonely. I put away my jewelry, pulled on a T-shirt, and crawled into bed. I was asleep as soon as my head hit the pillow.

~~~~

I was awakened from a sound sleep by the sound of my phone. I looked at the clock and it was six fifteen. I didn't recognize the number, so I let it roll into voicemail. Ten seconds later, the phone rang again. Since this eliminated salesmen and robo-callers, I picked up.

"Laura Black, this is José Luis. We met on Saturday."

Something about his voice sounded strained. His perfect English from Saturday was now heavily accented.

"I remember. What's wrong?"

"There's been an assassination attempt against Danielle. She's been badly hurt. Could you come meet us at the clinic? I'll give you the address."

Oh my God.

"I'll be right there."

"There's no need to rush. She just came out of surgery and will not awaken for an hour or two. But yes, please come to the clinic. He's asked to speak with you."

"Tio Francisco wants to talk to me? What about?"

"I assume it's about what happened last night."

I quickly took a shower and got dressed. Remembering how cold hospitals are, I put on long pants and a top with sleeves.

~~~~

I drove to the address José Luis gave me. It was a small private clinic in North Scottsdale. I parked and walked to the front door. A sign on the door said the clinic would be closed for the next two days due to a plumbing issue. I knocked and the door was opened by two beefy men.

"I'm Laura Black," I told the bigger of the two. "I'm here to see Danielle Ortega."

I waited outside while word went to José Luis that I had arrived. After about five minutes, I was ushered inside and then to an upstairs corridor.

Once upstairs, I was handed over to Señor Largo. He looked terrible. The side of his face had a large purple bruise. He had a wound on his forehead that probably needed stitches. He was also walking with a severe limp. He led me down the hallway towards a waiting room.

José Luis met me at the entrance and waved me into the room. Largo went back into the hallway to act as sentry. Tio Francisco was seated and looked more sad than upset.

"How is Danielle?" I asked José Luis.

"She came out of surgery about two hours ago. The doctors tell us her injuries were severe, but not life threatening. They believe if there're no setbacks, she'll be able to go home in a day or two."

I felt a wave of relief spread through me. "I'm so glad. What happened?"

"There was an assassination attempt at the house last night," Tio Francisco said. "The details are unimportant. Sergio made a desperate attempt to eliminate his competition for leadership of the group. Fortunately, he failed to kill his intended target."

"Why would Sergio try something like that? He knows who Danielle's father is. Escobar can't have things like that happen in his
~~~~

group."

"As I said, Sergio's attempt was made from a sense of desperation. It was the action of a madman."

As Tio Francisco was talking, I was getting a tickling in the back of my mind. Now that I knew Danielle was going to be alright, I was starting to ask myself why I was here. I couldn't come up with a plausible reason, but I suspected it wasn't good.

"Did you only bring me here to keep Danielle company when she wakes up?"

"Yes, partially. Danielle went through a very difficult event last night, it would be best if she had a friend at her side when she wakes. However, I also need to ask if you would do Danielle and myself a service."

Shit, here it comes.

"Sergio's attempt to assassinate Danielle may have failed, but he accomplished his goal. She won't be able to attend the ceremony tonight."

"Can't you postpone it until Danielle recovers?"

"No. By announcing that we will have a formal handover of leadership from Sergio to Danielle, it implicitly implies Sergio is still in charge. Even though he's now in hiding, he still leads the group. In my capacity as the brother and advisor of Escobar, I have some pull with the senior people here, but unless Escobar comes to Arizona himself, which he cannot do, the soldiers will take their orders from Sergio."

"Okay, what do you need me to do?

"I need you to take Danielle's place at the ceremony tonight."

What?

"You want me to pretend I'm Danielle and become head of the Black Death here in Arizona? In front of everyone?"

"I know it is asking much of you. But I don't know another way to resolve this. Danielle must be seen as taking charge. It's the only way."

"I'm afraid it was my idea," José Luis said. "We need Danielle to be at the ceremony and the two of you look so remarkably alike. If we change your hair to match Danielle's and hold the ceremony away from the group, like on a stage or something. I think we can make it believable."

I was trying to find a reason I shouldn't do it, when a doctor came in to say Danielle had woken up. He led the three of us to a private recovery room where she was indeed awake. She was surrounded by bags of IV fluids and wires connecting her to half a dozen machines. Her face was pale, but her eyes looked surprisingly clear for someone who had just woken up from major surgery.

"Hey," I said as I walked over and held her hand. "How are you doing?"

"I'm still here," she said weakly. "I wasn't so sure I was going to make it. Largo was brilliant. He took care of the assassination team singlehandedly."

I knew better than to upset her, but I wasn't sure how long she'd be awake. "Um, your uncle wants me to take your place at the ceremony tonight."

Danielle looked over at Tio Francisco, then back to me. "Yes, if the handover doesn't happen tonight, Sergio will still be in charge." She looked down at the wires and tubes. "I don't think I'll be leaving here for a while. You'll do great."

"But everyone will see I'm not you. Sure, I sorta look like you, but I don't look exactly like you. It's not only the hair, it's everything, including your voice. Plus, some of the guys have seen me before. Everyone'll see and hear the difference."

"You can fix the hair color. I bet Sophie would help. Add a little makeup and maybe a bandage or two and you'll look just like me.

Don't worry about talking. At the ceremony, you'll only be asked three questions and all you need to answer is 'Si' each time. Piece of cake."

I was going to try to argue my way out of it, but I knew it was no use. As always, when there's only one course I can take, I try my best to embrace it. "Alright," I said. "I'll do my best."

Danielle laid her head back on the pillow, her eyes already starting to close. "I know you'll do great," she whispered again.

I stepped out into the hallway with Tio Francisco and José Luis. "Where do you need me to go and when am I supposed to be there?"

"The ceremony is tonight at seven o'clock," José Luis said. "We're holding it at our corporate offices on Frank Lloyd Wright Boulevard. There's a big warehouse space there that will be perfect. If our information is correct, you've been there before."

"Yeah, once. I was there for the shoot-out that left Carlos dead and Tony DiCenzo wounded."

"Several people know Sergio mounted an attack on Danielle and that she was injured, but we've hidden the true severity. I'll need you here at six o'clock. There's a back stairway and Largo will let you in. We'll put you in a wheelchair and go out in front of everyone. We'll be on the move as a convoy to our headquarters at six-thirty."

"Okay, I'll be there. Um, what's the dress code?"

José Luis and Tio Francisco looked at each other. Finally, José Luis said, "It's, how you would say it, um, business casual."

"Okay, it would be best if I could wear one of Danielle's outfits. One everyone already knows about."

"Her purse is in the room," José Luis said. "I can give you her address and her apartment key. You can go over there and pick something out."

I walked down the corridor and headed toward the elevator. Señor

Largo was positioned at the end of the hallway, with a good view of the entire corridor. He still had his leather satchel hanging off his shoulder. From the look on his face, he hadn't slept in some time.

"Señor Largo," I said as I looked at the wound on his forehead, "you're injured. I hope you can take a few minutes and have that looked at."

"I'm fine. There's still much work to be done here before I'll see a doctor."

"I just talked to Danielle. She said you were wonderful last night. Thank you for protecting my friend."

Darkness and anger exploded out of Largo. I instantly regretted saying anything about it.

"No, I did not protect her," he said. "It's my fault she was injured. I acted too slowly when the team descended on us. Sergio's a fool. Even after everything he did, Escobar would have forgiven him. But now, his desire for power will be his death. I have many men looking for Sergio. It will not be long until we find him, then he will indeed be sorry for what he tried to do."

His outburst caused the gash on his forehead to begin to bleed. I reached into my bag, pulled out a travel packet of tissues, and handed it to him. "Nevertheless, if I have it right, you'll be needed more than ever for tonight's meeting. Things seem calm now. You should probably have it looked at before then. You're in a clinic, lots of doctors."

He grabbed three or four tissues from the packet and used them to dab at his wound. He seemed somewhat surprised at the extent of the bleeding. "Maybe you are right," he said. "I will have a doctor sew this up when I get a chance." He then looked at me. "I know what they asked you to do tonight. Are you with us?"

"Yes, Danielle's my friend. I'll do whatever I can for her."

"Your loyalty is good. This business with Sergio is ripping up the group from within, but Francisco is here. He will make everything alright."

"Do you think Sergio will try anything again?"

"I do not think so, but if he is so foolish it will be the last thing he ever does."

Yikes.

Chapter Thirteen

I made it out to my car before the reality of what I'd agreed to do hit me. I then sat motionless behind the wheel for almost five minutes. My thoughts were racing between wanting to pretend it didn't happen and wanting to drive out to California to get drunk on a beach and wait for the whole thing to go away.

When neither one of those options seemed like they would work, I did what I always do. I called Sophie.

"Hey, girlfriend," she said when she answered. "What are you up to today? Lenny's actually in a good mood today. He took off about five minutes ago and said he'll be out most of the day. He's probably off somewhere to think of a way to milk some more money out of Charles Barton."

"Sophie, I'm having a shitty day and it's going to get even worse. I need you to make me look like Danielle. I mean *exactly* like Danielle. And I need you to do it right away."

"Well, I can match your makeup to hers, but your hair's different. You'd need to change it."

"Would you be able to do that?"

"No, Danielle has great hair. If I do it, it'll look like crap. You'll need to get it professionally done. Her hair's four or five inches longer than yours. If you're serious about it, you'd need some extensions."

"Okay, you're probably right. Can we go somewhere?"

"When do you need it done?"

"By about five o'clock today, at the latest."

"It's too late to make an appointment. Let me call around and see if anyone has a cancellation. Are you going to tell me what this is all about?"

"You're right, sorry. Sergio tried to kill Danielle last night to prevent her from taking over the group. She'll be okay, but she's going to be in the hospital for a few days. There's no way she can move from her bed for the ceremony tonight. Tio Francisco wants me to impersonate Danielle and make it look like she really did take control. Then Sergio won't be in charge anymore and everything will be good with the group."

"What? They tried to kill Danielle? Shit. Is she alright? What happened?"

"I don't have a lot of details, but I went to see her at the clinic. The doctors say she'll be alright."

"What about Sergio? I mean if he knowingly tried to kill the daughter of the head of the cartel once, then he wouldn't have any issues going after her again, even if it's only you pretending to be her."

"According to Tio Francisco, Sergio's in hiding and won't be attending the ceremony. Largo and his men are looking for him and they aren't happy."

"Ouch."

"Yeah, I didn't ask for details."

"Good idea. Are you sure Danielle's going to be alright?"

"When I saw her this morning, she was waking up after the surgery. She seems okay and from everything I know, she'll recover."

"Yeah, but is everything still attached? Will everything still work? Did they say how long until she's up and around?"

"No, we didn't get much past the part where she's still alive and will recover."

"Fine. Let's work on making you look like Danielle, then maybe we can go up and see her."

~~~~

I got to the office and walked up front to reception. Gina was nowhere to be seen. Sophie was talking to someone on the phone, so I sat in one of the red leather chairs next to her desk. The reception area looked a lot better since Danielle had put away most of the stacks of files.

Sophie got off the phone and looked at me. "We're in luck. Adrianne at the salon has an opening for a hair coloring and highlighting, if you can come down right away. Extensions are going to be an issue, but she said she'll see what she can do."

Sophie forwarded the office phone to her cell and locked the front door. She hung a sign in the window that said the office would open again after lunch. She also grabbed her tablet so she could do her emails. We then walked out the back door. Sophie offered to drive, so we climbed into her Volkswagen.

Adrianne worked at one of the nicer salons in downtown Scottsdale. Sophie had been going to her for years and I'd gone to her once to have her do my highlights. I've never cared that much about my hair and couldn't afford to go to anywhere high-end in either case. I usually cut it myself or I'd go to a bargain family place in a strip mall by my apartment.

After we'd checked in with the receptionist, Adrianne came out to meet us. She was tall and thin with long red wavy hair. You could tell she put a lot of effort into it, always a good sign for someone who works in a salon.
~~~~

"Thanks for fitting us in," Sophie said. "We have an emergency hair coloring and highlighting."

"No problem," Adrianne said. "One of my regulars canceled." She looked at my hair. "What are we doing today?"

Sophie pulled out her cell phone and started flipping through pictures. She settled on two of them and showed them to Adrianne, who studied the pictures, then looked at me, then studied the pictures again.

"Alright," she said, "the woman in the pictures is between a chocolate brown and a walnut brown." She then looked at me again. "You're between a chestnut brown and an ash brown. I'd go with the walnut brown and we should end up in the right place. The woman in the picture has light gold highlights, so we can try to work those in. You both have the same basic hairstyle, so I'll only need to touch yours up a bit. You said you also needed extensions? The only walnut brown extensions I have in the shop are eighteen-inch virgin human and they're kinda expensive. To match the picture, you won't need all of that. I'd need to cut them down."

I inwardly sighed. It looked like the small amount I'd been able to save over the past few months was about to go back onto a credit card. "Do whatever you need to do," I said.

Sophie pulled out her tablet to set up a working area in the front while Adriane led me to her station in the back. This was the first time I'd had my hair colored in several years and I'd forgotten how much I disliked the procedure. The entire process of cutting, coloring, highlighting, extending, and styling took almost three hours, but when Adriane was done, I had to admit my hair was a close match. I went out to show Sophie.

"Oh my God," she squealed when I came out. "Your hair looks exactly like Danielle's. Once we do your makeup, no one will be able to tell the difference. She'll freak when we show her what you look like."

It was past noon and we decided to go to a Filibertos for lunch. I had my usual carne asada burrito while Sophie went with the camarones rancheros plate.

Even though I was hungry, I couldn't eat a lot. I kept thinking about what I'd be doing later in the evening. When I did that, it became hard to even chew. Sophie had no problem eating and after finishing her lunch, she happily munched on a basket of chips. We hadn't talked a lot about what was going on, but after looking at me for a moment, Sophie looked around to make sure no one could hear us.

"Um, are you sure about this?" she asked.

"About what?"

"About taking Danielle's place at a meeting like that. Do you really want to be the head of a branch office of a Mexican drug cartel?"

"Oh, I wouldn't really be the head. Tio Francisco explained it's just a ceremony, a formal thing that has to happen."

"I'm not so sure. Did he say anything about another ceremony, even an informal one, to transfer the title to Danielle once she gets better?"

"Um, no. I don't think so. He's going back to Mexico tomorrow."

"So, the entire cartel will think Danielle's the new head of the group, but we'll know it's really you? I don't know a lot about drug cartel rules, but I still think you'll be the real leader until something happens to switch it back to Danielle."

~~~~

We got back to the office about one thirty. It didn't look like either Lenny or Gina had been in yet.

"When do you want to get dressed and do the makeup?" Sophie asked.

"The sooner the better, I'm starting to get nervous about this."
~~~~

"Okay, I'll close up the office for the day and we can head over to Danielle's apartment."

"I hope Lenny doesn't mind no one's been here all day."

"Well, if he's worried about things like that, he should hire an admin. I keep telling him she'd be useful for things beyond filing, but he's too cheap."

~~~~

We drove to the address José Luis had given me. It was a nice apartment house near Indian School and Granite Reef. We found the apartment and went in. It was a creepy feeling, walking around someone else's apartment. We went to Danielle's closet and Sophie pulled out an outfit. I recognized it as one I'd seen her wear several times before.

"I've always thought Danielle looked good in this," she said. "It's nice, but not too fancy or over the top."

While Sophie raided the bathroom for makeup supplies, I looked through the closet until I found the shoes that went with the outfit. I quickly got dressed and was surprised how well everything seemed to fit. I then went into the kitchen where Sophie had everything lined up on the table. I sat with a bathroom towel wrapped around my shoulders while Sophie did my makeup.

After half an hour of trial and error, Sophie was satisfied. "Okay. Go look at yourself in the mirror."

Sophie and I went into the bathroom and I looked at my reflection. The resemblance to Danielle was remarkable and a little eerie.

"Well?" Sophie asked.

"With the hair and makeup, it's weird how much I look like her. Now, I just have to sneak into the clinic, take Danielle's place, and fool a room full of vicious hoodlums while I become the head of a violent drug cartel."
~~~~

"Well, yeah. But it's only the Arizona branch of the cartel, not the entire thing."

I put my old outfit in a bag and we headed out the door. It was only three o'clock and I wouldn't need to be at the clinic until six. Even with traffic, I wouldn't need to leave until five fifteen. Sophie and I decided to wait back at the office. Sophie's original idea had been to wait at a bar, but I knew drinking for two hours before I attempted the deception probably wasn't the best idea.

When we got to the office, Lenny was there, but his door was closed. If Gina had come in, she'd already gone out again.

We went up to reception and Sophie sat at her desk while I took my usual place on the red leather chair. A client call came in and Sophie spent several minutes on the phone straightening out a billing question. As I sat and listened to Sophie, I went over what I was about to attempt. The more I thought about it, the more nervous I got.

What was I thinking? Agreeing to act as a stand in for a mob ceremony? What if the police choose tonight to raid the place? What if another gang heard about the ceremony and decided this would be a good night to wipe out the entire group?

I was still deep in thought, when the door to Lenny's office opened and he came out, holding a couple of files. He walked up to Sophie's desk as she was hanging up with the client.

"Sophie, put these away and I need the file on the Bergman case. For the last couple of weeks, it's been the top file on a stack on the bookshelf here, but now it's been put away somewhere." Lenny looked down at me. "Not that I'm complaining. You've done a great job cleaning the place up. Feel free to stick around here until all the stacks in the conference room are put away. Maybe you can come back whenever the place starts to go to hell again."

Lenny then gave me a weird puzzled look. "Don't take this the wrong way, but it's creepy how much you look like Laura." He looked back to Sophie. "Get me the file?" He then turned and walked back into his office.

"Well," Sophie said. "That's a good sign. If we can fool Lenny, a room full of mobsters should be no problem."

"I hope you're right. If not, let Grandma Peckham know what happened. Someone will need to take care of Marlowe."

~~~~

Sophie drove to the clinic and we arrived right at six. Before we left the office, she'd wrapped my hair in a long scarf. It wouldn't hide my face, but without the hair showing it would be harder for someone to guess what we were up to. I had also put on a lightweight jacket to hide the outfit. As instructed, we drove around to the back where Señor Largo was waiting for us.

"Who is with you?" Largo asked me as we walked up. I noticed he now had a bandage on his forehead, likely covering up several stitches.

"This is Sophie. She's a friend of Danielle's and she knows all about what we're doing tonight. I thought it would be best to have someone stay with Danielle while I was at the ceremony."

Largo nodded as if he agreed. "So that you do not think I am careless, I pulled the man working this door so you could enter unseen. As soon as we go in, I'll place him back here." Largo then led us upstairs and into the room.

Danielle was awake and the top part of her bed was elevated. Her eyes were bright and the color had returned to her face. Largo then disappeared back into the hallway.

Tio Francisco was in a chair and José Luis was looking out the window. Standing next to the bed was a man I'd never seen before. He was in his mid-thirties and was cute.

I decided to make introductions. "Mr. Salazar, this is Sophia. Before last night, Danielle had been staying at her place. She knows
~~~~

everything about tonight."

"Sophie," Danielle said, her voice stronger than it had been in the morning. "I'm so glad you came."

"I am José Luis," the assistant said as he walked over and shook Sophie's hand. I'm glad Danielle has another friend here. It's a dangerous business tonight."

Sophie and I both looked at the man standing next to the bed.

"This is Roberto," José Luis said. "He also knows what we're doing and will stay in the room to protect Danielle while we're away. The guards working downstairs have only been told to see that no one enters the clinic and not to come upstairs."

"Roberto," Tio Francisco said. "Would you mind waiting outside while we talk?"

Roberto left and we walked over to the bed.

"Was that *the* Roberto you were talking about?" Sophie asked.

Danielle's face actually blushed red. "Um, Tio Francisco said I needed to have someone here I trusted. I chose Roberto. It was a bit of a shock when he found out who I was, but he handled it well."

"He's cute," Sophie said. "I'd say you made a good choice."

"Well?" Tio Francisco asked as he looked at me. "Are we going to be able to pull this off? Were you able to turn yourself into Danielle?"

I felt everyone's eyes on me as Sophie helped me remove the scarf and I took off the jacket. I kept my back to Tio Francisco as Sophie took a brush and put everything back into place. I then turned around and showed Tio Francisco. I heard José Luis let out a gasp.

"Amazing," Tio Francisco said as he stood to look at me. "Yes, this will work. We'll do this as a fast shuffle and no one will know the difference."

I turned to Danielle and she gave me a smile. "You look pretty close. Sophie, take off my necklace and put it on her."

Sophie did and I modeled the results for Danielle.

"Yes," she said. "Now we look exactly alike. I've always wanted a sister. We can go to a bar sometime and pretend we're identical twins."

José Luis looked at his watch. "We'll need to start down to the cars in about five minutes. I'll get the wheelchair."

~~~~

Ten minutes later, I was in the back of a huge SUV and we were driving towards the headquarters of the Black Death. I was sitting between José Luis and Tio Francisco. A man I didn't know was driving while Largo was sitting shotgun.

"The entire clinic is still closed," I said, more from being nervous than actually wanting to know. "Is that for Danielle?"

"Yes," José Luis said. "We own the clinic. After what happened last night, security was simplified by closing it for a few days."

"Tell me about the ceremony. Danielle said you'll ask me questions and all I have to do is say 'Si' after each question. Is that it?"

"Pretty much," Tio Francisco said. "If it will help, I can do the ceremony in English, except for the vows. It's traditional for me to say them in Spanish. But it will be no problem. Danielle was correct. I'll ask you three questions and you will answer each time with 'Si'. Can you do that?"

"I guess. What are the questions about?"

"It's an oath to be faithful to the group, to protect the secrets of the group, and to be willing to sacrifice your life to the group or suffer a painful death due to slow torture if you don't. It's all part of the formal ritual."

"Um, okay. Anything else?"
~~~~

"Yes, I will need to prick your finger with a ceremonial knife. It will only be a little cut."

"You need to cut me?"

"Yes. You'll first sign Danielle's name in a book. After I cut your finger, you'll place a drop of blood on the signature. It's an important part of the ritual. It needs to be done."

Shit. I hope Danielle appreciates what I'm doing for her.

"Alright, fine. But make sure you sterilize the knife before you do it. I don't want to end up in the hospital with an infection. Is that it or is there anything else I need to know about?"

"The group knows you were attacked and have needed to be in a clinic. Let us use the wheelchair to bring you in. I'll then help you to a chair on a stage we've built in the warehouse. Pretend you are stiff and sore after your attack, as if you have broken ribs or some sort of internal injuries. Don't talk during the ritual. Everyone would know you are not Danielle by your voice."

"Alright, what about Sergio? What if he tries another attack at the meeting?"

"Oh, Sergio," Tio Francisco said, a lighthearted tone to his voice. "Won't see him no more."

I looked up at Largo. He turned and briefly flashed a cruel smile. "It's been a busy afternoon."

"Oh."

We drove in silence for a moment when I had another thought. "Um, is Raul going to be there tonight?"

"Yes," Tio Francisco said. "Although he is only a junior member of leadership, his rank permits him to attend the ceremony. Will this be a problem?"

"I don't know. We have a history together. If anyone will see through this act, it will be Raul. Honestly, I don't think he's very stable. If he suspects something's amiss, I don't know what he'll end up doing."

"Very well," Tio Francisco said. We will be attentive."

~~~~

Ten minutes later, we arrived at the headquarters of the Black Death. As we pulled up to the main entrance, my stomach clenched and it became hard to breathe. I was swamped by a flood of memories from what happened the last time I'd been here. Memories of Tony being shot and Carlos being killed. Memories of being betrayed by Danielle. But mostly memories of hanging in a torture chamber, about to be sliced into pieces by that sick scumbag Raul.

Several men came out to meet us. José Luis helped me into the wheelchair while Tio Francisco stood next to me. Largo was standing guard over our group, even as he shouted orders to the men standing around.

I was wheeled into the warehouse portion of the building, then to a low platform that had a long table and a chair. The table had a red velvet tablecloth and there were a dozen lit candles in silver holders. A small book with a black cover was sitting open, directly in front of the chair. The lights had been turned down throughout the rest of the warehouse and it added a solemnness to the event.

A group of about twenty grim looking men stood in front of the platform. I felt their eyes on me as I was taken past them. From what Tio Francisco had said, this was the entire leadership team of the Black Death in Arizona.

José Luis stopped the wheelchair behind the platform and Tio Francisco helped me up. For the benefit of the men watching, I softly grunted with pain and effort as I was led to the chair. As I sat, I slightly contorted my face with pain. I tried to be subtle, but to still show I'd been injured. I hoped my performance would be enough to convince the men I was the genuine Danielle.

Tio Francisco stood next to me and began to speak.
~~~~

"For the benefit of our new American members, I will do this in English. We are now an American company. It is good to speak English, no?"

Everyone laughed. It struck me that this could have been a meeting at any company.

"Okay, to business. We are here tonight to recognize Danielle Ortega as the new head of the group. Although Sergio was a capable leader and did valuable work for our organization, he did not ultimately have the temperament to lead our group and has been removed."

At that, there were several knowing glances between the men in the group. Several of them looked over at Largo, now standing next to the platform. I again hoped the police didn't decide to swoop in tonight for a mass arrest.

"My brother, Escobar, has appointed Danielle to take over. Assisting her as the new head of security will be Señor Largo. For those of you who have not met Largo in person, he was the man in charge of training Carlos. And we all know how much respect Carlos had in the eyes of Escobar."

As Tio Francisco continued to talk, I looked out over the men. I got a sudden shock of fear as I realized Raul was standing in the back of the group. Even in the dim room, I could see his eyepatch. Apparently, he was still blind in the one eye from the wasp spray I'd shot in his face the first time he'd tried to kill me. What had caused the fear was the look he was giving me. He was staring at me with an intense concentration, as if he was having an inner debate with himself on what he was seeing. As our eyes made contact, there was a look of shock and recognition on his face.

Shit.

My own look of shock must have shown, which seemed to confirm his suspicions. His good eye opened wide with surprise.

I felt a hand lightly touch my shoulder and I jumped. I looked up to see Tio Francisco.

"You will now take the oath of leadership," he said. He then slowly said the first line in Spanish. Even not knowing the details of what he said, I could tell it was a very solemn and serious question. When he was done, he looked down at me.

I took a deep breath. "Si," I answered, trying to sound as much like Danielle as I could.

Tio Francisco asked the second and then the third question. Each time I responded with "Si."

As Tio Francisco was asking his questions, I watched as Raul slowly drifted up to the front of the group. His eye had lost the look of surprise. It had been replaced with cold hatred. It was the same look he had the last time he'd tried to kill me.

"You will now sign the book of leadership," Tio Francisco said.

He handed me an old-fashioned ink pen, one with a long metal tip, and pointed to a spot on the page where I should sign. I looked and saw the name above it was Carlos Valentino. There was a bloody fingerprint over the last name. Seeing it gave me a shudder. Ignoring the stare of Raul, I carefully signed Danielle's name. Fortunately, I'd seen her sign credit card receipts before and I knew the basics of her signature. I hoped my quick forgery would be close enough.

"You will now verify your signature in blood." Tio Francisco said as he picked up a silver knife that had been lying on the table.

Inwardly cringing, I held my hand out. He took it and I felt a sharp stab of pain. He then took my finger and pressed it against the page. There was a black cloth on the table and he gave it to me to wipe off my finger.

Tio Francisco then stood and addressed the crowd. "With the oath of leadership taken and the signature verified in blood, I proclaim you, Danielle Ortega, the leader of…"

"You!" Raul suddenly shouted as he raised a finger towards me.

"It's you. I know it's you. You bitch!" He then pulled a pistol from under his shirt. "Not this time. Never again!"

Time went into slow motion as Raul aimed the pistol at my chest. The barrel opening in the front of the gun was huge, likely a ten millimeter or even a forty-five. His finger tensed as he squeezed the trigger.

I closed my eyes and waited for the inevitable. Oddly, I didn't panic or even think about trying to escape. Instead, I felt strangely at peace. It was as if I knew all along this was going to be the outcome of my attempt at a deception. What had I been thinking? Agreeing to take Danielle's place at a Black Death ceremony? It had been foolish and now I was about to pay for my stupidity.

As if from far away, I heard the blast of the pistol. I held my breath and waited to feel the pain of the bullet as it tore through my body. My only hope was that death would come quickly and I didn't have to suffer for too long.

There was an eternity of three or four seconds while I waited for the pain. Which part of my body had taken the hit? It wasn't my head, because I was still thinking. Was it a gut shot, so I would slowly bleed out, or was it a chest wound, which would kill me before help could arrive?

When I didn't feel anything, I slowly opened my eyes. I looked down but didn't see blood anywhere. I then looked back at Raul. He was crumpled on the floor and his pistol was several feet from his outstretched hand. His other hand was clutching at a bright red spot that was rapidly growing on his chest.

Señor Largo took a step forward, his smoking revolver still pointed towards Raul.

"Stop this foolishness at once," Tio Francisco shouted angrily. He then went into a two-minute tirade in Spanish. As he was admonishing the group, two men came and dragged Raul away.

"This meeting is over," Tio Francisco said. "Everyone go home.

We'll decide what to do with him later, assuming he lives."

~~~~

No one said anything on the drive back to the clinic. For the benefit of the men in the lobby, I used the wheelchair to go back up to the second floor.

When we got into Danielle's room and closed the door, I felt a huge rush of relief. Although it had been close, I'd made it through the night. Sophie and Roberto were standing next to the bed. Danielle was sitting up and she seemed to be focused and alert.

Danielle looked at us and could sense something was wrong. "What happened?"

"You are now the leader of the group," Tio Francisco said. "Unfortunately, Raul figured out the truth. He attempted to kill a person he viewed as being a threat to the organization and was badly wounded as a result.

"What do the rest of the men think?" Danielle asked. "Did anyone else see through the deception?"

"I do not think so," Largo said in a matter-of-fact voice. "I was watching them all, very carefully. The only one who seemed to take notice was Raul. The loss of a soldier is unfortunate, but this is not altogether a bad thing. The men will know how seriously I take your protection. It will stop any future attempts."

I went into a room down the hall and changed back into my outfit from earlier in the day. I somehow felt better being me again. As I was walking down the hall to the room, Tio Francisco stepped out.

"A moment of your time before you go back in."

I immediately got a knot in my stomach. I didn't know what he wanted, but I suspected it wouldn't be good.

"Sure," I said. "You want to talk?"

From a pocket of his jacket, he pulled out a thick white envelope.
~~~~

"This is for your efforts tonight. It was very brave of you to go through with it. Few people could have done so well."

I opened the envelope and it was stuffed with hundred-dollar bills. Easily ten or twelve thousand dollars' worth.

Damn.

I thought about what I could do with it. I certainly had some bills to pay, including some new ones over the past few days. But I knew I could never be comfortable taking money for what I'd done, especially money coming from the sale of drugs. Instead I handed the envelope back to him.

"Thank you for the offer. But I did what I did out of friendship, not to gain from it. Please don't take this the wrong way, but I don't want to be a paid member of your group."

Tio Francisco looked at me for a moment, then nodded his head. "Yes, I understand. I know you and Danielle have a somewhat complicated relationship. Perhaps the exchange of money would make it more difficult. But please, I know you had some expenses today. Let me take care of those." He reached into the envelope and extracted a few bills. "Will this cover it?"

I thought about the credit card bill I had coming from the salon and took the money.

We went back into the room and I gave Danielle her necklace. Sophie and I then said our goodbyes. On the drive back to the office, she wanted to know all the details about what happened, but I didn't want to talk about it yet and only gave out the basics.

"Raul?" Sophie asked. "Isn't he the one who threw the hatchet at your car, and who set off the cake bomb at the wedding, and who was going to gut you like a fish that night?"

"Yup, I think that's why he recognized me. We sort of have a history together."

"And he's dead?"

"I think so. He got shot in the chest and was bleeding pretty badly."

"But you didn't actually see him die?"

"No, they took him away somewhere and we left right after that."

"So, maybe he's still alive and will get better?"

"Maybe, but even if he lives to tell the story, Danielle will be better by then and no one will doubt who she is."

"I was more thinking about you. Even if no one else believes him, if he lives, he's still going to find a way to take it out on you."

"Maybe, but it's been a long shitty day. I can't worry about that tonight."

~~~~

Sophie dropped me off at my car and I drove home. Even though I really hadn't eaten all day, I still wasn't hungry. I stood in front of the bathroom mirror and removed the makeup. I felt better seeing my face again in the mirror. I then stripped off my clothes and pulled on a T-shirt. I lay in bed for about ten minutes, thinking about the day, then fell asleep.
~~~~

Chapter Fourteen

When I woke up, I lay in bed for almost an hour, enjoying the sensation of not having to be up for an assignment. I was exhausted from everything that had happened over the past couple of weeks and I hoped nothing new would come up for a while.

I made a pot of coffee and got dressed. Not having anything else to do, I decided to go down to the office. Before I left, I found my old Arizona Diamondbacks baseball hat. I put my hair into a pony tail and pulled it through the back of the hat. I decided I was too tired to answer a lot of questions about my hair. Hopefully Gina wouldn't say anything about the darker color.

When I parked, everyone's cars were there. I walked up front where Gina was talking to Sophie. According to Gina, both Charles Barton and Mindy had been appearing all over the TV for the past two days, discussing the finding of the Lost Sister. Gina said Mindy had a real talent for speaking on TV.

Lenny had been thrilled when he first got to meet Charles Barton. Caroline had agreed to pay all the legal fees Mindy had rung up, even though Lenny shamefully padded them. But according to Sophie, he'd been sitting in his office most of the morning with the door closed. He'd apparently come out a few times, but Sophie said he looked and sounded down. Gina's theory was that Lenny was depressed because he couldn't figure out a way of getting any more money from the billionaire. It seemed reasonable to me.

~~~~

By eleven o'clock, Gina was back out on an assignment. I'd just come back from across the street, where I'd grabbed a couple of coffees. When I handed Sophie her peppermint mocha, she had a huge smile on her face.

"What happened?" I asked. "You look like you got some good news."

"I've been poking around the secret software for the past couple of days and I finally found what I've been looking for. It was hidden pretty well, but I found the 'restore' function. I typed in all the information and I'm back on the internet. I looked on Facebook and it's back to the way it was. Although, I think I need to clean it up. I'm friends with about three hundred people and I don't know who half of them are."

"I'm glad you're back on the grid. But if you didn't know them, why'd you accept them as friends?"

"It sorta seems rude not too. I mean, what if I really did know them at some point, then refused their request. That's the sort of thing that could piss somebody off for years."

"Good point."

"Have you heard anything more about Danielle?" Sophie asked as she sipped her coffee.

"Not a word. I assume everything's still okay."

"Let's go see her after lunch. I don't think Lenny will come out of his office all day."

"Don't you think he'll mind if you aren't here for most of the afternoon?"

Sophie shrugged her shoulders. "Like I said, if he's concerned about things like that, he should hire an admin. What are you doing this weekend?"
~~~~

"I'm supposed to have a date tomorrow with Max. Now that everything's finished up, I'm hoping nothing else comes up before then."

"When you say a date, are you only talking about dinner and a movie?"

"The plan is to meet him somewhere tomorrow night and then spend the weekend together."

"That's my kind of date. Last time was San Diego. Where's he taking you this time?"

"I don't think we're going anywhere. We're probably staying in a suite at one of Tony's resorts. Even if we can manage the entire weekend together, I don't think Max wants to be too far away, in case something comes up."

"Not quite as romantic as strolling down the beach in San Diego, but it sounds like a date with lots of room service. It's been a long time since I've had a room-service weekend."

"What about you? Is Snake in town this weekend?"

"No, they're playing in Green Bay and Snake isn't high enough up in the pecking order for me to travel with the wives. But if Max is going to be busy all weekend with you, I bet that'll free up Milo. He probably won't be able to travel outside of Scottsdale either, but Tony has a lot of nice resorts and I think Milo gets an employee discount. Maybe I can have a room-service weekend too."

"That would be great, but don't get the room next to us. That would be a little weird."

"No shit. I make a lot of noise and I'd hate to think someone I knew was listening to it."

"Really? What about your neighbors in your apartment?"

"They're mostly old and they don't hear so good. Besides, it's my apartment, I live there. What are you going to do?"

Sophie looked at me. She then cocked her head to the side. "If you're about to have a weekend with Max, why don't you seem happier?"

How does she always know?

"I had a talk with Tony the other day. You can't tell anyone, but he's thinking about retiring and giving the company to Max."

"Is that a bad thing?"

"According to Tony, if Max takes permanent control, he likely won't ever be able to date me, at least not openly."

"Well, that sucks. You're telling me if Max gets to be the boss of a huge crime family, you'll be out a boyfriend?"

"That's what Tony thinks."

"Looks like you maybe should have stayed with Reno after all."

"Shut up. I'm depressed enough about this. Besides, Reno seems happy with toe-fungus woman."

"Well, don't let it ruin your weekend. Who knows, it may be your last one with Max."

"Are you actively trying to make me feel like crap?"

"I'm just sayin', you never know. Live for today, tomorrow may never come."

"Is that supposed to help?"

Sophie's eyes got big and she started to giggle. She kept going until tears came into her eyes and she had to fan herself.

"Okay. What's so funny?"

"I just realized. The head of the Black Death is going to spend the weekend having sex with the head of Tough Tony's group." She started laughing again. "And no one has the slightest clue."

"I'm not head of the Black Death."

"Oh yeah? You have your fingerprint, in your own blood, in the Black Death book of leadership. Hopefully the police never get their hands on it. Some people might think that's close enough to count."

"How do you know about the book of leadership?"

"Danielle told us all about the ritual while you were gone last night. It sounded really cool. I wish I could have seen it."

"Do you want to go to lunch?" I asked, changing the subject. "I'm still hungry from not eating yesterday. I could use some tacos."

~~~~

We walked down the street to Old Town Gringos. We got one of our favorite tables, close to the street, and I had my fill of carne asada tacos, along with a couple of Coronas. It felt great not having to rush away to work on anything.

After lunch, we walked back to the office then out to the back. I offered to drive, but Sophie only looked over at my car.

"When are you going to get a new car? That burnt license plate gives out waves of sadness."

"Hey, my car has personality," I said.

"Your car should be abandoned somewhere out in the desert."

"Fine, we'll take your car."

We drove to the clinic where the note on the door said the building was still closed for a plumbing problem but would reopen the next day. I took it as a good sign for Danielle.

We knocked and eventually one of the henchmen from the night before came to the door. He recognized me but wouldn't let us in until he checked with the people upstairs. Fortunately, Señor Largo was there and he came down to escort us up.

When we made it to the room, Danielle was awake and sitting up in the bed. Roberto was standing next to her. She smiled when we
~~~~

came in.

"I'm glad you made it," she said. "They're letting me out in a couple of hours."

"Are you going to be okay on your own?" Sophie asked. "You could stay with me until you feel better."

"Thanks," Danielle said. "But now that I'm head of the group, I'll be staying at the house in North Scottsdale. I'll have people to see to my needs until I'm up and around. They tell me I should be back on my feet in about a week."

"So, how are you?" I asked. "Is everything going to be alright?"

"The doctors say I'll make a full recovery. They tell me in two or three months, it will be like it never happened."

"I'm glad," Sophie said. "We were a little worried about you."

"Thank you for doing what you did yesterday," Danielle said as she looked at me. "I've been hearing about it all day. You were very brave and they say you did great."

"Thanks, but I hope I don't ever have to do anything like that again."

"Yeah," Sophie said, looking at me. "You should probably also do something different with your hair. It was creepy as shit seeing the two of you together like that."

~~~~

The next day, I was back up front at reception, talking with Sophie and Gina, when Professor Mindy walked through the front door. She was again dressed in brown cargo pants, a khaki shirt with big pockets, and a beat-up leather fedora. She even had a brown leather satchel hanging by a long shoulder strap. As with the first time I'd seen her, all I could think of was Indiana Jones.

We gathered around her as we said our hellos, then made it over to Sophie's desk.
~~~~

"How are you doing?" I asked. "We hear you've been busy."

"My head's still spinning," Mindy said, as she sat in one of the wing chairs. "I was in New York yesterday and gave four interviews."

"I saw you on CNN last night," I said. "You looked amazing."

"Thanks. They had a professional makeup artist and hair stylist work on me for almost two hours before the interview. When they were finished, I could hardly recognize myself. The last few days have been a total whirlwind. Since Charles gave that press conference on Tuesday night, we've both been giving interviews to everyone."

"I saw some of his interviews," Gina said. "He's pretty much saturated the networks and the cable channels. He's quite the showman. He's built up your discovery to be the archeological find of the century. Although, I noticed he's making it sound like he planned and financed your expedition from the start."

"I know," Mindy said, "but I'm not going to quibble. There's more than enough credit to go around with this. Science magazine has already contacted me about publishing the article about how I found the Lost Sister. You'll both have to let me know if it's okay if I use the pictures I took of the two of you."

"You mean the pictures of us after we'd climbed up that big ass mountain and had those helmets on?" Sophie asked. "I'm sure we both look like crap."

"Not at all. You both look like archeologists."

"Oh," Sophie said. "I guess we can live with that. What do you say? I think this calls for drinks."

Sophie led us into the conference room, walked to the wet bar against the far wall, and started dropping ice cubes into glasses.

"Are you sure it's okay for us to be doing this?" Mindy asked.

"Who do you think's in charge of both cleaning up and ordering the booze in the first place?" Sophie asked. "Lenny's out for the rest of the day. If nobody tells, who's even to know?" I noticed as she said this, she was looking at Gina.

"I'll take a gin and tonic," Gina said with a smile.

"Scotch for me," I said. "As long as Lenny's buying, make it a good one."

"I'll take a margarita," Mindy said. "Top shelf."

"My kind of woman," Sophie said as she started pouring. "I'll make it two."

After Sophie made everyone a drink, we rearranged the stacks of unfiled folders enough for us all to sit at the conference table.

"What about the legalities?" Gina asked as she sipped her drink. "I know the permits were filed several days ago, but Lenny hasn't said anything about their status."

"We've now got both the treasure-trove and the excavation permits," Mindy said. "The university received final approval for everything yesterday afternoon."

"Really? I'm surprised you got the approvals so soon," Gina said. "I understood those were going to take several weeks, if not months."

"I had a meeting with Caroline last night, in between the CBS News and the CNN interviews. Apparently, Charles knows somebody high up at the Department of Agriculture, that's the department that oversees the U.S. Forest Service. We now have retroactive permission to excavate the cave and to direct the artifacts to an appropriate museum. As part of the agreement, Caroline said when the statue isn't on tour, it'll be on permanent loan with three of her sister statues at the National Museum of Anthropology in Mexico City. It's a gift from the United States to the people of Mexico. Charles is already working out the details of a world tour of the Seven Sisters. He says it'll be the largest archeological event since *The Treasures of Tutankhamun* tour back in the nineteen eighties."

"I can understand the museum wanting the get the Lost Sister back to where it came from," Gina said, "but I'm surprised the Mexican government would be so willing to let the statues travel."

"From what I understand, Mr. Barton has already pledged to build a new wing to the museum to house the Sisters. They'll probably even name it after him. His only condition was that he could borrow the museum's four Sisters whenever he wants them to go on tour. Those tours can be quite lucrative and I'm sure the museum will get its share."

"What about the money?" Sophie asked. "The million-dollar donation Caroline promised would be in your name. What happened with that?"

"You saw Charles give the check to the president of the university during the press conference on Tuesday night, right after I gave him the statue. But yes, Caroline was as good as her word and I now have the paperwork showing the money was donated in my name. I'll have a nice tax write-off and the university will get a major upgrade to its anthropology museum. Caroline's foundation even offered to publish a book on my discovery of the Lost Sister and sell it in the museum gift shops during the tour. They think it'll add to the authenticity of the piece."

"What about the finder's fee Caroline promised?" Sophie asked. "After everything you've been through? Are you saying you got squat?"

"Well, not exactly. They slipped a provision into the dig permits saying I can keep any non-native minerals found at the cave, as long as they aren't culturally significant."

Sophie looked puzzled for a second, then her eyes opened wide. "Are you talking about the gold?"

"Yup," Mindy said. "I get to keep all of the gold we pulled out. That's the finder's fee."

"Holy shit," Sophie said. "Seriously?"

"We recovered a little over eight hundred and fifty ounces," Mindy said. "At current prices, that's roughly one point one million dollars."

Wow.

"That's so wonderful," I said as I stepped forward and gave Mindy a hug.

"What are you going to do with it?" Sophie asked.

"I've already identified the most interesting and significant pieces of gold. I'll donate those to the museum here at ASU and to the museum in Mexico. They'll also get the wooden box with the cross on it and the lock. All of that will be part of the traveling exhibition."

"Not that," Sophie said. "What are you going to do with the money?"

"Oh. I was thinking, after I pay off my student loans, I'm going to get a house. Something on a hill, not far from Scottsdale. Nothing too big or fancy, but somewhere I can live for a long time."

"Make sure to invite all of us over when you have your housewarming party," Gina said.

"I will, but I also came over to give everyone something." She took the leather satchel off her shoulder and started digging through it. She took out something hard, the size of a small potato, wrapped in a piece of white cloth. She set it on the conference room table with a thud. She pulled off the cloth to reveal a shining gold nugget. We were all momentarily transfixed at the raw beauty of the lump of shiny gold.

"I have one for each of you," Mindy said, as she reached into her bag and pulled out two more large chunks of gold. She sat each one down on the table with a thud.

Sophie let out a loud squeal and her hand shot out to grab a nugget. Her hand bobbed up and down as she felt the weight of it. "Oh my God," she squealed again. "It's so heavy."

"Each of these is about fourteen troy ounces," Mindy said. "They're worth about eighteen thousand dollars each."

"That's very generous," Gina said. "But you don't have to give us anything. You've worked for ten years to get these. You should keep it all."

Sophie frowned and gave Gina a sideways look, but Mindy only laughed. "No, I want you to have these. Each of you put yourselves in danger to help me find the Lost Sister. Besides, I picked out the pretty ones to give to everyone. You can mount them as a keepsake of our adventures, or if you want to sell them, go ahead. Other than a few of the more unusual nuggets I'm keeping or donating to the museums, I'm going to sell the rest."

Gina looked at me and I nodded my head.

"Alright," Gina said. "But it's still a very generous gesture."

"This will take care of my credit card payments, once and for all," Sophie said. "Thanks, Professor." She then stood up and gave Mindy a long hug.

"What are you going to do with yours?" Mindy asked as she looked at me.

"I don't know," I said as I picked up a nugget. "I should sell it and use the money to get a car that works. But you're right. It's pretty and would make a great keepsake."

"What are you going to do with your time now that you've found the Lost Sister?" Gina asked. "You must feel kind of let down after all the excitement."

"I've been thinking about that," Mindy said. "In my studies of the region, I've come across another legend of a cave full of stolen treasure. This one's in Colorado, near the old mining town of Durango. I've always been meaning to look further into it, but finding the Lost Sister always took priority. It turns out the college in Durango was looking for a Professor of Archeology for the summer semester and I've already been accepted. I'll do some additional research over the next few months, then spend next summer in the mountains around Durango. Who knows? Maybe I'll get lucky twice."

~~~~

I went home about three o'clock and packed. I wasn't sure where we were going or what we would be doing, so I packed two different bags. One for if we stayed in town and one if we ended up going somewhere.

~~~~

I drove north to the Tropical Paradise and parked in the visitor's lot. I assumed this is where we'd be staying for the weekend but, just in case, I left my bag in the car. I was a little early, so I casually strolled up one of the sidewalks next to a manicured lawn and a big tropical foliage display. I had butterflies in my stomach and a rising sense of excitement for what the weekend would hold in store.

I thought back to the first time I'd ever been to the resort. It was long before I knew it had anything to do with Tony DiCenzo or organized crime. At the time, I only knew it to be a beautiful and peaceful oasis from the world. I'd even wondered what it would be like to live in a place like this.

I walked up the hill to the main lobby. As I did, Tony's words started echoing through my head, intruding on my carnal hopes for the weekend. *Once Max takes over, he won't be able to have a steady girlfriend, even if he wants to.*

I was having mixed feelings as I stood in the middle of the beautiful tropical rain forest that was the hotel lobby. I wanted to be with Max, but I didn't want to keep sneaking around to see him. I wanted him to be happy, but I also didn't want him to be the target of the police or the other gangs. But what I knew for sure was that I didn't want to do anything to mess up the weekend. Max had enough on his mind without having to deal with a moody girlfriend.

I was dwelling in this state of confused frustration when Johnny Scarpazzi walked up to me.

"Miss Black, it's good to see you again. Hopefully you're feeling better than last week."

"Thanks, Johnny. I'm feeling much better. I hadn't exercised that hard in years and I was pretty wiped out. But now, everything's mostly back to normal."

"I'll be taking you back up to the terrace. I've already let Max know you're here and he'll be waiting for you."

"Um, do you happen to know what we're doing this weekend?"

"Not officially, but I've heard a reliable rumor you'll be staying in the Grand Canyon suite. It's probably the nicest one in the entire resort."

"Thanks. I packed two bags and I wanted to know which one I'd be using."

Johnny led me through the second-floor offices, then into the private elevator. When we got out, Gabriella was at her usual place at the end of the hall. I think I caught the faintest trace of a smile as she opened the door to let me in.

Max was standing on the balcony, overlooking the city. The sun was on the western horizon and it made him look like a dark figure silhouetted against the light.

When the heavy door clicked shut, I knew we were alone. I ran the best I could towards Max, then flung my arms around him. I hugged him with a feeling close to desperation.

"Wow," he said. "Are you alright?"

"I've missed you. That's all."

His eyes softened as he looked down at me. It gave his face a beautiful glow. I reached my hand up to the back of his head and pulled him down for a kiss. The kiss started out light and slow, but rapidly built. My breathing became faster and deeper as I pressed myself against him. The feel of his skin as I ran my hands over his body was pushing me into a zone of arousal. Max held me tightly and his kisses also became more passionate and urgent. I could tell he wanted me as much as I needed him.

Thoughts of Max becoming head of the group and what would happen after that started to recede. What was replacing it was the warm excited glow of being with a wonderful man and the knowledge we'd be together for the entire weekend.

"Your hair," he said when we took a break. "That's new."

"Do you like it?"

"It looks great."

"Thanks. I thought I'd try something different for a while. Give me a month or two and it'll probably go back to normal."

"Either way, you'll look beautiful."

"What's the plan. Dinner up here?"

"Yes, after last time, I wasn't sure if I should chance it, but we'll start out with champagne and dinner here."

"And after that?"

Mmm, maybe a king-sized bed?

"We have both the rooftop terrace and a beautiful suite for the weekend. It may not be the beach, but it'll at least be private."

"If we're together, it doesn't matter where we are. I'm turning off my phone and hopefully yours won't ring too much."

"Let's have the weekend to ourselves. Something's about to happen at work that'll keep me busy, at least for a while. But for this weekend, Tony assures me that my phone won't ring, not even once."

Why is he bringing this up now?

"Really? Um, what's going to happen at work?"

"Let's talk about that next week. All I want to talk about this weekend is you and me."

Max pulled the bottle of champagne out of the bucket and began to peel off the foil. As he did, I took a moment to look around. We were alone on a lovely private terrace in one of the most beautiful resorts in Arizona. I was with a gorgeous man who I'd been lusting over and fantasizing about for months. I wanted him and he seemed to want me as well. I know I should have kept my mouth shut and simply had a nice weekend. But, ultimately, that's not me.

"I should probably tell you" I said. "Tony and I talked this week and I think I already know what your big news is."

"Really? I should have known. Tony's very fond of you. I know he's worried about how all of the changes will affect us."

"Tony thinks we won't be able to date after you become head of the group. He says he hasn't been able to become close to anyone in years."

Max stopped what he was doing, walked over to where I was standing, and wrapped his arms around my waist. He looked down into my eyes and I got a warm erotic shiver.

"I'm not Tony. I don't care if I'm head of the group or a guy parking cars at one of the resorts. We're finally together and nothing's going to interfere with that. This new role will have its own set of challenges. But if you're game, let's make it work."

Waves of different emotions hit me all at once. Relief that this weekend wasn't going to be our last time together. Happiness that Max thought we could make it. But mostly it was a feeling of wonder. Max was the first man I'd ever been with who hadn't run away when things turned tough. My ex-husband never understood me and Reno couldn't even last a full year before things went to hell.

Max poured two glasses of champagne and handed one to me. I

clinked my glass against his.

"To the start of a wonderful life?" he asked.

"A wonderful life seems like a great place to start."

Yes.

Epilogue

It took several months to get the Seven Sisters together so they could begin the tour. A series of bizarre accidents and illnesses pushed back the opening date and there was even talk of canceling the tour all together. Caroline, and a few of her colleagues from the Barton Foundation, eventually stepped in, and at last the Seven Sisters were reunited.

The first time they all were together was in London's Natural History Museum. As the event curator set the final Sister into place, in a custom-built, bullet-proof glass display case, all the Sisters began to glow with a faint blue sheen.

The effect lasted for almost three hours and the head curator at the London museum took several pictures and videos of the unusual phenomenon. She also reported there was a high-pitched humming noise, almost like singing, coming from the statues.

To date, no one has ever explained why the statues had glowed blue or why they never glowed again. A conspiracy theory website claimed the whole thing was a made-up hoax, simply to draw publicity to the tour.

Interestingly, after that unusual event, the tour went smoothly, and the bad luck seemed to disappear. People reported that seeing the Seven Sisters together filled them with hope and a sense of optimism. The Seven Sisters became famous the world over and the tour went on to become one of the top money makers of all time.

As a special bonus, here's the first chapter of *Scottsdale Shadow*, the seventh book in the Laura Black Scottsdale Mystery Series

Scottsdale Shadow

Chapter One

November is a time of change in Scottsdale. The slow and measured pace of the hot summer months changes to a high-pitched frenzy as paradise weather returns to the Valley of the Sun. The Beeline Highway becomes clogged with thousands of winter visitors, or Snowbirds as the locals call them, streaming down in their RV's from parts of the country that have already been hit by a blizzard or two.

Thanksgiving is known as the official start of Snowbird season. In anticipation of this, the trickle of Northerners in October becomes a flood in November. Once the Snowbirds arrive, they all want to eat at the best restaurants, play at the best golf courses, and shop at the best stores. This is great for the Scottsdale economy, but plays havoc on us working girls who are only trying to get along. Snowbirds don't know how to drive, how to call ahead for a reservation, or how to stand in line. Good luck trying to get a doctor or a dentist appointment when the winter visitors are in town. By the time Thanksgiving rolls around, I start wishing for Easter, the official end of Snowbird season.

~~~~

"Why am I doing this?" Sophie asked, for about the fifth time.

"I keep telling you," I said as we stood in the living room of a beautiful sixth floor apartment, located a little north of the Scottsdale Fashion Square. "My spy cameras normally broadcast the video with
~~~~

radio waves. But there's something about this building that won't let the signals through. I've already wasted three days trying to make them work. I needed to switch to the type of camera that keeps the videos on memory cards. But with these cameras, the batteries are only good for one day at a time. I need to come here every day to change out the memory cards and put fresh batteries in all the cameras."

"I get that part," she said. "I mean, why am I here with you? Why can't you do this by yourself?"

"I told you, the husband, Chet, works from home. Every day he goes out for cigarettes and lunch at around eleven-thirty. He's only out of the apartment for twenty-five or thirty minutes. I almost got caught yesterday when he came home early. I need a faster way to change everything out. I'll show you where the cameras are and tomorrow you can do half of them. I'll do the other half and we'll both get out of here with plenty of time to spare. Besides, I thought you liked getting out of the office."

"I do like getting out of the office, but how long are we going to have to do this?"

"Until we get videos of him together with his girlfriend. The wife thinks she's an instructor named Angie who works at the Pilates studio they own. The wife thinks Angie comes over to the apartment during the day while she's at work. Once we get proof of Chet having the affair, we're done. Why are you so grouchy? You know how this works."

"Yeah, I know how it works. But you're the one who likes to go out and do the spy stuff. I like it when we can do something fun and exciting, like the time we went on that road trip to Mexico to find Jackie. That was great."

"The only reason you thought it was fun was because you spent the entire time drinking margaritas and sangria."

"Well, yeah, that helped. But sneaking around somebody's house isn't a lot of fun. I can see why you always grumble about it so much."

We walked into the den and I showed Sophie where I'd hidden the camera, slightly behind a Boston fern on a shelf facing the desk.

"After you replace the memory card and the battery, make sure the camera's facing the couch, or the bed, or wherever looks like the most likely place for sex."

"I can do that. How many of these camera things are in here?"

"Seven. I put one in every room."

Sophie picked up the camera and looked at it. "Hey, this camera's cute. It looks like a little cat statue. He'll never know it's a camera, even if he happens to see it on the shelf."

"That's the idea. I have cameras that look like statues, picture frames, and tissue boxes. He'll assume the wife bought everything and put them on the shelves."

For the next five minutes, I showed Sophie how to change out the batteries and where to insert the fresh memory cards.

"Okay," Sophie said as we finished up the camera in the bathroom. "Where next?"

"One in the master and one in the living room. After that, let's get out of here. We're being slow as it is."

We both froze as there was the distinctive sound of a key going into the lock in the main door in the living room. Sophie heard it the same time as I did.

"Thirty minutes?" she said in an annoyed whisper. "That couldn't have been more than fifteen minutes, tops."

"Maybe he forgot something. Let's hide and wait for him to leave again."

We slipped into the guest bedroom and I slowly closed the door.

Sophie was giving me a look that said she still wasn't happy about being a spy.

We heard someone making noise in the living room. I silently hoped he didn't need to come into the guest bedroom to get whatever he'd forgotten. We then heard a woman's voice. Chet answered her and the voices grew louder as they walked back towards the bedrooms. Sophie's eyes got big as we waited to see which room they'd end up in.

We heard more noises as they moved into the master and I breathed a sigh of relief. We then sat on the bed and waited for four or five minutes, hoping they'd leave. Instead, we began to hear the unmistakable sounds of a woman's needs being attended to.

"Wow," Sophie whispered. "She's really loud. At least they didn't come in here."

"But we haven't changed out the battery or the memory card of the camera in the master bedroom. I doubt we're recording a thing."

"You mean they're in there right now having sex and just because you don't have a working camera in the room, we're going to have to keep coming back over here every day until you do happen to catch them?"

"Yeah," I whispered. "There's nothing else we can do."

We sat on the bed for another five or six minutes. If anything, the woman's moans were getting louder. In addition to the moaning, she'd started slapping her hand on the bed and doing the "Oh my God, Oh my God," thing.

"You know," Sophie said. "Listening to her in there is sorta getting me worked up."

"Yeah," I said. "It happens to me too. I get visions of Max whenever I hear it."

"Damn. I'm thinking I might have to call one of my honeys tonight for a quickie."

We sat on the bed for another three or four-minutes, listening to the woman pound on the bed and moan.

"You end up doing this a lot, don't you?" Sophie asked.

"Yup," I said. "But this time isn't so bad. The last time I was stuck in a closet and it was really hot."

"What about the camera in your cell phone? Let's walk in and catch 'em in the act."

"We can't do that in an apartment. It wouldn't be safe."

"Hey, didn't you and Gina do the exact same thing, like a month ago, with Timothy and Crystal in the gym?"

"That was different. It was a public place. I don't want this guy to pull a gun out of the nightstand and shoot us as home invaders."

"I think you're worrying too much," Sophie said as she pulled her phone out of her purse. "I don't know about you, but I don't want to have to keep coming over here every day. It's going to mess up my lunch hour."

I saw her setting the camera to video mode and knew what she was about to do.

Shit.

"Fine," I said. "If you don't mind getting shot at, let's get this over with."

I pushed open the guest bedroom door and we walked out into the hallway. The door to the master was open and we crept down until we got an unobstructed view of both of them on the bed. We then stood there for almost five minutes shooting video.

After the initial shock of watching two naked people having sex, I was able to get a handle on what I was seeing. The woman was about our age, maybe a few years older, had straight blonde hair, and a body that was incredibly toned. She was riding him cowgirl and was still making a lot of noise. Chet was older, pale, and a little pudgy. Clearly, he was someone who didn't get out of his apartment a lot.

We'd started to slowly back up to return to the guest bedroom when Chet noticed we were in the hallway filming them.

"What the hell!" Chet yelled as he pushed the woman off. She got off the bed and looked back and forth between him and us, visibly confused.

Why do I keep having arguments with angry naked people?

Chet sat up on the bed and seemed stunned. His eyes were darting around the room, like he was trying to process what was happening. I knew I should say something before his jumbled thoughts turned violent and things got out of hand.

"We're here with the permission of your wife," I said. "We work for her attorney at Halftown, Oeding, Shapiro, and Hopkins."

"Why are you taking pictures of us?" the blonde girl, who I assumed was Angie, asked.

"Before they got married," Sophie said, "Chet and his wife signed a pre-nup that would give his wife jack squat when they divorced. Unfortunately, the agreement also had a clause that voided it if Chet wasn't faithful. You'd be surprised how many guys let the woman slip that one in. We get 'em all the time."

Angie looked over at Chet. Her hands were on her hips and she was starting to get angry. "You said you were going to keep everything after the divorce."

"Oh, that was with the pre-nup," Sophie said. "Now he's blown that and everything goes back to plain old Arizona family court."

"What does that mean?" Angie asked.

"It means they split everything fifty-fifty and the wife will likely get all the good stuff, seeing how the husband's such a low-life scumbag and all."

"What about Chet's company, the Pilates studio? Who'll get that?"

"Well," I said. "The business amounts to about eighty percent of the marital assets. There's no way one side or the other would get the entire thing. Chet and his wife will either need to agree to run it together or more likely, the judge will make them sell it and they'll split the proceeds."

"There's no way in hell I'm handing my company over to my wife," Chet said, now coming back to reality. "I'll run it into the ground before I let her have any of it."

"Of course," Sophie said to Angie. "From what I've read, Chet here's already taken out a ton of loans against the company. I don't think either side will get a lot out of it when they sell it."

"Well shit," Angie said. "I was hoping to run the place after the divorce. I have a finance degree and Chet's completely inept when it comes to business."

"What?" Chet stammered as he looked at Angie.

Sophie looked between Chet and Angie. "Sorry, but I'm thinking that's not going to happen now. But if you really want to help run the place, maybe you could contact whoever buys the studio after Chet sells it. They'll probably need help getting the finances back in shape."

"That's a great idea," Angie said. "I already know the business better than anyone."

"Angie?" Chet asked in a whiny hurt tone.

I had a thought. "If you could get a bank to loan you the money, maybe you could buy it yourself?"

Angie thought about it for a few seconds, then smiled. "Yeah, you know, I bet I probably could. My credit's pretty good and I have a paid-off house I could use as collateral."

Chet seemed to have pulled himself together and was becoming angry. "What if I grabbed your phone and tossed it out the window?" he asked in a snotty voice. "Then you'd have nothing. It would be my word against yours."

"Oh," Sophie said, "while everyone was standing around talking, I uploaded a copy of the video to our computer at the law office. You can break the phone into a thousand pieces and it won't change anything." Sophie held it out to him. "Here, if it'll make you feel better, go ahead and smash it. The battery's starting to go and I wouldn't mind if my boss bought me a new one."

Hearing this seemed to deflate Chet. He let out a long sigh and slowly fell back against the pillows.

Angie looked at Chad and then over to us.

"Um, I'm on my lunch hour at the studio," she said. "After I get dressed, can I get a ride back with you guys?"

"Sure," Sophie said. "As long as you don't mind being seen in a piece of crap car."

"Hey," I said. "That's my car you're talking about." I looked over at Angie. "I'll be glad to give you a ride, but would you mind taking a shower before we go? You know, eeewww."

~~~~

The next morning, I was sitting in the reception area of the law office, talking with Sophie. Getting evidence of Chet being unfaithful had been my only assignment. With Sophie's video safely stored on the office computer system, I was free for the day. I figured I'd stop by the office and see if Sophie or Gina would be around for lunch.

"Was it just me?" Sophie asked. "Or, yesterday, did Chet seem a little pudgy for someone who owned a Pilates studio?"

"Yeah," I said. "I was thinking the same thing. I guess I was expecting someone who looked a little more motivating. Maybe that's why the finances of the place were in such bad shape."

I looked around the office. In the week since I'd last been in, the stacks of files on Sophie's desk and on the end-tables had started to
~~~~

grow again. I looked into the conference room and the piles of file folders were again covering the conference table. "Are you still protesting Lenny not getting another admin in to do the filing?"

"Yup. My work load here keeps growing. He knows that. He didn't have a problem hiring Annie to help me over the summer. She was great. She kept the place looking good and I was able to concentrate on the paralegal and the billing. But when she quit, Lenny suddenly didn't want to pay to have anyone else help me. He even started to bitch when Danielle was here for those couple of days last month. If he doesn't want to pay to have the files taken care of the way he likes, I'll use my own system. The important files are on my desk. The ones I'll need soon are there on the coffee table. And long-term storage is on the table in the conference room."

"How do you keep track of everything?"

"As long as no one moves anything, I can pretty much remember where I put what I need."

"Well, I hope Lenny gets someone in for you soon. It looks like a disaster in here."

Sophie looked at me and I could see her thinking. "Why are you being so grumpy today?" she asked. "You finished your assignment in under a week. That's like a record. You should be all like: 'Sophie, you were great yesterday. You helped me get the video I needed.' I thought you'd be thrilled."

"Sure, I'm done, but the only reason I'm done is because you decided to go rogue and film them having sex directly."

"Hey, it worked. I'm thinking you should make it part of your standard procedure. Hide in the house and pop out with your camera whenever you hear someone having sex. It would save you a lot of time."

"Yes, but it would eventually get me shot or at the very least get me into fist-fights with sweaty naked men."

Sophie paused, stared into space for a moment, then got a slight smile. Apparently, fighting with sweaty naked men was something she'd never considered before. After a moment she shook it off. "So, that still doesn't explain why you're so glum. Normally you're happy between assignments. Is it because you changed your hair back? I loved the way it came out when you were trying to make yourself look like Danielle. You two looked like identical twins."

"I know and that's part of the reason I changed it back. I didn't want someone on the street mistaking me for the head of a vicious drug smuggling gang. Actually, I'm glad my hair's back to the way it was. I didn't mind the color so much, but the extensions felt weird. Besides, Lenny kept looking at me. He never said anything, but he could tell something was up."

"So, why so moody?"

"Honestly, it's because each new assignment is as bad as the last. Sometimes I get tired of hiding in closets and filming naked people having sex. It's frustrating and a little depressing. Every once in a while, I'd like to have an assignment that was different, maybe had a little adventure."

"What, like James Bond or Lara Croft? Are you looking to go somewhere exotic and dangerous? Meet some hot men then get into all sorts of life and death situations? Maybe you'd like to have some gun battles and high-speed chases, then kick the bad guy's ass and save the world?"

"I'm not trying to save the world, but I'd like to do something where I could actually make a difference and really help someone. Sneaking around with a camera isn't cutting it so much for me anymore."

"You helped our client yesterday when we filmed her husband having sex with Angie. That should count as a good deed. Besides, last month we got to help Professor Mindy recover an ancient Mexican statue. That was sort of like an adventure and the Mexican government was able to recover an artifact that was stolen like five-hundred years ago. Besides, I'd be careful on what you start wishing for. You might get it."

"You're right. I'm probably overthinking things again."

The door to the street opened and a woman walked in. She looked around the office and took a tentative step inside. She was in her mid-twenties, medium height, and was relatively thin. Her hair color was somewhere between dark blonde and light brown and hung down to her shoulders. She wore flat comfortable shoes, dark slacks, and a long-sleeved cotton top, the typical outfit of a woman who worked in a Scottsdale office.

"Hello," Sophie said, in her friendly talking-to-a-client voice. "How can I help you?"

The woman took another two steps towards Sophie's desk. She then paused as she looked at the file folders stacked everywhere. "Um, I need to talk with one of the lawyers. I'm not sure which one. I guess I could start with any of them. Do I make an appointment or how does this work?"

"Well," Sophie said, "we only have one lawyer now, so that part's simple."

The woman looked more confused than ever. "But your sign says there are four of them."

"There used to be four," I said. "One retired and two died. We've never gotten around to changing the name of the business. Leonard Shapiro's the last one."

"Um, well, if he's the only one, I guess I'll need to talk with him."

"I'll be glad to set something up," Sophie said. "Could I get your name?"

"Oh, sorry, it's Susan Monroe."

"Hi, Susan," I said as I walked over and held out my hand. "I'm Laura Black and this is Sophia Rodriguez. I do investigations and

Sophie's the paralegal. Gina Rondinelli also does investigations but she's not here at the moment."

"Are you looking for someone to take naked pictures of your husband while he's having sex with his mistress" Sophie asked.

"No, I'm not married. Do people want that a lot?"

"You'd be surprised," I said.

"I need to talk with your attorney about a case your law firm handled a long time ago."

"Okay," Sophie said. "Lenny's in the office today, but I don't know if he has any free time. Let me check."

Sophie walked over to Lenny's door, which was open, and went inside. Thirty seconds later she popped her head back out. "Lenny's able to see you now, if you have time."

We walked into Lenny's office and made introductions. He took one look at Susan, who was now visibly trembling, then asked Sophie to pour him a Beam on the rocks. He pointed to the wet bar and asked Susan what she'd like.

"Oh, actually a white wine might help. I didn't realize how stressful coming in here would be."

Sophie poured the drinks and handed them out. As usual, Lenny didn't offer anything to either Sophie or me. Not that I needed a drink before lunch, but it would've been nice if he'd at least asked.

Susan looked at her glass for a moment, then downed about half of it in a long gulp.

"We might as well get started," Lenny said. "Sophie says you have some questions about an old case of ours. Have a seat and tell us a little bit about who you are and what we can do for you."

"There isn't a lot to tell about me. My name's Susan Monroe. I've lived in Scottsdale my entire life, well, except for a year after high school when I shared an apartment in Mesa with a girlfriend. I have an associate's degree in business technology from Maricopa Community College and I work as an admin at an insurance office in Tempe. I've been there for almost three years. I'm taking courses in information technology at ASU and I hope to have my bachelor's degree next spring. From there, I'm hoping to get a more serious job in I.T. I've always had a thing for computers."

"Alright," Lenny said. "How can we help you?"

"Did you once represent someone who called himself William Southard? This would have been many years ago."

Lenny sat back and stared into space for several moments.

"That name doesn't ring a bell. Do you have any details of the case? Can you narrow down the year?"

"I don't have a lot of information on it. My mom said it had something to do with a company he owned. Apparently, he sold it and his former partner, Kathleen somebody, thought she'd been treated unfairly and decided to sue him. It was right before I was born so that would have been about twenty-six years ago."

Lenny did a quick calculation in his head to come up with the correct year. "The name doesn't match, but the timing and details sound about right for a case my former partner, Paul Oeding handled."

"Oh, then maybe I could look up Paul and ask him directly?"

"Unfortunately, you can't. Paul died a few years ago in a skiing accident."

"Oh, of course. I understand. Are there still records of the case available or is there anyone else who might know about it?"

"All the records from back then are in long-term digital storage. We'll need to search through all the cases from back then to come up with the right one. However, assuming it's the same case, I still remember some of the details of it. May I ask your interest in the matter?"

"I have reason to believe William Southard's my father."

"You no longer communicate with him?"

"As far as I know, he doesn't know I exist."

"So, why are you trying to find him? At the time we represented him, and you'll have to remember that was many years ago, he was a very wealthy man. Are you perhaps hoping to get ahold of some of his fortune?"

She smiled and slowly shook her head. "No, I'm not interested in that."

"Well, what then?"

"He and my mom were only together for a few months, but he turned out to be the one true love of her life." Susan was talking very fast, as if this was something she'd been thinking about for a long time.

"After he left, mom hasn't ever gotten close to anyone else. She always said she didn't have time for a man, since she had me to take care of. But I remember she used to go out on a lot of dates. The funny thing was, she never went out on more than two or three dates with any one guy. I think she was looking for someone as special as my dad, but she never found anyone. I was hoping if I could meet him and explain things, maybe he'd give her a call. They wouldn't need to get back together or anything, but I know it would mean the world to my mom to hear his voice and know he was okay. I think if she had some closure on it, she could start to move on again."

"Again, the names aren't matching up, but you're saying William Southard is your father. Do you have any proof of that? Does your mom also believe he's your father?"

"No, no actual proof. And mom always denies he's my father. But I don't believe her. I think she's only trying to protect me."

"Do you know where he's living?" Lenny asked. "If you'd like, we could set up an introduction based on our prior association with him.

But, honestly, it would be a lot quicker for you to send him an email, explain who you are, and maybe ask to meet face-to-face. I'm sure he's on social media, everybody is these days. He'd likely have where he works listed. You could probably call up the business to set up a meeting. You may have to go through an admin or two, but it probably wouldn't take too long."

"Unfortunately, it's not that simple. About five years ago, my mom tried to track him down. She thought if they could meet again, everything would be like it was. Sort of like in the movie *Mama Mia*."

"I take it she couldn't find him."

"We hired an investigator, but all they could discover was William Southard wasn't his real name. Back when they were together, he told my mom his entire life's story. Unfortunately, when the investigator checked, he wasn't born where he said he was born, he didn't go to school where he said he went to school, and he never lived where he said he lived. It even turned out the company he said he owned never existed. It was all made up."

"Alright, that would explain why things aren't matching up for me either. What do you have to go on?"

"Not a lot. Mostly pictures. He and mom are in a lot of pictures together. Mom remembers right before he took off, he had some sort of legal issue come up. My mom used to own an art gallery across the street from here and you were the only lawyers she knew of. She recommended you and that's how he ended up here. I was hoping you'd have some records of his case. If he was doing something with the court, I was thinking he would have needed to use his real name. Then I could use that as a starting point."

"Was the art gallery called Desert Vistas?" Lenny asked.

"That's right. My mom, her name's Olivia Monroe, closed it down about fifteen years ago. She said she couldn't afford the rent in Old Town Scottsdale anymore and had plans to open another gallery in downtown Tempe or Chandler. Unfortunately, some financial problems came up and she never did open the new gallery. She still talks about doing it, but after fifteen years, it's pretty obvious it's not happening."

"I remember the woman who ran the gallery," Lenny said. "I never talked to her, but I often saw her going in and out. Tall and thin, with blonde hair down to her waist?"

"Yeah, that was how mom looked back then. She's not quite as thin and her hair's shorter, but you'd probably still recognize her."

"Sure," Lenny said. "We can do a search and hopefully find the original records. If we can do that, we may come up with some clue as to who your father really is. It shouldn't take a lot of digging. However, researching something like that will have some costs associated with it."

"I live with my mom, drive an old car, and my expenses are low. I've been able to put some money away. My aunt knows what I'm doing and said she'd help with the expenses. I have two weeks of vacation coming up, so I can be gone if I have to go out looking for him."

"Why now?" Lenny asked. "You said the other investigation was five years ago."

"Ever since the first investigator came up empty, it's been a goal of mine to find my dad. I keep thinking if he could talk to my mom one more time, maybe things would start to go better for her. For the last six months mom's been more moody than usual. She's been spending a lot of time on the couch watching TV. You don't know her, but that's unusual for my mom. She usually on the go. I've asked her what's wrong, but she says it's nothing. A few weeks ago, I came home and found her flipping through her old scrap books, the ones with the pictures of her and my dad. It was the first time I'd seen her happy in months. I think this obsession with my dad is starting to get to her."

"Alright," Lenny said. "This first part will be fairly straightforward. Compile a list of everything you know about him. Where he said he grew up, where he lived, and the places he worked. We'll assume that none of the information is correct, but it'll give us a place to start. It would also be helpful if we could get a copy of the report the previous investigator put together. Again, we'll know all his leads were dead ends, but it may keep us from going over the same territory twice. I'll go through the old records of when he worked with us. All of that should give us a starting point."

Susan, Sophie, and I went back into reception. Sophie opened her desk and gave Susan a multi-page new-client form. "Let's schedule an appointment for you to come back tomorrow afternoon. I should have all the old records first thing in the morning, so by tomorrow afternoon we should have some more information. Then you and Lenny can go over the fees for whatever you want us to do."

"Thanks," Susan said. "I'll fill these out when I get home tonight."

She was about to leave when Gina came up to the front from the back offices. We made introductions, then asked Susan if she'd like to go to lunch with us.

"Unfortunately, I can't," she said. "I came here on my lunch hour and I'm already late. Maybe another time?"

She disappeared out the front door and Gina looked to us for an explanation. Sophie gave her the thirty second download.

"She seems nice," Gina said. "I hope we can help her out. Where should we go for lunch?"

"Anywhere," Sophie said. "I had to watch Lenny and our new client sip drinks for half an hour. That was just mean. I think I need a margarita for lunch."

"Street tacos at Old Town Gringos?" I asked.

"Sounds perfect," Gina said. We haven't been there in a couple of weeks.

About the Author

Halfway through a successful career in technical writing, marketing, and sales, along with having four beautiful children, author B A Trimmer veered into fiction. Combining a love of the desert, derived from many years of living in Arizona, along with an appreciation of the modern romantic detective story, the Scottsdale Series was born.

Comments and questions are always welcome.
Email the author at LauraBlackScottsdale@gmail.com

Made in the USA
Monee, IL
24 February 2020